So Ma͟n ͟͟ͅts

Lynda Blakesley

First Published in 2022 by Blossom Spring Publishing
So Many Secrets
Copyright © 2022 Lynda Blakesley
ISBN 978-1-7396277-8-2
E: admin@blossomspringpublishing.com
W: www.blossomspringpublishing.com
Published in the United Kingdom. All rights reserved
under International Copyright Law. Contents and/or
cover may not be reproduced in whole or in part without
the express written consent of the publisher.
This is a work of fiction. Names, characters, places and
incidents are either products of the author's imagination
or are used fictitiously.

To my beautiful granddaughter Natasha who read my
first draft and encouraged me to publish.

To Deborah
& Bob

Best Wishes
from

Lynda X .

Chapter 1

It was an unusually warm September day with a clear blue sky, but even so, a chilly wind blew down the platform as Lucinda waited at the station. Stations always seemed cold somehow, even when the sun was shining. She stepped from foot to foot and buried her leather-clad hands into the deep pockets of her cashmere maxi coat, looking up and down the platform and willing the train to arrive. At last she saw the engine coming into view, and nervously positioned herself in what she hoped would be the best place to board. Checking her bag for the first class ticket, her heart began to beat quickly and her mouth felt dry, until licking her lips and breathing deeply, calmness returned and the pulse pounding in her forehead steadied. Recalling the events of the last few months left her feeling unsettled yet excited at the prospect of the new life ahead of her. The days leading up to her departure were chaotic and frenzied leaving her completely over-burdened with the thoughts that filled her head. In the cold bleakness of the grey station, she tried to make sense of everything that had happened in her young life.

The decision she had made to make the journey to London alone and by train had been strongly disapproved of by her grandmother. Lady Agatha was against her leaving home but to travel without a chaperone was completely unacceptable. Realising that she was fighting a losing battle, the old lady knew she couldn't prevent her granddaughter from taking up her place at the college but she would not allow her to travel alone. Well-bred young ladies needed protecting.

"If you persist in this irresponsible behaviour, child, then you must take the limousine."

Lucinda smiled wryly and simply shook her head.

"Henry will drive you."

But she was a determined young woman and she had decided to take the train and that was that. Nevertheless, she felt so sorry that her last words to her grandmother had been so forceful and harsh and as she stood alone on the crowded platform, they echoed in her head. Re-living the whole emotional farewell scene that had taken place between the two of them left her feeling close to tears.

"I can't and won't ask Henry to drive me to London. It wouldn't be fair."

"Nonsense, girl."

"It's totally unnecessary and it would take forever to get there." Infuriation was evident in her voice as she continued, "It makes much more sense for me to go on the train."

The sound of carriages rattling along the tracks broke the silence that existed between them.

"I'm eighteen, I'm not a child anymore."

The old lady pursed her lips and clicked her tongue and even though she didn't utter a single word, her expression said it all. Raising her eyes to the heavens, Lucinda persisted, "It's 1968, Grandmother!" She paused, taking in a long deep breath that expressed all the frustration that had been building up inside her for so long. "You're so old-fashioned; you live in a world that doesn't exist anymore."

"Mind your manners, young lady."

Lucinda studied the tight lines around the mouth and the coldness in the old grey eyes but nothing would deter her from her ambition.

"I'm sorry, I don't mean to be rude but I'm leaving and I'm going on my own." Her face was set with a hint of the same arrogance that Agatha wore as armour against the modern world. "Nothing you say or do will change my mind."

Having made the decision, there was no turning back and her grandmother could only express her disapproval at every opportunity, up to the very moment she arrived at Newcastle station with Lucinda. Sitting together in the depressing tearooms, Lady Agatha Addington looked disdainfully at the huge mug that contained something resembling tea. Pretending to take a sip, she curled her lip and then put down the mug on the sticky tabletop and frowned. She instinctively began straightening her ridiculously large and embarrassingly old-fashioned hat while looking down at Lucinda through spectacles that perched precariously on the end of her nose. She looked so out of place sitting here in this busy station cafe and her granddaughter couldn't wait for her to leave. People were staring at them. Women like Agatha Addington didn't drink coffee from heavy white earthenware mugs and hats like hers were only ever worn at weddings and only if it was a posh 'do.' Lucinda felt uncomfortable and avoided the eyes that scrutinised the two of them. Her grandmother seemed oblivious to the whispers and sniggers as she continued to inspect the room, taking in the shabby décor and the awful drabness of the place. It was unfortunate that her natural demeanour meant that she habitually appeared to have a bad smell under her nose and Lucinda heard a comment from behind the counter.

"Wonder what Lady Muck's doing here. Must be slumming it today!"

A fat man laughed loudly making his belly wobble and his mug of tea spill onto the floor.

"This is quite ridiculous, child; we'll forget all about this nonsense and return home now."

"Why won't you listen?"

"We don't belong here. The car is parked outside.

Come along, dear, come now!"

There was an urgency in her voice as the old lady guided Lucinda out of earshot of the gawping onlookers and out into the busy station. Undeterred, her granddaughter drew on all her courage and strength to defy the woman who had dominated her since she was a small child. She arched her back, thrusting out her small but well-shaped breasts and took in a deep breath of the pungent air that filled the railway station. The heady mix of steam, oil and coal dust made her splutter but she recovered quickly, determined to stand her ground.

"You just don't understand, do you?

The edge in her tone had been developing over the past year, ever since she had decided that she would take control of her own life. Stinging tears began to smart underneath the long lashes.

"It's not like when you were a girl! You're an old woman. What do you know?"

The words cut deep into the soul of her grandmother, who visibly bristled with an anger that she struggled hard to contain. "Lucinda, I will not be spoken to in such a manner. What would your father say if he could hear you address me so disrespectfully?"

The girl straightened, reaching her full 5 feet and 4 inches with her head held high and her little turned-up nose pointing skywards. The image she portrayed was truly noble, if also rather comical. "My Father would be proud of me and you know it as well as I do."

"I know nothing of the sort."

"I'm going to study art just like he did."

There was such an air of authority and determination in the young woman's words, that her grandmother was impressed with the way she stood up for herself, even though she would never acknowledge the fact. Her words had brought back many memories, but even as she

4

reflected on the past, she ordered Lucinda to behave herself in her usual brusque fashion.

"I am quite aware that you are to study art, my dear girl. I am paying for that privilege, something that I fear you do not always remember!"

"Oh, believe me, I haven't forgotten!" Lucinda prickled, "Once I'm established, I'll pay back every penny."

She genuinely intended to repay the debt as soon as she was able and there was more than a hint of pride in the way she stood up to her grandmother. It was clear in her ladyship's mind that this little thing was a veritable Addington through and through, even though it was another's blood that flowed through her veins. Softening slightly at this notion, tears almost sparkled in the old woman's hard-dark eyes as she remembered Arthur, the son who had died in 1951 just a few years after the war had ended. He too had been a student at the Royal College of Art when he was called up. On his twenty first birthday, the whole nation celebrated D-Day and Lady Agatha thanked God that her son had come through all the horrors of those years. However, her joy was short-lived, as only a few years later he was involved in a fatal car crash with Lucinda's mother, Vera, an aspiring young actress. She had been a drama student at RADA during the time Arthur was studying in London and they had literally bumped into each other at Lyons Corner House Café. As his portfolio spilled its contents of half-finished sketches and quick studies made in charcoal, she knelt to help him pick up his embryonic masterpieces.

That was the beginning of a whirlwind romance that saw them married within six months in a magical summer wedding attended by everybody who was anybody in the county. His mother didn't approve of the marriage but realising that she was powerless to stop it, she was determined to put on a show that would be talked about for years to come. But she would never accept her new daughter-in-law. She would never be an Addington and Agatha refused to acknowledge her as such. As it turned out, she didn't need to; very soon events were to eliminate the unwelcome addition to her family.

Try as she may, Vera couldn't win over her mother-in-law and an air of polite hostility existed between them. Even when she became pregnant, Agatha failed to show any real emotion and when the child was born, she instinctively tried to take over her upbringing. But by then Vera had developed a shield; a thick skin that kept her mother-in-law at a distance. However, neither of them could have foreseen the tragic end to the relationship which saw both Vera and Arthur die in his brand-new Jaguar XK120. As they returned home from a trip to London, the car veered off the icy road into a tree. They had gone to see Howard Keel in the musical Oklahoma at Drury Lane. It was her last chance to catch the show as it was coming to the end of its long run after a wildly successful premiere in 1947. Vera had once worked with the now famous actor and against all obstacles she was determined that she would make the trip to the capital with or without Arthur. Now musing over the tragic facts, Agatha wished with all her heart that her son had been a more dominant husband. Vera was headstrong and poor Arthur could deny her nothing.

Never really recovering from the heartbreak of the disaster, Agatha grew bitter and even more distant. At first, she found it impossible to take to Vera's child, but she was such an adorable little girl that it only took a short while for her grandmother's heart to melt. It was difficult for the old woman to express her feelings; a cold arrogance, which stemmed from a heightened sense of her social position, stifled her. Her life was very privileged in all respects, but she had experienced the same despair as many of those wives and sweethearts who lost their loved ones in the Great War. She had only been married a few short years when her husband was killed at the Battle of the Somme and since that day her life had been empty and devoid of love. There had been no real romance in her life; even her marriage had been an arranged affair, but she had loved her husband in her own fashion. No-one could ever say she was a particularly pretty woman, although her aristocratic looks gave her a certain air which was attractive in its own way. Of course, there had been many fortune hunters who had all tried to ingratiate themselves through insincere flattery, but Agatha was a highly intelligent, independent individual and so she resolved to remain a widow.

Lucinda was only a year old when her mother and father were killed, although she had faded memories fired by all those below stairs who had revered and respected the golden couple. Wonderful tales of the parents she adored became more and more embroidered, founding endless evenings of entertainment for the kitchen maids as they sat by the remains of the fire in the servants' hall. Her mother, the most beautiful glamorous lady she could ever imagine, was the heroine of the stories and her father a talented artist, the handsome hero. She could only imagine her parents as they were never mentioned by her grandmother. Paintings and sketches of Vera were all hidden away from view in the attic until little Lucinda discovered them one day when playing hide and seek with Dossie, her nanny.

"Who's this lady?" she asked, with wide innocent eyes. "She's pretty."

"Mmm. What lady?" Looking through the darkness in

the attic, Dossie spied a painting of a handsome young man and the child's words disappeared into the rafters.

"This lady!"

Dossie turned to face the little girl.

"Look here in the picture! Is she a film star?" she whispered breathlessly.

"My word, a film star indeed!" Dossie laughed out loud.

"That's it, isn't it, Dossie, she's a film star, isn't she? I know she is!" Excitement made the child jump on the spot.

"Calm yourself, Miss Lucinda. You'll make yourself sick with all that jigging about!"

Staring long and hard at the painting, a thought popped into her head and she asked with some puzzlement. "But why do we have a picture of a film star. Why is she here in our attic?"

"A film star!" chuckled the little girl's nanny, remembering Vera.

"Grandmama doesn't like going to the picture house, does she, Dossie? She never lets me go."

The little girl's bottom lip stuck out petulantly and she huffed noisily but Dossie wasn't listening. She was gazing at a self-portrait of a handsome young man with a shock of auburn hair and eyes the colour of the sea; deep and unfathomable. Not quite blue yet almost green with tiny flecks of brown; they were alive and real, drawing her into the painting. Pulling out the canvas from its place against the wall, she stood it in front of the child with a dramatic flourish and a proud smile. "Look, Lucinda, this is your father."

"My Father? Daddy!"

"Oh yes, he was a wonderful man, pet, so full of talent and life. He was a real artist, Lou; a real man!"

Dossie's words meant little to the child who was only

really interested in the glamorous woman in the picture.

"Was he really my Daddy?" The little girl looked both curious and excited as she tapped her foot forcibly on the wooden floorboards, "But who's the pretty lady? Tell me. Who is she? I want to know!"

Dossie didn't answer, remaining focused on the portrait of Arthur Addington. He was undeniably handsome and with an ambition that saw him set to follow his dreams and never those of his mother, who could see no future in painting or drawing. Lady Agatha may not have been the most maternal of women, but she was indulgent when it came to Arthur and she was eventually persuaded to allow him to become a student at The Royal College of Art. But when it came to her granddaughter, she would not be so tolerant, not after the grave mistake she had made with the child's father. She was determined to create a life for the girl that was appropriate to her station, ensuring a suitable marriage to a young man of similar background. There was no way that she would allow any relationship that she disapproved of to develop and to achieve this goal, Lucinda must be kept close to home.

But the harder she tried to restrain the child's spirit, the stronger she grew. She was Vera's daughter after all, and it was her blood that flowed through the whole of her being and not the blue blood that surged through her ladyship's veins. Lucinda knew that the path that her grandmother had mapped out for her was not what she intended to follow and not what her parents would have wanted for her. She instinctively knew that her father would wish her to follow her dream to become whoever she wanted.

And so, it had been a long hard war of wills between the two women over the past months but now the battle was coming to an end and it looked like Lucinda was going to be the victor. Standing face to face with her only living relative there on that cold platform waiting for her train, she had never felt so strong in all her short life.

"I'm so sorry; believe me, I love you dearly, I really do, but it's my life and I will live it my way." The young girl's eyes were full of pain, but they remained focused as she made a final plea, "Please give me your blessing! If you love me, let me go. Please Gran."

"Oh for goodness' sake, Lucinda, I am not your Gran. I am your Grandmama!"

"Right," she said, finally grasping how antiquated her grandmother really was. Everything about her was from another era; the way she dressed, the way she spoke. If she didn't leave now, she'd probably end up in Switzerland at some posh finishing school or worse still, incarcerated in the mausoleum they called home. She had no intention of ending up like Agatha Addington.

"Your life is not for me, Grandmother. I am not you!"

Realising that she was facing defeat, Agatha sucked in her cheeks making her old face look skeletal and as she slowly closed her eyes, the crepe-like skin on her lids looked dark and as thin as tissue paper. She suddenly appeared incredibly old. Unable to speak, she merely shook her head whilst wringing her hands. She refused to cry. Well-bred ladies did not cry in public and besides, she would never demonstrate such an expression of weakness. Reaching up to kiss the old lady on the cheek, Lucinda genuinely felt a surge of deep affection for her grandmother and tears rolled down her face. Agatha wrapped her in her arms very briefly before turning her back on her, leaving her cold and alone waiting for the train to London. The girl watched as she strode purposefully out to meet Henry who was polishing the bonnet of the car. He instinctively knew that Lady Agatha would be returning alone.

A whistle blew in the distance and Lucinda shuddered, shattering the unpleasant memories that almost made her change her mind and race back to the woman who had ruled her life for so long.

Chapter 2

Suddenly the thoughts that flooded her head disappeared as the train pulled into the station and came to a noisy halt. Picking up the bag that she'd packed the night before, she rushed towards the first-class carriage door. A young man with floppy brown hair opened it before she reached the step and as their eyes met, he flashed the most enormous smile, taking her bag and ushering her into the carriage. Strangely, Lucinda felt no sense of anger or fear at his actions, only a strong feeling of amusement. Her eyes crinkled and she laughed out loud, shaking her head and covering her mouth with the gloved hand.

"Well, thank you very much for your help, Mr... er... Mr...," she paused and looked directly into the smiling hazel eyes, "I think I can manage quite well on my own from here!"

"No problem, it's a pleasure."

Suddenly this stranger somehow lifted her mood and she was amazed at how differently she felt. It was if a light had been switched on inside of her, illuminating all the dark shadows of the previous months. It was incredible what a smile could do. He brushed the hair from his face, revealing a few red highlights, the exact same shade as her own. She turned to look into his handsome face as he continued to follow her into the corridor.

"Please don't bother yourself. I really can take it from here!"

Her words belied her true feelings as she secretly wished for him to follow her onto the train. He would be the perfect diversion, but she was more like her grandmother than she would ever admit and there was no way she would ever reveal her emotions to a stranger.

"Honestly, it's no trouble."

"I can manage."

Completely ignoring Lucinda's words, he continued to carry her bag, guiding her firmly into the carriage. "Forgot to get a newspaper."

"What?"

"A paper."

"Oh, did you get one?"

"Thought I might have time to grab one from the kiosk before we set off! Trains never leave on time, do they?"

Winking cheekily, he was glad that a forgotten newspaper had led him to such a lovely girl. He'd left his grandfather to find his seat before jumping back onto the platform to get the old man his paper and bumping into Lucinda.

"You were risking it, weren't you?" The girl blinked.

"You gotta take risks, baby."

"Baby!" Lucinda screwed up her face. His attempt to sound cool failed miserably but he was right. She, herself was about to take the biggest risk of her young life.

Not giving up, the young man persevered, "I'll have to get back to my seat in the cattle truck sharpish, though, but not until I find out your name, pretty lady!"

Thoughts of the newspaper totally gone, they both tumbled into the compartment and Lucinda almost fell into the olive-green plush seat as the train lurched forward. In that same second, the young man sat down heavily at the side of her. Smiling that infectious smile again, he held out his hand and introduced himself.

"Hi, I'm David and I'm very pleased to meet you."

Recovering herself, Lucinda stood up now that the train was steadier and she started to lift her case onto the rack above their heads. Completely forgetting her impeccable manners, she simply mumbled her name which immediately disappeared into the sleeve of her coat. Grabbing the bag from her grip, he continued to hoist it into place, repeating the name he thought he had heard.

"Melinda, what a beautiful name... suits you perfectly." He threw the cashmere coat that she had casually removed onto the case. Stretching out his hand towards her again, he waited for the effect of his well-versed flattery on this fabulous creature.

"How lovely of you to say so!" she laughed, teasingly, as she took his hand in a most polite handshake, "But my name is actually Lucinda, though you can call me Melinda if you want to. Does it suit me, do you think?"

Suppressing a giggle and with a twinkle in her eye, she looked directly at the boy, delighting in his embarrassment as he coughed nervously and ran his hands through his hair. He wasn't used to this treatment; girls usually fell hook, line and sinker for his boyish charms and his tried and trusted chat-up lines. This one was different and thoroughly perplexing. Sitting down again, this time by the window, Lucinda finally ignored David's obvious discomfort and stared out onto the rows of terraced houses that flashed by. Trying to imagine the families who lived in these tiny boxes, she thought of the stories that Dossie, her grandmother's maid and her nanny, had told her about living in a mining village. She smiled to herself as she imagined sitting in a tin bath in front of a roaring fire and then blushed as she caught the young man staring straight at her.

"I suppose you should find your seat. You do realise this is a first class carriage, don't you?" The words spilled out automatically without much thought to his feelings until she pulled herself up sharply, inwardly scolding the snobbery she loathed.

But before she could say another word, he quickly countered, "I much prefer it here, if you don't mind. I'll face the conductor when the time comes, or I could always hide in the baggage rack under your coat."

David seemed oblivious to any sense of superiority that she felt she'd conveyed in those few words and she was impressed with his confidence and self-assurance. She smiled, smirking to herself at the image of this lanky youth perched under her coat in the luggage rack but she continued to stare with great determination at the long rows of little houses flashing by.

"Can't imagine yourself living down there, can you, milady?" His eyes narrowed slightly, and Lucinda wasn't sure if he was mocking or genuinely interested in her feelings.

Lucinda didn't acknowledge his words, continuing instead to stare hard out of the window. No, it was impossible for her to imagine what it must be like to share a two-up two-down with a whole family; to walk down to the bottom of the garden when you needed to go to the lavatory and to worry about all sorts of things, including if there was enough money to get you through the week. To some people, it seemed she had led a charmed life, living in a grand house with servants to take care of your every need and more clothes and possessions than most would ever see in a lifetime. And yet she had been brought up by an elderly grandmother whose views were more Victorian than 20th century. Her life was not charmed but it was about to become so, she told herself.

"Dossie lived in one of those houses!" she blurted out as if in retaliation to his accusation. "I know what it's like."

David let out a low whistle, "Dossie... fancy that! You won't believe this, but I actually had a Great-Auntie called Dossie."

"No."

"Never met her or anything but my Ma talked about

15

her a lot when I was a nipper."

"Really."

"Yeah. It's an unusual name, don't you think? Fancy us having that name in common. Who is your Dossie?"

"Well... she's not really my Dossie!" she stammered

How could she tell him that her Dossie was a servant? "She used to live with us, but she's really just a... a... friend of mine, a good friend."

Dossie was indeed a friend to Lucinda. She had comforted her when her parents died, protected her from her grandmother's coldness and watched over her as she grew up. Stretching his long arms above his head, David leaned back into his seat and sighed. He thought about this enchanting creature for a minute or so, collecting his thoughts and making his own assessment of her. He suddenly realised he didn't really know much about her at all apart from her name and the fact that she was high class, quite different from the usual dolly-birds he associated with.

"So, I know your name, I know you're well-to-do for sure and I know you have a Dossie just like me!"

"Well-to-do... what do you mean by that?" she retorted.

"Well just look at you, dressed in the best of gear and that accent; we don't hear many of those beautifully rounded vowels around here. Not in Geordie-land we don't!" he teased.

Looking down in embarrassment at the Mary Quant smock dress she was wearing, she crossed her cream lace clad legs and wriggled her toes in the patent leather Mary Janes that had been left polished and shiny outside her bedroom that morning. She hadn't really noticed a strong north-eastern accent but now that she thought about it, it was quite clear that David spoke in that lovely sing-song way that Dossie soothed her with when she was feeling low. With narrowed eyes, David scrutinised the girl, staring hard at her downturned face until she lifted her head and her beautiful eyes fleetingly met his. He quickly looked away as her long dark lashes fluttered against her flushed cheeks. Turning to face her again, he spoke with an assertiveness that impressed the young woman.

"But there's something a bit bohemian about you!" the words broke into her thoughts, reinforcing her own feelings about herself.

She was a free spirit; she was an artist and she was going to London! She would never be the sort of grand lady her grandmother wanted her to be. It was the sixties and things were changing. Nobody bothered about class anymore. Working class boys like The Beatles and David Bailey became famous and rich and girls like Twiggy and Jean Shrimpton made a fortune simply because of their looks. Staring at the young stranger in front of her, Lucinda imagined him with an electric guitar strung round his neck. She wondered if he was a musician or possibly it wasn't a guitar but a camera that hung on his neck. Yes, he had a look of David Bailey about him. She pondered for a few minutes, deep in her reveries.

He coughed nervously, bringing her back to reality.

"And what do I know about you then, Georgie Porgy, apart from the fact that you have a Great-Aunt Dossie!" she joshed with a flirtatious glimmer in those beautiful enticing eyes.

"I'm not bohemian, that's for sure… too down to earth for that. But you know my old grandma was a bit of a dreamer. Wanted to draw and paint and stuff."

"Was she an artist then?"

"Well she always dreamed of going down to London to some art college. She was desperate to soak up all that arty paraphernalia. Had a lot of talent, so I'm told!"

"Well, well," a tantalising smile played around her

mouth.

"You know what I mean. Stop it!" he appreciated her teasing and smiled back.

"Arty paraphernalia, eh?" The words were articulated very precisely and slowly whilst her eyes twinkled mischievously. "Did you swallow a dictionary for breakfast?"

"I'm not entirely ignorant, you know," he sounded quite indignant, but the good humour never left his face.

"I didn't think for one moment…"

"Actually I'm a student like you. Nothing as innovative or ingeniously creative as art, though. I'm training to be a teacher. Told you I'm very down to earth. Teaching is a good sound respectable job or so my grandfather tells me."

Secretly, David was proud of the way he was dropping in a couple of words from the dictionary he'd had for breakfast! This was unreal. She hadn't mentioned the fact that she was on her way to take an art course in London. He didn't know that she was an art student. How could he possibly know? It took a while but then it dawned on her. Some people were just very intuitive and made clever guesses. She looked down at the portfolio case resting against her seat. It was a burgundy leather folder containing some of her drawings.

"You are such a fake, David! Your dear old Granny was a bohemian just like me and your great-auntie was called Dossie. I bet you've never even come across anyone called Dossie!"

Lucinda felt a real idiot. He certainly must think her a fool to fall for such a contrived chat-up. Suddenly her mood changed and she turned on the boy.

"I'm sure your apparent coincidences work on some gullible Geordie girls, but I don't fall for all this guff. If you want to impress a woman, just try being yourself!"

David looked genuinely hurt and bewildered. He frowned at the girl, who was now fiddling with the strands of red hair that fell over her pale freckled brow.

"OK, then," he gulped, clumsily fastening up the toggle buttons on his duffle coat. "I'd better go and find my seat but for your information, your ladyship, I admit I might use stupid chat up lines, but I don't lie. I just wanted to get to know you a bit better but thinking about it, you're probably not worth it."

Getting up to leave, he turned to face Lucinda and added pointedly, "You're just a spoiled little rich girl pretending to be some kind of hippie but you'll never fool anybody wearing those expensive clothes. Goodbye, milady."

His words hit home. It was true, she was pretending to be somebody she wasn't, but she was so desperate to break free from her grandmother's clutches, she didn't even realise it herself. Somehow this stranger had got under her skin. He seemed to know her better than she knew herself and it bothered her. Totally frustrated by her mixed emotions about this fascinating young man, her usual good manners deserted her for a moment.

"Oh do sit down and shut up, you idiot!" All the authority of her breeding came through in this simple command which she delivered with such a confident air that it seemed a natural thing for her to say, even to a stranger. Nevertheless, she was totally surprised at how powerful she felt in that instant.

Without a moment's hesitation, David sat down immediately and obediently, utterly amazed at the effect Lucinda had on him. Completely dumbfounded by his total compliance, Lucinda stared open-mouthed at the boy, not knowing whether to laugh or apologise for her unacceptable rudeness. David stared back without uttering a single word and for a few moments they contemplated each other curiously until they both collapsed in a fit of hysterical laughter.

"You can call me Lou!" she giggled.

Chapter 3

Ernest Lowes was at the end of his tether. After trudging almost, the length of the train, looking for his grandson, he was shattered, totally drained by the effort. They were on their way to Doncaster for the races – a trip which David had arranged as a special birthday treat for his grandfather. He was studying at teacher training college just outside of the Yorkshire town and was lodging with his grandpa's brother Lance who lived in High Melton. After the races, they had planned to visit Uncle Lance and stay the night. Ernest hadn't seen his younger brother and his wife for some time and David thought it would be nice to get the family together.

After leaving his grandfather in the corridor, David had jumped off the train to get a newspaper, but now Ernest was alone and wondering whether he had managed to get back on in time or whether he was still somewhere on the platform. He was an old man and although still quite sprightly, he relied on his grandson for quite a lot of things these days.

"Where the hell is that lad? I'll have his guts for garters when I find him!"

A ticket collector stopped and asked if he was alright, "Can I help you, old timer? You seem a bit lost."

Without replying, Ernest pushed brusquely past the uniformed man, his brows furrowed and his face apprehensive. How dare the man! He was no old timer, just a little forgetful at times. Searching for his ticket, he panicked as he failed to find it in his top pocket. He couldn't remember whether David had held on to them both or had given him his own. His memory wasn't quite as good as it had been, although he remembered the old days with brilliant clarity. A shrill whistle signalled the start of the train's departure from Newcastle. Well if the lad had been left behind, there was nothing he could do about it now, but he had a feeling that he was somewhere on this train. He just had to find him. As he passed into the first class carriage, Ernest felt a sudden pang of anxiety. What if the conductor asked him for his ticket? He knew his place only too well and it wasn't up here with the nobs. Where was that lad when he needed him? Ladies and gentlemen, carrying leather suitcases pasted with exotic labels bustled past him to get to their seats, leaving him disorientated and confused.

The train rattled speedily down the track and the corridor began to shake, making it almost impossible for Ernest to stay on his feet. At that moment, the old man stumbled into the doorway to the compartment where Lucinda had begun to doubt whether she was right about David. He had looked just like a little boy, hurt and downhearted when he sat back down so obediently and then they had both chuckled like silly schoolchildren. Now though, his mettle returned in an instant, and he stood up with such energy and power as he readied himself to steady his grandfather. Just as the old man began to lose his footing, David grabbed him and led him to a seat where he gently sat him down, kneeling in front of him with a look of genuine anxiety on his handsome face.

"What are you doing, you old duffer? You gave me such a shock."

"What am I doing?" Ernest asked with a wobble in his voice. "Where the bloody hell have you been?"

Breathing deeply, he recovered himself sufficiently well to realise that there was a young woman sitting opposite him in the compartment. His was the generation when it was unthinkable to blaspheme in front of a woman and he put his head in his hands and dragged his fingers through the little wisps of auburn hair he had left.

"Excuse my language Miss, apologies for my behaviour just now. Hope I haven't offended you too much!"

"Not at all, don't worry about me," soothed Lou with real regard for Ernest. "How are you now? Do you feel better?"

The voice from the opposite side of the compartment was soft and caring, willing the old man to lift his head and face her. As he did so, he caught his breath, exhaling loudly and rubbing the back of his neck. A sudden pain spread from his arm into his chest, leaving him exhausted and white as a sheet. Both Lucinda and David rushed to his side, with apprehension and trepidation, one on either side of him. As they cradled his trembling body, their hands touched, and their eyes met with a genuine feeling of concern for the old gentleman. David loosened his grandad's tight shirt collar while Lou pulled down the window to let in a gust of air.

"Grandad, are you alright? Speak to me."

"Stop fussing boy, I'm fine... just fine. I've had a bit of a shock that's all!"

Thinking that Ernest had been upset by his absence, David whispered gently into the old man's ear.

"I'm so sorry. I shouldn't have left you like that. I've been really selfish." A look of real concern flashed across his face as he spotted the same alarm in Lucinda's eyes.

Taking the old man's hand in hers, she gently patted it, trying desperately to do something that might help. She felt quite useless and was suddenly struck by the foolishness of her action. He wasn't a pet Labrador. Recalling Dossie's cure-all, a sweet cup of strong tea, she sprang into action.

"David, I'll go and get him a cup of tea from the buffet car. You take care of him; don't leave him!" she instructed.

"That's it! Nice cup of tea Grandpa, eh... how about that?"

But Ernest Lowes wasn't listening, continuing to stare at the lovely stranger as she made to leave the carriage. That face, that beautiful face! The shape of the nose, the fullness of the lips and the eyes were all familiar to him. He knew this face so well; framed by the short helmet of hair... a bob, they called it. The colour was intense and fiery, too red but there was no mistaking it was her all the same. It was the face of the woman he had cherished for the whole of his life. Lucinda smiled at the old gentleman with genuine concern in her eyes as she turned to reassure David. Her fingers lingered softly on his shoulder for just a moment before she stroked the grandfather's brow and she was gone.

In that mystical moment, Ernest was transported back in time. Gazing into space, his old eyes sparkled with the magic of it all. He had always loved her from the first moment he had seen her all dressed up to the nines for her mother's wedding to Jack Dawson. Not quite a woman but more than a child, a girl so lovely and beguiling that his heart missed a beat the moment he saw her. Of course, she had realised the effect she had on him from day one and had played him like a fiddle, flashing him an entrancing, almost seductive smile before turning her back on him and floating away; a vision in pink. He remembered her words the day he naively asked for her hand and the crushing feeling in his belly when she told him she would be no man's wife; would never marry. Real passion and affection had replaced the lust that he had first felt for her, but she was elusive, playing games with his head, every now and then making him think there was still a chance for him. But his heart was finally shattered the day she told him there was somebody else and his thoughts swung between suicide and murder. He remembered the despair as her voice echoed in his head, destroying his hopes for the future with the woman he loved.

"I'm going to get married, Ernie. I know now, that's what I want. I love him with every part of me and he loves me; I know he does!"

"No."

"Please... please don't hate me. I don't know why but things have changed."

"What's changed?"

"Everything."

"So you lied to me."

"I just feel so different now; more grown up."

"You made a fool of me."

"No, I just wasn't ready. I wanted more."

Her words had cut into him like a knife and it was all too much for Ernie as he broke down, falling to his knees, begging her to come back to him. The image of that moment brought a lump to the old man's throat and a sense of shame and humiliation so strong he could still taste it.

"Please don't do this to me. You know I love you. You can't marry him. He's no good for you. He'll only hurt you; believe me, he can't love you like I do, no-one can!"

She had drained him of every drop of self-respect and left him a hopeless and broken man. The hurt was so real that even now, so many years later, he felt the same sharp pain that had wracked his body all those years before. Clutching his chest, Ernest tried desperately to eliminate the rawness of the memory. Blinking furiously, the feelings slowly began to subside until his breathing returned to normal and his body once more relaxed. But she was still there and no matter how hard he tried; he couldn't erase her image. An ice maiden with a heart of gold. It was true enough, beneath that cool facade there was indeed a softness within her that she could never really conceal. No matter what had happened between them, she'd really been just as sensitive as this sweet, lovely stranger whose face was at this moment swirling in his subconscious; a beautiful young girl whose eyes were filled with such tenderness and concern. He'd seen that look so many times before on the face of the woman he had always known had cared for him and for him alone. In spite of everything she said, her true feelings for Ernest Lowes had been real and pure. There had been an ardour that flickered like a candle in her heart even though she tortured him mercilessly. Her head was turned by silly notions of romance and excitement and he knew he could never compete with her idealistic picture of life and love. He could offer stability and respectability and undying adoration, but could he ever thrill her the way she craved? He knew the answer only too well. Their relationship had been a bittersweet affair and he would never forget the overwhelming sense of joy she brought into his life as well as the sorrow.

Vivid memories of how she'd comforted him the day she broke his heart teemed back into his mind. It had been a cold winter's night the first time they'd made love. They loved each other so passionately and powerfully that he could remember every single detail, every stirring even now, over fifty years later. He ought to have hated her with every ounce of his being but somehow his infatuation had grown despite himself. He knew even then that she would one day be his; that he would possess her body and soul as she possessed him. There was never any doubt in his mind that she would eventually be his wife, his soulmate for ever and ever.

As the painful scenes from the past played out so

realistically in his imagination, a single tear welled in his eye and to avoid it being seen, Ernest turned his face to the window. He was unaware of the young girl now standing over him holding out a plastic cup of hot sweet tea.

"I've brought you some tea, please try to drink it while it's hot."

"Grandpa, drink your tea. It'll make you feel better."

But Ernest was completely lost in time. Her face had transported him back to his youth and every detail was so clear and intense that it could have been yesterday. Every word and action remembered so accurately that the present no longer existed for him. Staring out onto the rows and rows of miners' cottages that had avoided the demolition men, Ernest began to feel dizzy watching each little dilapidated terraced house with its tiny back yard flash by. As they all blurred into one, his head began to spin and then everything went black.

Chapter 4

The gas lamps flickered and then spluttered in the cramped front room of the cottage as the little girl bent over the table and rested her head on her hands. It was late and her fine blonde hair was curled in candy striped rags ready for the morning. Tiny strands of red gold escaped from the strips of cloth that wound round the curls and tickled her eyebrows. Brushing aside the fine hairs from her face she stuck out her tongue and licked the corner of her mouth, catching the last drops of the cocoa that lingered on her lips. Fiddling with the fringing that edged the thick green chenille table cover, she yawned noisily and then smoothed down the shiny oilcloth protecting it. The part roll of wallpaper, which had been left over when the pit manager's house and offices were being decorated in the modern style, had been given to the child when she went with her Da to collect his pay packet one Friday. A skivvy was about to throw it into the tin dustbin in the yard under the metal steps when she noticed the tiny little thing staring at the pattern on the roll.

"It's pretty, isn't it? Do you want it, pet? You could cut out the flowers and stick them into a book."

The child replied sweetly, beaming all over her face, "Yes, please Missus."

But she wouldn't be cutting out any flowers, she had other ideas.

The roll stretched out over the tabletop with the pattern facing down and with her pencils lined up neatly in graduating hues at the side. Looking at the grey grainy paper, she smiled as the drawings she had made filled her with pleasure and pride. Princesses and fairies skipped and flew gracefully from the roll until her father burst into the room, black-faced with coaldust clinging to his eyelashes and moustache. He roared like a wild animal, loud and rough so that the sound echoed through the tiny house, sending shivers down his wife's spine. She dreaded her man coming home in this state. It always signalled trouble but at the same time she worried when he stayed away. She knew with certainty what that meant and it always involved another woman. She bore the shame with such dignity, but it didn't stop the village gossips or the pitying looks. Luckily, her two girls knew nothing of his adultery, only his brutality and indifference.

As Edwin Ramsey's eyes searched the room, he spotted the drawings. "Get that rubbish off table, where's your Ma?" Not waiting for an answer, he bellowed, "I want my dinner, woman, get your arse in here now, you lazy cow."

His huge form shook as he threw down the filthy grey coat that he ripped from his bulky frame. A checked cap that had seen better days followed swiftly and landed on top of the coat that lay in a heap on the red and blue peg rug. There was a distinct smell about him; a heady mixture of beer, tobacco and coal dust that always conjured up a picture of some mythical monster in his little daughter's vivid imagination. As if to give credence to this image, he had a long thin blue mark stretching from his hairline to his eyebrow from where he was caught by a falling lump of coal. Miners' scars often healed with a tell-tale blue tinge from the black dust that couldn't be completely cleaned from the wound.

At that moment, a small busy woman appeared instantly from the scullery, powdery white flour covering her flushed cheeks and robust arms. She was clutching a tea-stained checked cloth in one hand and flicking her faded gold hair out of her dull eyes with the other. In an instant she had gathered up the coat and cap and hung them on the peg at the back of the door into the kitchen.

"Won't be long, pet." Her voice trembled as she watched him violently sweep the paper roll and pencils onto the floor as the child looked at her prized possessions roll in all directions across the mat.

Annetta, or Etta as her Mam called her, bent nervously to pick up her pencils and watched as her father threw her precious princesses and fairies onto the fire that blazed in the black leaded hearth. Tearfully she quietly and invisibly crept into the back room and crumpled onto the horsehair mattress that sat on top of the little brass bedstead. Wiping away the silent tears from her cheeks and licking away the few salty drips that were left clinging to her soft pink lips, she sat upright, hugging her scrawny legs to her chest. In a few years, she thought to herself, she could leave school, she would be twelve then and she would get a job and take her mother away to a nice place, a place where princesses and fairies might live. She had no thought of the man who was her father, a bully of a man who terrorised her mother and ignored her. It was strange to feel nothing for someone who should be a hero in the eyes of a daughter, but she hardly knew him and what she did know was something to be forgotten.

Most of his time was spent in the pub or worse and Minnie saw little of the man she had married when she wasn't much older than her eldest daughter, Doreen. Not that she complained; the less time she spent in his company, the less chance there was of her being beaten to a pulp. She had taken the beatings and the abuse over the years without complaint as she accepted her lot when she took her wedding vows. Like many others, Minnie saw marriage as sacred, no matter what the circumstances. There was only one thing she would not tolerate and that was violence towards her bairns. Mercifully, Edwin

Ramsey had never once struck his daughters, although his verbal abuse was equally as painful. Etta's only escape was through her vivid imagination and she fancied how things could be very different for them. She visualised a family where there was love and happiness, where her fairies could live. As the snow fell and settled in the yard, she saw their feathery wings flutter against the bedroom window and a faint smile landed briefly on the child's lips.

Christmas was only days away but there was little joy in the house. Minnie tried her best and helped Etta with the paper chains. The one thing they both looked forward to was seeing her sister again. Doreen, or Dossie, as she was known, had escaped as soon as she could to go into service. She had secured a nice position with a wealthy lady and her harsh life with her unfeeling father was almost forgotten. But she couldn't forget her mother and sister, almost physically feeling their pain and she would be home on Christmas Eve, no matter what.

The little girl was delighted at the news that her sister was coming home. "Will Dossie bring me a present, Mammy?"

"Oh, I'm sure she will, my pet," Minnie knew very well that her eldest daughter had bought some new coloured pencils and some proper drawing paper for her little sister.

"I'll help with the dinner tomorrow."

"Bless you sweetheart."

"I can go down to the allotment and get some potatoes and there's still some cabbages, I think. They haven't gone rotten yet."

"You're a good lass, our Etta."

"We'll make it special for our Dossie, won't we, Mammy?"

Words tumbled out of her sweet little mouth while

Minnie listened with great amusement, "I've got some Christmas crackers, Mam."

"Have you, pet?" Minnie wasn't really listening as she wiped her hands on her apron.

"Yes, we made them at school last week."

"Well, fancy that."

"They won't bang and there's nothing inside but I don't think that'll matter, do you?"

"No... no, sweet pea," Minnie said reassuringly. "That's lovely, Etta and I've got a surprise for you."

"What is it?"

"Guess."

"Tell me, Mammy, what is it?" the little girl demanded.

"It's a plum pudding!" there was a real sense of satisfaction in her voice as she waited for the response.

Etta clapped her hands, skipping round the kitchen at the thought of a sweet sticky dollop of Christmas pud.

"Will we have some cream?"

"Oh yes, you can't have Christmas pud without real cream."

"Goody goody gumdrops. Real cream, not tinned stuff. We're posh, we are!"

"You silly sausage, go on with you!"

The pair of them laughed until they fell into each other's arms and for a short time, things seemed so good.

But within weeks, a tragic event was to alter their way of life for better or worse, it was difficult to say. On Tuesday 16th February 1909, a muffled explosion rocked the little mining village and about a minute later there was a second explosion with flames shooting into the sky. The West Stanley mine had exploded. Panic followed and people headed towards the pit head where, in no time, thousands were gathered at the stricken colliery.

"What the bloody hell's happened here?"

The anxious voice was almost trembling as Mr Fairhurst, the manager of one of the other local collieries, arrived on the horrific scene. Stephens, the colliery engineer was closest to the explosion and looked down the north shaft, where there was a red glow.

"Not sure yet but colliery manager's not around. That's why you were called out. But I'll tell you this; it's not good and no mistake!" his voice was thick with emotion as he imagined the devastation.

"Hell fire." As they stood back a ball of flames leapt into the sky then the smoke was sucked back down into the pit. The explosion killed almost 200 in the three seams: some of them little more than children.

The explosion in the Brockwell seam where Edwin Ramsey was working left Etta and Dossie fatherless and their mother a widow. This was the biggest mining disaster in British history and many thousands of mourners and onlookers filled the town to bursting point. The funerals were headed by banners from the Durham Miners Association and the West Stanley Colliery. Hordes of bereaved, grieving women and children, family and friends crowded every road until a river of misery flooded the streets. The mass graves were in the form of long trenches and several widows, overcome with grief, fell trance-like into them. Others let out haunting wails that echoed through the village.

"Come away, hinnie, don't step too near."

The voice was female and seemed to come from nowhere but the tone held a certain authority and three or four women did exactly what the voice demanded. Minnie Ramsey simply watched, frozen faced, with Etta by her side as The Durham Light Infantry fired a volley of shots at the last funeral. As they played the Last Post, she finally broke down, grieving for all of those young men who'd been taken.

"What a wicked shame," she sobbed. "Bairns with no fathers, women without menfolk. What's to become of us all?

A very tall handsome woman, dressed in a flamboyant black hat pushed her way to the front of the crowd, dragging two young boys behind her. One of the boys was quite big for his age and looked the image of his father. The other was older and slightly taller still with same dark looks, but his cheeks were swollen, and he looked sickly. The mother looked down her long sharp nose at Minnie.

"Are those tears for your man, for Edwin?" the words hissed aggressively from the red stained lips." It's my bairns that'll suffer; you want to cry for them."

"What?"

Minnie stretched herself to her full five feet, barely reaching the other woman's shoulder and stared up into the cold grey eyes.

"You, you whore, think I didn't know about you and your little bastards!" Minnie's voice was full of venom and Etta looked on in disbelief. Such ugly words and from her sweet Mam!

Everyone in the village knew about the Barker woman and Edwin Ramsey but it was never spoken of in front of Minnie. Instead, folks looked on with weak sympathetic smiles when they saw her. But she knew and had done for an awfully long time; from the time their first child was born a girl and the look of disappointment showed in Edwin's dark brooding eyes. He spent his nights away from the home and Minnie would catch the smell of cheap scent on his best collars. She knew what he wanted and even though the love had gone out of their marriage she tried for another baby, hoping that it would be a boy this time. It took a long while before Etta came along;

another girl and soon after her husband changed completely towards her, blaming her, spurning her, and the sparkle went out of her pretty face and she became old and tired before her time.

Mrs Barker only smiled at the insult, "I gave him what he wanted, what you couldn't!"

Hot angry tears began to blind Minnie and she was about to pounce on the hussy when...

"Hey what's going on here?" A pretty young woman grabbed Minnie by the arm. "Mam, I've been looking for you for ages. You'd left by the time I got home."

The girl turned towards Mrs Barker, "Who's that then, who is she, Mam?"

Minnie was relieved to hear the familiar voice as the tall woman stepped back towards the crowd with her boys in tow. Beaming at her daughter, she carefully tucked the stray strands of hair back into the bun at her neck. Pulling her close, Minnie kissed her eldest softly on the cheek and then shook her head, ashamed of her behaviour towards the Barker woman. "Don't ask, pet. She's nobody!"

Dossie was nearly sixteen and already in service in the big house at Cranfield Hall on the Newcastle Road, she'd come home for the funeral and to help her mother and sister in whatever way she could. But as a housemaid, she only earned £12 a year, so there wasn't a lot to spare. Fortunately, all the miners were members of the Northumberland and Durham Permanent Relief Fund, which meant that the widows received five shillings per week and two shillings for each dependent child. At least for the time being, Annetta and her mother could eat.

"What's the matter, Ma?" Dossie was concerned to see her mother so angry. She had never seen such hatred in her face before. "Who is she, what's she said to upset you?"

"Forget it, Dossie, it's not worth bothering about. It's all forgotten."

"No, just tell me, Mam. What's it all about?"

Dossie knew it wasn't all forgotten. She glanced behind her at the woman who had turned to stare at Minnie. Her eyes were narrowed, and her face was set in an ugly snarl that was intended to threaten and intimidate.

Dossie certainly wasn't a big woman but she wasn't going to stand there and allow her mother to be treated in such a hostile way, so she marched up to Mrs Barker, who was a good head and shoulders above her.

"I don't know what you think you're doing but my Ma hasn't done anything to you, so leave us alone and bugger off and take your brats with you!"

The tall woman huffed and snorted in such a derisive way that Minnie pulled her eldest daughter away before anything more could be said.

"Leave it, sweetheart, she's a bad lot that one. We don't want anything to do with her or her offspring."

Once more dragging her daughter by the arm, she almost ran down the street, with Etta, a bewildered and frightened little girl weeping hysterically behind them. Struggling and spluttering, the younger girl kept looking back at the tall woman with the two boys at her side. One of them must have been about her own age and one a bit older, both with very dark eyes and hair. They appeared as mystified by the dreadful scene as she was but neither of them cried or looked upset, both remaining stony faced as they clung to their mother's skirts. Once they were safely settled in their own little home, Dossie tried to quiz her Mam for more information about the unpleasant incident she had just witnessed. But secrets were buried only to be uncovered much, much later. The next few years were hard, even with Dossie's help. Minnie's hands grew gnarled and rough, covered with red weeping burns as every day she scrubbed at washing with carbolic and then heated up the iron on the range to smooth away the creases in white cotton shirts and sheets. A strange smell seemed to permeate the house, sometimes pleasant and warm and then raw and sickly sweet. Taking in washing helped stretch out the meagre relief money and there were sometimes a few pennies left to buy Etta's pencils. She escaped with her princesses every night, her drawings becoming increasingly precise and creative. They helped her to block out the pain that she didn't really understand. Her mother never spoke about what had happened that day at the funeral, even though she asked and asked until eventually she stopped thinking about the woman's cruel words.

Chapter 5

Six years flashed past, by which time Minnie Ramsey was working at Picktree Lane Garage in Chester-le-Street. There were quite a few automobiles about by then, and they needed petrol and parts, so the garage had sprung up to meet the needs of a new and modern age. The men were all at war so it meant that women could take on men's jobs without any stigma attached. It was a godsend for her and Etta as the job paid good money, meaning that life was at last a little better for the two of them. Etta by now was nearly sixteen and had found a job of work in Dawson's Confectioners shop and Café on the corner of Front Street and Middle Lane and would often meet her mother after work with a bag of Black Bullets. The women always enjoyed a bag of sweets together, sucking endlessly on the little chunks of sugar on the omnibus home at night, resisting the urge to crunch them. Their cheeks swollen with the sweet confection, they would attempt to tell each other about their day and then collapse into fits of giggles.

"How was the shop today, Etta?" Minnie would ask. "How was Mr Dawson, is he well?"

The conversation always went the same way. "Busy as always, run off my feet today I was." Still sucking on the sugary sweetie, which stained her tongue a hideous purple, Etta's words were almost incoherent.

"And how was Mr Dawson?" Minnie would repeat the question again, trying to sound politely uninterested.

"Oh, he's just the same, you know how he is, doesn't say much really."

Every time she wished to hear more and more about Jack Dawson and what he said, hoping that he might give away some clue as to his feelings for her but each night her face expressed the disappointment at her daughter's response. All this time Etta remained completely oblivious to her mother's interest in the shopkeeper and both women smiled as they waited for the omnibus. By the time they reached home, the sweets were eaten and both women exhausted and ready for bed. They had endured the horrors of the war years together and thanked God for their lives and for their few blessings. They were both fit and healthy, had a roof over their heads and food on the table. It was more than some poor souls, they reminded each other.

The next few years saw Etta grow into a beautiful young woman and her princesses transformed into baby girls and boys as infants with cherub faces and wonderfully chubby toes and fingers emerged from the pages of her drawing pad. She watched as friends and neighbours went courting with boys who had come back from the battlefields in Northern France. Some of them were so scarred, both physically and emotionally, that it was impossible not to feel a strong longing to take away their pain in whatever way a young girl could. Etta was no exception as her hormones kicked in and let loose the inner yearning that began to consume her. She was her father's daughter in that respect and even at her tender age she had thoughts that would make her sister blush. Girls she knew became pregnant and were shunned by their families, finally disappearing from villages all over the north east. Annie Hogarth was one such girl, a good friend and work mate. Every day they worked together behind the counter and the sweetie jars at Dawson's, chatting girlishly in between customers until one day, Annie whispered into Etta's ear, "We did it last night, me and Seth, we did it, you know, did it!" Etta wasn't sure at first what she meant but after looking long and hard at the ever-reddening face and the smirking pink lips, it dawned on her what 'it' was. Annie was an innocent and it was her first time, but she didn't intend to let Etta know. As far as she was concerned Annie was a woman of the world.

"You didn't! You mean... What was it like, did it hurt?"

"It did a bit," then suddenly realising what she had said, she bustled towards her workmate and sniffed, "No, it doesn't after the first time."

"What if somebody finds out, Annie?" There was a sense of shame in what she said but the other girl only smirked.

"I don't care one jot!" boasted the girl and filled with pride, she grabbed her friend's hands and spun her round until they were both quite dizzy.

Recovering from the spinning sensation that nearly caused her to lose her balance, Annetta had a sudden thought that made her panic so much she grabbed hold of Annie and stared hard into her brazen brown eyes.

"You might be expecting, haven't you thought of that?"

"Oh Etta, I love him, I really, really do. He told me not to worry about things like that; said he'd make sure... well you know what I mean?

Etta didn't know what she meant at all. Her face was vacant as she continued to stare in complete bemusement.

"We're going to get married anyway and married women know how not to get caught."

She giggled and clutched her tight little stomach as she doubled over in a fit of nervous laughter, remembering the experience the night before. Not really believing what she said, Etta's mind was buzzing. There were so many things she didn't understand. She was more of an innocent than Annie had ever been, but she was intrigued, and a sexual awakening prompted her to discover more of what went on.

"What do they do then, married women I mean, how, what happens?" Etta probed even harder, both anxious and curious at the same time.

"Well!" Attempting to look more grown up, Annie stood up straight, throwing back her shoulders and stretching to her full height. But not really knowing what married women did she simply pursed her lips, eyes twinkling and nodded in a knowing way and then giggled again.

"Go on!" Etta urged the girl on, fascinated to hear all the smutty details.

"Well, I don't know everything. I'm not married, not yet anyway!" she bristled and realising she was losing her new disciple, she returned to the titillating details that had enthralled Etta so much.

"Oh, it was lovely last night, I'll never forget it," sensing the interest returning, she went on with obvious delight. "We kissed just like film stars and well, things just happened, you know what I mean!"

"What things? What happened?" Suddenly conscious of the butterflies crashing together in her belly, she could hardly wait for what came next. Encouraging Annie to reveal more, her eyes widened as the sordid little story unfurled with no real regard to authenticity. It had only been a dirty drunken fumble in the alley outside the local dance hall in the town on Saturday night after Seth Austen had rolled out of The Black Horse. Of course, he told her he loved her!

"He told me he loved me!" She smiled coyly and continued, "And then he pulled up me petticoats with his strong manly hands until his fingers slid up between my legs and then…"

Etta's eyes widened and her jaw dropped until a voice made her jump.

"Girls," shouted Mr Dawson, "back to work this minute!"

Etta felt hot and the strange feeling fluttered again low down in her stomach. Her bodice began to stretch across her chest and the high starched collar bit into her neck as she struggled to breathe in the tightly laced corset that Mam had made her wear. She had never really thought of Seth Austen as strong or manly, not even his hands. In fact, he was a bit of a daft youth she thought, although any man doing that to her made her feel quite giddy.

She couldn't wait to finish the day and hear the rest of Annie's story. A feeling of guilt washed over her, and she wondered what her mother would think if she could hear them talk about such smutty things, but she felt excited, and her breathing quickened as she grabbed her friend's arm and snuggled close to hear what happened next. As the story unfolded with images of popped trouser buttons and dangling braces, Etta almost laughed out loud but then thoughts of the young man who came into the shop every day to buy a couple of ounces of violet creams crept into her head, forcing her to bite her lip. His long sensitive fingers always touched hers as his pennies dropped into her hand. A tingle shot down her spine as she imagined him buying the delicious confectionary for her, instead of for his special girl. Little did she know that the chocolates were for his mother, whose apron strings bound the young man extremely tightly.

"I like the boy who buys the violet creams," she blurted out. "You know, the one with the lovely smile."

Annie recalled him very well, "He's a bit wet - a mammy's boy. There's no doubt about that! You wouldn't do it with him, would you Etta?" The words almost spat out of her curled lip and she couldn't stop the look of disgust from spreading across her face.

After listening to the things Annie had talked about

today, part of her wanted to be close to any boy, or to a man. Suddenly a new feeling swept over her, a feeling that had nothing to do with love or romance. Losing interest in the silly boy with the violet creams in an instant, her thoughts turned to the men she knew. There was no doubt that she was beginning to be noticed by many of the male customers who came into the shop, and she was just discovering how she could become even more attractive to them. Annie Hogarth had unwittingly been instrumental in Etta's education. A desire to possess, to taunt, to tease, germinated inside the young woman and it didn't matter who it was, any one of the many admirers would do. It was the power she desired; to be coveted and craved for by a man. Mr Dawson was old, older than her mam probably, but there was something about him that made her tingle when he spoke to her. Maybe it was the distinguished silver strands that glistened amongst the dark hair and those eyes that seemed hard and shiny, like the Black Bullets she sucked on her way home at night that made her so excited.

"What do you think of Mr Dawson, Annie?

Annie laughed like a fishwife, making her chubby cheeks flame up and her brown eyes water until tears trickled down her face.

"He's an old man; you can't really like him, can you?"

She didn't know who or what she liked but she was a woman now and she had feelings. New emotions were beginning to have a funny effect on her, making every part of her feel strange and at the same time very pleasant. But Etta had grown into a strong young woman, hardened by a bully of a father and years of poverty and she vowed never to allow any man to dominate her. If she were to succumb to such temptations, it would be on her terms, and she would be the one pulling the strings. A long time ago, she finally understood the truth about what had happened between him - she couldn't bring herself to call him Father - and that woman and she promised herself that she would never fall in love like her poor Mam did; never ever! But sex was different.

"Yes, I think I do like him, but I don't love him. I love no-one 'cept Mam and our Dossie and never will! She was adamant and to prove it, added, "And I think you're stupid to think yourself in love with that Seth Austen. He's just a big fool."

The wind had been taken out of Annie's sails and Etta's words hurt and angered her. "Well you're just jealous. I've got my man and you'll end up an old maid, an ugly old maid, you will, Etta Ramsey!"

Annie flounced off into the back room as Etta shouted after her, "Mr Dawson likes me, might even want to marry me, what do you think of that then, Annie Hogarth?"

The friendship between the girls was never the same again after that and the atmosphere in the shop became strained and difficult. It was true Mr Dawson was always very friendly with Etta and especially so when Minnie came in after early shifts at work to see her bairn and walk her home. He certainly seemed to take her side if any disagreements cropped up in the shop and it wasn't long before Annie was sent packing. In her naivety, Etta had failed to notice the swelling belly and the sickly pallor on the other girl's face and proudly assumed her dismissal was down to Mr Dawson's loyalty to her. That was the last she ever saw of Annie Hogarth. As the weeks went by Etta's fantasy had grown to hero worship and her employer became a lover as well as a father figure in her fevered imagination. She began to sidle up to him at every opportunity and hoped he would notice the scent she had bought at Woolworths, the one in the pretty blue bottle that she kept in the top drawer with her best silk chemise.

One afternoon just before early closing, she took her chance as they both stacked boxes of treacle toffee in the stockroom. Pretending to stumble, Etta fell into Mr Dawson's arms and attempted a kiss. His bristly greying moustache scratched roughly against her cheek as he pulled away and grabbed her arms.

"No you don't, lass. You can't go round kissing folk like that!"

"Why not?" She stared into his eyes and made towards him again.

"What the blazes are you thinking, girl, what on earth are you about?"

Blustering, he pushed her away and dashed into the public area of the shop. Etta followed, deflated and embarrassed, tears welling up forcing her to quickly pull out a prettily embroidered handkerchief from her apron pocket. As she dabbed gently at her eyes, her body began to shake, and then real sobs totally consumed her. Mr Dawson was taken aback; not knowing how to deal with such a situation, he vigorously patted her back as though trying to bring up a swallowed boiled sweet. However, the more the tears flowed, the more he softened and as Etta threw herself into his arms, he cradled her as though she was a crying baby.

"There, there, Etta. It's all forgotten," his soothing voice was soft and gentle, leaving the young girl feeling safe and warm.

They were both visible through the clear glass pane in the shop door and were oblivious to the face that stared in on the cosy scene. The bell rang loudly as Minnie bustled in and Mr Dawson suddenly but gently pushed Etta away.

"So!" murmured Minnie "It's Edwin Ramsey all over again and this time with my own lassie!" Her voice was shaky and noticeably quiet as though she was surprised that she had spoken the words aloud. The man she had grown to love and whom she believed had returned that love had betrayed her. Their relationship had blossomed over the time they had known each other, and her heart was broken to realise that he wasn't the man she thought him to be.

"How could you do such a thing?" Wrestling to get the words out between sobs, Minnie smeared the tears across her cheeks. "I thought you were different; I thought you were a respectable man, Jack Dawson, but you're no better than Edwin Ramsey!"

"Listen."

"Don't bother."

"Minnie, pet, listen," Jack Dawson struggled to explain. How could he tell her what had happened? He approached the woman he had grown to admire but she rushed off into the twilight and was gone.

Turning to Etta, his face ruddy and contorted with pain and anger, he took her shoulders and shook her until she fell to the floor in a crumpled heap.

"I was wrong."

"Yes, you were bloody wrong; too true and look what you've done now."

"But I thought…"

"You didn't think, you stupid child? Me and your Mam, we're to be wed." He paused and lowered his head, stroking the back of his neck with his big hands, "Were to be wed, before you ruined everything!"

The man, broken and near to tears himself, sat down on the bentwood chair reserved for customers in front of the highly polished counter. A silence encompassed the two of them as they remained motionless in the fading light. Dumbstruck, Etta eventually struggled to her feet. She had no idea that her mother was in love with the shopkeeper, not even when the colour had returned to her Mam's cheeks and strands of gold sparkled in her slightly greying hair. She had not once spoken of her feelings and certainly marriage had never been mentioned. Left with her thoughts, Etta began to recall the many times in the shop when her mother had called in. Now she remembered how flushed and pretty her mam had looked, how attentive the shopkeeper had been. The bags of strawberry creams that were so often offered over the counter, the boxes of Turkish Delight given to Etta to take home to share, it all began to make sense!

"I'm so sorry, I know I'm a silly fool." She put her hands to her wet face and wiped away the tears until her cheeks were red and streaked with the rouge she had powdered on so heavily that morning.

"Yes, a proper little fool."

"Sorry."

"Sorry won't put things right, you've ruined everything."

"But I never guessed. I'll talk to Mam; tell her... it was all me. It'll be alright, I promise."

Chapter 6

That night, the two women sat in front of a roaring fire and the whole story spilled out alongside tears, apologies and laughter. The daughter realising that what she thought she felt for Mr Dawson was fleeting and childish, was now overjoyed for her mother. However, it was harder for Minnie to realise that her darling Etta was a grown woman with those sorts of feelings. In her mind, she was still her little girl; a fragile child who had been hurt so much that she dare not share her happiness in case it all went wrong again. How could she speak of her love for the man who Etta knew as Mr Dawson, the confectioner, the sweet shopkeeper? Minnie found it hard to understand what had been going on in her daughter's mind to make her be so foolish as to imagine that he could love a child like her when all the while his true feelings were deepening. His affection for Minnie had strengthened with every day but for a long time he had kept it a secret and so had she.

But now it was time to share everything - secrets, dreams and a new life together with Mr Jack Dawson. She would speak to him tomorrow and put things right. After all, it was her own fault, she should have told the girls sooner, but she didn't know how they would react to her getting wed again. Jack finally saw the funny side of it as Minnie relayed her jealousy at thinking he was interested in young Etta and they both chuckled at the absurdity of it. She was nothing but a child. Once a date for the wedding was decided upon, Jack insisted that the girls be the first to know. Minnie had asked her elder daughter to come for tea on Sunday so she could tell her the news that she was getting married and both she and Etta waited impatiently for her to arrive from Cranfield. The table was set with the best china, the set with the gold rim, and her Victoria sponge cake took pride of place. Hoping that Dossie would be happy to welcome Jack into the family, Minnie asked Etta if she knew whether her sister liked Mr Dawson.

"Oh, I think so Mam, but look, she's here now, you can ask her yourself."

"Oh, Mother, I think it's just grand. He's a good man and…"

Dossie hesitated to mention it but after a pause, carried on with a hint of pride in her voice, "Well he's got a bob or two, hasn't he? You won't go short and it'll be one in the eye for them old crones that we lived aside of, wont it?"

Etta listened, suppressing a giggle.

"You're right, we won't go short. Not of sweeties, anyway!"

"Give over, you two, you're both a disgrace," Minnie retorted, but her face was lit up with a warm smile that told the girls how happy she was.

"And our Doreen, I've told you before to watch how you speak now that you're working up at the posh place. Talk proper and like a lady and you'll go far."

"What about me, Ma? Do I talk proper? Will I go far?" Etta already had a pleasant, refined tone to her voice and always tried extremely hard to find the right words like some of those classy young ladies who sometimes came into the shop. She intended to go far, there was no doubt about that, and she knew she could learn to speak like a real lady. She would need to if she were to go to London. But Minnie was no longer listening to either of the girls' idle chatter. Her thoughts were elsewhere.

At last, the day of the wedding arrived as bunches of flowers, bundles of ribbons and heaps of love filled the house. Minnie Ramsey was to become Mrs Dawson, a woman with a future, with a man so unlike Edwin Ramsey that she felt dizzy and dreamy. She scrutinised herself in the looking-glass that stood on top of the cast iron washstand in the room she had once shared with the brute of a man she had married as a young girl. Tilting her head in disbelief at the reflection, she saw a radiant, golden-haired woman looking back from the mirror. Elegant in her coffee-coloured taffeta and ostrich feathers, she carefully adjusted the wide-brimmed brown hat so that plump pink roses perfectly framed the serenity of her face.

"You look beautiful, Mam." A vision of loveliness in pastel pink muslin hugged her mother and gently placed a kiss on her cheek. Fragrant yellow flowers mingled with the fairness of her hair that had been precisely dressed into a mass of curls at the back of her head.

"You do, Mam, really lovely," echoed the older sister, picking up the cloche hat that she had bought new for the occasion.

Dossie pulled the red felt down until it almost covered her eyes. Her long brown lashes almost touched the brim and her brow was hidden by the fashionable headwear. Curls of chestnut hair escaped from under the hat, complementing her plump pink cheeks. She was a pretty enough woman with a buxom figure, but at twenty-two, there was still no sign of romance in her life. Too busy for that sort of thing, she had concentrated on her duties at the hall and had risen from housemaid to lady's maid in her years in service. Her days were filled with the pleasant task of attending Lady Addington, which meant that she was surrounded by the most stunning gowns and precious jewellery. Sometimes her ladyship would give her a trinket or two to reward her dedication and hard work. As she fingered the little gold locket, studded with a tiny diamond, that circled her throat, she remembered how she had admired it every time she put away her ladyship's jewellery. It was a small inexpensive piece and her mistress had long ago tired of it but Dossie treasured the necklace, only wearing it on special occasions. Today was indeed a special occasion - her mother's wedding day - and without thinking, Dossie unclipped the clasp on the locket, letting it trickle into Minnie's hand in a pool of gold.

"Here, Mam, I want you to wear this, to have it for your own. You deserve it - you deserve all of this!" and she waved her hands in the air as if scooping up the peonies and the daisies that filled the room.

"I know he'll make you happy, Mam - he's a good man and he'll give you and our Etta a good life!"

Minnie, now extremely near to tears, turned her back to her elder child and felt the cool golden chain settle against her neck as she fastened the clasp securely.

"My sweet girl, thank you. I'll wear it today, but you must have it back - it's too precious and it's yours, my love. I can't keep it." Tears filled her eyes. "It'll be my something borrowed, Doreen, I already have something blue and my beautiful outfit is brand new."

Dossie smiled at hearing her Sunday name, no-one ever called her Doreen anymore, but it felt right that her mother should use her birth name, today of all days. Remembering the old rhyme, she imagined her mother wearing a saucy blue garter and giggled.

"Something borrowed? We'll see!" Dossie smiled before picking up a small bouquet of sweet peas and rosebuds and sniffing in the heady scent of the summer flowers. She carefully threw the pretty bouquet to her sister who caught it as she noticed the horse and buggy pull up outside.

"Mam, it's time to go now, the carriage is here and...

You'll never believe it, our Dossie, but the horse is wearing a bonnet with flowers in it!" Etta jumped up and down on the spot, sending her curls in all directions until they settled like rolls of spun gold against her head. "Look, Mam, its ears are poking through the straw bonnet!"

All three women collapsed into fits of laughter and Minnie quickly grabbed her own posh hat before it fell over her eyes.

"Now look what you've done," she gently scolded her girls before adjusting it so that she looked perfect again.

The three of them squeezed through the front door, arms locked together with smiles on their faces that came from a deep love of one another. The street was full of well-wishers and gawkers as Minnie was helped into the carriage by Etta and Dossie. She looked a picture of elegance in the expensive outfit that Jack had bought from one of the big shops in Newcastle and a whisper spread amongst the women who had all come out into the road to join in the spectacle. It was unusual to see such finery in this little pit village and jealousy meant that not everyone shared in the family's happiness.

"Fallen on her feet, that one has!" the old woman from the end house tutted, as she wiped her hands on the dirty pinny that covered her worn black dress.

"She's no better than she ought to be!" agreed several other hard-faced matrons with tight lips and sharp eyes.

"God bless you, Minnie," came a friendly voice from the other side of the street. "You look a picture pet, a picture!"

"Are we all set, Ma'am? Asked the young lad who sat in front, holding the reins. Without waiting for an answer, he turned to Etta and shot her the most seductive smile before adding, "And Miss Ramsey, are you warm enough in that flimsy frock?"

Dossie bristled before replying for them both, "Both Misses Ramsey are just fine, thank you very much young man, and don't be so impudent!"

Etta giggled coquettishly until both mother and sister gave her such a disapproving look that she bit her bottom lip to stop herself from disgracing herself any further. And with that, the little family group set off on the short journey to St Thomas's Church at the top of the hill. She a widow and Jack a widower meant that the Reverend Batty was only too happy to join them in holy matrimony. They arrived at the church to catch a glimpse of Jack and his brother Daniel, who was stubbing out a cigarette between his fingers outside the big oak door leading into the nave. The sound of the horse's hooves startled him and both men quickly dashed back into the church.

"She's early, isn't she?" Dan had been about to light up again when they had spotted the bride, sending him scuttling through the huge oak doors and now, he really felt in need of a smoke to calm his nerves. He fiddled nervously with his collar stud and then loosened his tie. It was too tight, and he really wasn't used to wearing a collar and necktie anyway.

Jack, on the other hand, appeared perfectly calm and he stood at the front of the church in total silence as he waited for the woman he had grown to love. The carriage pulled up outside St Thomas's and Minnie and the girls were helped down by the young driver, whose eyes were drawn to the vision in pink. Etta felt his eyes burning into her as he guided her onto the path, his hands lingering on hers for a much longer time than on Minnie's lace-clad fingers or even on Dossie's soft skin. As his strong hands curled round the older girl's to help her down from the carriage, she smiled and her eyes flashed with an energy that sent sparks flying. He couldn't ignore the signal and returned the smile, even though his thoughts were firmly on the younger sister. Aware of the effect she was having on the young man, Etta flashed him an entrancing, almost seductive smile as she turned her back on him and floated like one of her wallpaper fairies into the church behind her mother. It seemed like a lifetime ago since she had brought her princesses and fairies to life with her beautiful drawings. Maybe she would start drawing again now that they were all settled, even start painting. She knew she had a talent. At school, all the girls used to crowd round to watch wonderful images appear as if by magic on the paper in her exercise books and her pictures were prized by scholars and teachers alike, but as she had grown older, she dismissed her talent as childish and of no use in the real world.

Putting such notions aside, she followed her mother, who was holding on tightly to Dossie's arm, down the aisle. She stared affectionately at the face of her new stepfather, who had turned to take in the lovely vision that was his handsome new bride. He was a kind man and Etta knew he would someday give her some special responsibility in the shop, even make her manageress but was this what she really wanted; to work in a sweet shop for the rest of her life? She was sure of one thing, she would be like her sister, and she would never marry. No man would ever possess her, not even someone as kind as Jack.

An image of the gallant young driver, who was even now waiting outside for the wedding party, popped playfully into her mind. He was muscular and tanned with the summer sun and outdoor work and she felt a stirring in her loins. It was true she told herself, she never wanted marriage, never wanted to fall in love but sex was different. Etta was a very modern 1920's girl and she knew her appetite for life would one day make her break with convention. She could go to art school and there she would meet some dark and brooding bohemian, who would... All sorts of fantasies crept into her brain, transporting her to another world, making her head spin and her mind leap with the sheer excitement of what could happen one day. But then, just as quickly, a sense of pessimism descended as her dreams were brought back to the reality of her humdrum life.

"I do." Her mother's quaking voice broke into her steamy thoughts and suddenly Etta stood to attention and immediately smoothed down her dress, guiltily wiping the sweat from her palms as she did so.

"I now pronounce you man and wife." The vicar's words were very loud and clear, and preceded a loving kiss between the two of them.

Dossie and Etta instinctively put their gloved hands together and clapped and then everyone in the small congregation joined in with the applause. Minnie's face flushed with a mixture of happiness and embarrassment as she whispered into her new husband's ear, "Can you believe it pet? I'm Mrs Dawson, a respectable married woman!"

Jack laughed nervously and shifted uneasily in his new leather boots, each step announced by a loud squeak, which made him laugh even more. Minnie beamed at her man with a huge sense of pride and fondness that had flourished over the past year of knowing him.

As the newly married couple were bustled out of the church amongst a host of brothers and sisters, cousins and friends, the two daughters remained apart from the crowd at the front of the nave.

"Well, our Etta," sighed Dossie, "this is it, a new life for you both and a good 'un, I'll bet."

"What do you mean?"

"Well, Mr Dawson will take care of you both, he's not

without. You should be comfortable enough."

Irritably, Etta glared at her sister, "I don't want to be taken care of. I want my own life!"

The older girl was taken aback by such an angry and unexpected response and she bent her head while taking in a gasp of air. Sometimes, she just couldn't fathom out what went on in her sister's pretty little head. She was obviously in one of her moods again and it was best to leave her to work out for herself whatever was bothering her. Her frame of mind had been strange for most of the day, swinging from almost childish excitement to dark melancholy. There was one thing she knew for sure; that handsome boy who drove them today had turned her head. Shaking herself free of her irritation Etta blushed appealingly as she beamed at her sister.

"I'm sorry Dossie, didn't mean to speak harshly but I want to be like you, you are your own woman, no man to take care of you, to tell you what to do!"

Dossie snorted at her sister's words. "My own woman, I'm not my own woman, you silly lass. I dance to her ladyship's tune and as for a man to take care of me, well, if one asked me tomorrow, I'd say yes and you can be sure of that."

Etta's eyes widened in disbelief as the words hit her like a bolt from the blue. Dossie, reading her sister's face, carried on with more than a touch of melancholy in her voice.

"No man has ever asked me and I'm not beautiful like you so... I'll remain an old maid for the rest of my days. I'm a spinster in service Etta; you really don't want to be like me!"

The words cut into the younger woman's heart like a knife and she turned, running to join the throng of folk all congratulating and cheering on the contented twosome, whose high spirits radiated happiness and joy. Etta, trying desperately to blank out Dossie's words, sniffed loudly and then hugged her mother, salty tears beginning to well up in her beautiful eyes. Jack was touched at the obvious display of emotion and patted his stepdaughter gently on the arm. As he did so, she turned and embraced the man, producing a sense of well-being within him that made the day even more memorable than ever.

"You're my bairn now, lass, as well as your Mam's," he whispered, making Etta's face flush so that her cheeks were as pink as the roses she carried.

"But I'm not, Mr Dawson."

He looked aghast at her response until she added, "I mean, I'm not a child anymore, I'm older than Mam when she married Da. I'm a woman, Mr Dawson!"

He smiled knowingly, remembering the incident in the stock room that day, which now seemed so long ago. "I know you are, pet, and now do you think you could call me Jack instead of Mr Dawson?"

She laughingly took his hand.

"I think so or do you want me to call you Daddy?"

It was his turn to laugh now as he pulled her along by the hand towards Dossie and Minnie, who were waiting by the flower-strewn carriage.

"Come on, you two" squealed Minnie, like an excited slip of a lass. "They're expecting us at The Black Bull; we have a delicious wedding cake to cut!"

Jack spun his new wife around to face him, holding her in his arms, both quite oblivious of the others around them. Pulling her to one side out of sight of the girls, he pressed his lips to hers and breathed in the sweet perfume from her neck. A heady mix of his favourite aromatic tobacco and a slight smell of the pomade he had used to sleek down his hair filled her nostrils in return. It was a while before he released her, by which time she was giddy with the excitement of his embrace and the exhilaration of the whole enchanted day. Etta was the first of the wedding party to reach the carriage and Ernie the young trap driver caught her eye as she stepped up into the carriage. Flashing her a wide smile that lit up his handsome face, he watched as Dossie joined her sister on the black leather seat facing the horse. The animal was still wearing the straw hat and Ernie nodded his head cheekily towards the flower-strewn bonnet. Pulling a face, he tore it from the horse's ears and plonked it on his own head, sending Etta into hysterics. Dossie tutted as her mother approached with Jack and Ernest swiftly resumed his previous proper demeanour and was a picture of decorum by the time the happy couple joined the girls. Etta's eyes were still full of fun and as she stared at the back of the auburn head of the young driver, she correctly predicted the same cheeky glint that gleamed in his.

A dozen or more guests were already enjoying the occasion, knocking back the pints of ale and the tiny glasses of sherry wine that Jack had paid Bob Armstrong to provide in the upstairs room at the pub where he was landlord. A wedding tea of boiled ham and pease pudding was laid out on the trestle tables that had been set up with crisp white tablecloths and in the corner, atop a little card table in pride of place, was the three-tiered cake that Minnie had proudly baked herself. It had been delicately decorated with royal icing and piped with miniature rosebuds and swirls by the lady who provided the cakes for Jack's little tea-room. Cheers and whistles heralded their arrival and Jack and Minnie almost ran into the room, taking up their position at the head of the top table. Dossie sat down on the chair that Dan had kindly pulled out for her next to his. He theatrically produced a silver cigarette case and offered her one before taking one for himself.

"No, thank you kindly, Mr Dawson," she refused and after sensing a disapproving glare from his brother Jack, Dan pushed the little tube of tobacco behind his ear for later.

The place next to Minnie was empty and she was busy looking round for her younger daughter, who was nowhere to be seen.

"Jack," she said, "where's our Etta?"

Etta was still outside with the attractive boy who had driven the carriage. All the way to the pub, he had been aware of her sitting prettily behind him and he preened like a peacock, sleeking back the thick red hair and holding himself straight and tall with the reins held strongly in his tanned hands. It was impossible for Etta to ignore the animal magnetism of this young male and she felt weak at the knees, experiencing the familiar stirring low in her belly. She knew he would take her hand and hold it for longer than he needed as she stepped down from the carriage when they arrived at their destination. She knew, too, that she would hold his gaze with her sensuous eyes, half closed and fringed with thick dark brown lashes, until she set him ablaze with desire for her. And then she would leave him, turn her back and smile knowingly as she stepped out with her dress swaying provocatively so that glimpses of her well-turned ankles were seductively visible.

Minnie stood up, looked anxiously at Dossie and raised her eyebrows, "Where's your sister?"

At that moment, Etta was in full embrace with the fetching stranger she had met today for the first time. As he furtively looked up and down the empty street in front of The Black Bull, Etta giggled and pulled him into her, feeling his manliness, blatantly oblivious to the fact that they were in full public view. She knew that she had aroused him and as his hands were just about to gently fondle her sweet young breasts, she pulled away and ran up the stairs to the room above the pub with a satisfying sense of achievement.

"Where have you been? We've all been worried sick."

Etta smiled knowingly without uttering a single word.

"I thought you were behind us. Where were you? What have you been doing?" The words tumbled from her mam's mouth as Dan shushed them all into silence and they reluctantly settled into their places.

Minnie reluctantly ended the conversation, but her eyes burned into her younger daughter's back as she turned away to face her new uncle.

"Time for me to say a few words about me brother and his new lass." He fiddled with the cigarette behind his ear and went on nervously with his speech.

All the while he was speaking, Minnie was staring at Etta's flushed face. She began to worry about her second child, but she didn't really know why. Dossie, too, wondered about her sister but she guessed where she had been. She may be a spinster, but she had been only too aware of the electricity between Etta and Ernest Lowes. She knew him well, although he hadn't recognised her at all. He regularly collected her from the hall to take her into town on her Sundays off and brought her back; in fact, she looked forward to his company and made a special effort with her chestnut hair when she knew he would be in charge of the pony and trap. Ernie always had a smile for her and a cheeky wink, but he didn't even acknowledge her today. His twinkling eyes had been captivated by her sister and her alone. More than a touch of the green-eyed monster overcame Dossie as she flashed a disapproving look in Etta's direction just as Daniel Dawson raised his glass of ale to toast the bride and groom.

"Here's to Minnie and Jack, long may they reign!"

Raucous cheering and clinking of glasses followed as the whole room filled with good wishes for Mr and Mrs Dawson.

The noise flooded out into the street, startling the horse and breaking the silence in the street. Still waiting and becoming more frustrated by the minute, Ernie sat on the pavement looking up at his grey mare.

"She's a proper little teaser that one, Nellie, but I tell you, lass, I'll have her; I will, and by God, she'll cry out for more!"

As they prepared to leave for their new home in the rooms above the shop, Minnie and Etta gathered up the flowers and the remnants of the fruit cake, the daughter nibbling on the icing swirls that fell into her hand.

"How are we getting back, Mam? Is the carriage still outside?"

She was really wondering whether Ernie would still be outside. Of course, she knew he would be waiting with his firm lean limbs still fired up from the closeness of her soft rounded bosom and the heady scent of her sex. She felt a strong surge of lust that made her body quiver and her brilliant blue eyes widen in anticipation.

Chapter 7

Lucinda sat in her room, pondering over her work. Lectures had gone on somehow and she found her mind wandering from the Renaissance masters, thinking ever more about the young man she had met on the train. It was her first term at college and she was settling in well, enjoying learning about the history of art and beginning to recognise the various styles of the great masters of the past. But sometimes, like today, she couldn't quite concentrate on her studies.

She was an incredibly attractive young woman with her red hair falling seductively over her blue eyes but not enough to conceal her perfect features. Even so, for some reason the boys at the art college seemed oblivious to her charms, or so she thought. Nothing could have been further from the truth, as she was lusted after by nearly every young man on the campus, as well as a couple of tutors, but there was something about her that warned them all off most emphatically. The way she held herself and the almost arrogant way she spoke to people was a bit off-putting. However it had been instilled in her very effectively by her grandmother and she was totally unaware of the effect she had on others, particularly men who felt quite intimidated by her self-assurance. In fact, she longed for a real relationship: to be close to someone who she could share her thoughts and feelings with and feel wanted. The truth of it was simple enough. She wasn't really looking for sex, not even romance; what she craved was a family. Her whole life had been empty of affection and apart from Dossie, no-one had shown her any real love. Growing up with a grandmother who was cold and distant left Lucinda with a real craving for intimacy. She desperately needed to belong; to feel part of a unit but at the same time, her hormones were beginning to send her senses reeling and as David's face swirled in her memory, she imagined herself in love. She couldn't help but laugh as she remembered the way he had taken offence so easily and then the memory of their fit of giggles actually made her chuckle out loud.

"What's tickling you, Lou?" A voice came from behind the open door as Sandy, her room-mate fell into the space carrying a huge blank canvas and a string bag full of tinned beans and a loaf of bread which represented tea for the girls. Sandy was a domestic goddess in Lou's eyes, and she was in awe of her new best friend. The difference in their backgrounds didn't matter to either of them one bit.

"Come on Lady Lou, share the joke with Auntie Sand!"

"Oh, it's nothing. Just ignore me," she replied and then added what she knew her flatmate would appreciate. "I need a man. You haven't got one tucked away in that bag of yours, have you, darling?"

"You're sex mad, you are. All you posh birds are the same. Suppose it's that repressed upbringing."

"What me – sex mad? You, my girl, are the one who wears skirts up to her bum and flirts with anything in trousers."

Sandy pretended to be offended, staring at Lou with innocent green eyes that widened and then crinkled in amusement. "My mini skirt is quite respectable, thank you very much – much longer than most these days. And anyway, there's no real talent here so there's no-one to flirt with!"

Her words were thick with that lovely Liverpudlian accent that so attracted Lucinda and made her think of her favourite pop groups. Tugging at her skirt, she straightened the fabric across her canary yellow-clad legs and then collapsed into an old wicker chair that had been painted the same bright colour as her tights.

"You are right there, dearest girl! We ought to go to the King's Road one Saturday. That's where all the action is."

Lucinda imagined all the flamboyantly dressed young men parading down the road in their flares and trendy jackets with the sound of The Beatles booming out of all the shop doorways. But each one seemed to have David's face. It was weird how she could still remember so vividly how he looked even after so long. Unable to shake his image from her brain, she went over every detail of that strange meeting on the train. He had been so sweet, helping her with her bags and his chat up seemed so innocent now that she remembered it. He certainly wasn't one of those puffed up toffs her grandmother seemed intent on introducing to her, nor was he one of the chinless wonders who pursued her incessantly. She had been so impressed with the way he cared for his grandfather and she recalled how upset he'd been at the hospital when the old man collapsed. He was just the sweetest boy she had ever met. She hadn't thought twice about breaking her journey and going with David to the hospital. However, it wasn't just for him. She had taken to the old man immediately. He was so genuine a person and never having a grandfather of her own, she couldn't fail to like him. There had never been anyone in her life quite like the old gentleman, surrounded as she was by women.

"I wonder how he is?" she mused under her breath.

"What did you say?"

"Oh nothing, forget it. I'm just in a very funny mood today."

"Mm, you can say that again. I couldn't fail to notice it, darling." Sandy laughed out loud, grabbing her friend's hands in hers. "But I know what you need, my girl!"

Smirking, she flicked her long black locks over her shoulder and winked in such an exaggerated way that her long lashes fluttered on her cheek.

Lucinda returned the look with a naughty grin and a cheeky lilt in her voice, "You know Sand, you're right but I don't suppose I'll see the boy I'm hankering after ever again."

"Love of your life, was he, then?" The strong Liverpudlian accent made the words sound even more mocking than intended as Sandy stared into her friend's lovely face.

"He was just an enigmatic stranger whose image one day I shall recreate in one of my famous paintings."

At that, Lucinda pressed the back of her hand to her forehead in such a melodramatic way that it had both girls fall about in stitches. Sandy stretched out her hands to grab Lou, spinning her round until she was quite dizzy. Both girls slipped down onto the flokati rug, catching the long white pile between their fingers until the room stopped spinning. As they both lay flat on their backs, their legs twitched jerkily to the sounds of The Beach Boys coming from Sandy's little portable turntable that sat on the sideboard.

David was feeling utterly miserable, the strain showing in his handsome face, making his attractive eyes seem dark and cloudy. It was so unlike the young man who was usually so full of life and fun. Everything was incredibly grey at the moment, even the weather. The sky was black and heavy with rain which cast dark shadows over his whole life. College seemed dull and boring and David had no interest in all the pretty young dollies who made such an effort to grab his attention. Only one girl tempted him and she was totally unobtainable. Even his favourite Beach Boys album failed to cheer him up. A shout from the kitchen eventually broke into his thoughts.

"I'll be down in a minute, just changing out of these school things."

"You must be in a dream world lad; you've been ages getting changed. Have you got a young woman up there that we don't know about?" Uncle Lance joked, completely unaware of David's real feelings.

Taking off the respectable white shirt and tie he had worn that day, he washed and then pulled on a pink cotton Ben Sherman shirt over his head. He fastened down the collar and turned up the cuffs on his sleeves, revealing dark hairs on his tanned muscular arms. Lance had shouted him again for his tea, but he didn't really feel like eating. It had been the first day of his final teaching practice and he found it quite stressful. He had prepared all his lesson plans meticulously, but he found the kids' behaviour challenging and was beginning to wonder if he had chosen the right profession. Teaching hadn't been his first choice at all, but it seemed like a safe option and it certainly pleased the old man. He enjoyed the theory and was totally absorbed in his subject as history had always been something he enjoyed but the actual teaching bit was quite different. Teenagers these days weren't easy and a student teacher was easy meat. The girls particularly had given him a tough time as they flirted without mercy, fluttering their eyelashes at the gorgeous young teacher who reminded them so much of Paul McCartney. Lads stood around with their hands in their pockets begrudgingly complying with his requests for order.

"How the hell do teachers focus on their work?" he asked himself.

Besides all that it was also difficult to concentrate at the moment as all his attention seemed centred on his grandfather. He needed to get home to look after him now that he was due to be discharged from the hospital. There was no-one else but that wasn't the only reason David wanted to go home. His grandfather was very special to him and he would never desert him, no matter how hard the old guy tried to reassure him he was fine. He had already decided that he would make an appointment to speak to his personal tutor and ask for special leave for family reasons. Under such circumstances, he was sure that there would be no problem. After all, he could always do another year if necessary. His grandfather's illness and his collapse were just too important to ignore.

The memory of that day was always with him, bringing mixed feelings, tormenting and delighting him in equal measure. The old man's heart attack was traumatic, making him sick with worry but different deep emotions also stirred inside him as he remembered the way that beautiful stranger made him feel. The elation he felt when he thought of Lou brought about a guilt so heavy that he tried to eliminate all thoughts of her from his brain. If he hadn't been so involved with her, his grandfather may never have collapsed.

However, the harder he pushed her image out of his head, the more her smiling face taunted him. It wasn't even just that he fancied her; it was more than that. He had the greatest respect for the girl who showed so much concern for his grandpa. She was the kindest, most caring person he had ever met. He told himself he would never see her again and even if he did, they were from such different backgrounds he was convinced nothing could ever come from it. There could never be any relationship between Lucinda Addington and David Lowes.

"Right, get your glad rags on, Sandy. I've decided it's

time for some real fun. Forget the beans on toast, I'll treat us both to a slap-up meal in the West End and then we can go on to a discotheque. And who knows what we can look forward to for pudding!"

The other girl blushed a pretty pink, then guffawed loudly, "Whatever do you mean, Lady Lucinda Addington?"

Lucinda banished all thoughts of the boy on the train from her head, as she looked forward to an evening on the town, where she would meet as many handsome young men as she could wish for. "We are artists, my sweet friend, and I intend to seek some adventure. I have a life to live, there's no point in living in the past."

"That's my girl!" The flatmate finished spitting onto the block of black mascara before lifting the gungy brush to her eyelashes. "Give me five minutes, Lady Lou, and I'll be ready for all those hooray Henry types that lust after you!"

Lou only laughed, thinking to herself that those upper crust dandies left her totally cold, but she knew how her flatmate felt about them. Sandy loved their beautifully rounded vowels and their arrogance. The fact that most of them were loaded also held a certain attraction, of course. She was fond of Sandy but was well aware of her potential as a fully-fledged gold digger.

"Oh, I don't know what to do with you darling; you just blow me away!" Lucinda poured a glass of bubbly and gulped it down before filling another glass for her friend.

"It's so good being your mate, Lou." Sandy took the glass of champagne and chinked her glass against Lucinda's. "No-one in Liverpool drinks champers like you do!"

"You only like me for my money!" laughed Lou, as she threw back another glass of Moet.

David picked at his evening meal before downing a glass of lager, which helped to lift his spirits slightly. The froth left him with a snowy moustache before he licked it clean. Denying himself a second glass, he wiped his mouth with his hand before grabbing a towel from the bathroom. Staring at his reflection in the mirror, he smoothed his long hair which reached his collar and bared his teeth revealing perfectly straight pearly whites. Lifting both arms, he sniffed at his armpits which thankfully smelt of something pleasant and slightly musky.

"You're all spruced up, lad, in your best gear so get yourself out there and have a good time. You're only young once, my lad, and don't you forget it." Uncle Lance patted him hard on the back. "And don't go mooning over one lassie when there's plenty of lovelies just waiting for a smashing chap like you!"

"Aye, you're right, there's no point in wishing for something you can't have!"

And so, miles apart, two young people went out on the town that night each seeking the same thing in a bid to forget each other.

Chapter 8

After the excitement of her magical wedding to Jack, it took Minnie a while to come down from the ceiling. But as the months passed, Mrs Dawson settled into a comfortable routine of working mornings in the shop and afternoons looking after her new husband in every sense. Etta became more and more uncomfortable with the situation. Her mother was too old for all this romance and stuff and anyway it wasn't right that her Mam was savouring delights that she wasn't. Shortly after the wedding, she had come face to face with Ernest Lowes over the cinder toffee that he had suddenly started craving every day after his work was finished. Of course, it really wasn't the toffee he desired, it was Etta and as the days passed, he succeeded in breaking down her barriers.

At long last, he felt that he had managed to get past the flirtatious games she enjoyed playing and they began a courtship that completely entranced him. Etta, on the other hand, continued to enjoy playing with the young man's emotions and she would lead him on until he felt he would burst. Each night would end in the same way. A walk in the park and then home and as they stood together on the doorstep, the same old scene would play out.

"Etta, you know I love you, more than any other lass I've ever known," Ernie breathed the awkward words into her ear as his hands fumbled with her petticoats.

"You do, do you, my lad?" she murmured softly, nuzzling herself closer into his grasp, wriggling and pressing her thigh against his. And then as she swelled out her chest, she suddenly pulled away from him, "Well, it's late, Ernest Lowes, time we were in our beds!"

Ernest would watch, miserable and dejected, as she

ran into the house, slamming the door in his face. It was clear that she enjoyed teasing him; watching him squirm as she sent him into raptures that she had no intention of satisfying.

But the fascination for Ernest Lowes was short-lived and sordid. Etta began to feel disgust at the way she was behaving and thought back to her old friend Annie Hogarth. Vowing to improve herself morally and emotionally, she threw all her energy into working in the shop and decided to end the relationship that was blossoming between them.

"You're looking glum, my girl," Jack noticed one day as Etta returned from a clandestine meeting with Ernie, "What's the matter, pet?"

She smiled her glorious smile and shook her shoulders to reassure him, "I'm very well, Jack, take no notice of me!"

But Jack took great interest in his young charge as he often grandly referred to her. Although he wasn't her real father, he had already begun to love her like a daughter, introducing her as Annetta Dawson to all and sundry, even though, of course, she had no legal right to the name. He felt a responsibility to her and to her mother and was unhappy at the way the relationship with her young man was going. In his day, a suitor did things the proper way, courted his girl in a respectable way. He knew that Etta was a modern miss and often laughed at him for his Victorian ways. But he hated the way they sneaked around, kissing and touching in public. It hadn't gone unnoticed by the busybodies in the town and Etta was certainly giving the gossips something to talk about. Minnie seemed unaware of what was going on around her and he determined to speak to the girl at the first opportunity.

Etta stood in front of the long mirror that adorned the wardrobe in her bedroom, tilting her head one way then another. She looked a picture of innocence with her blonde curls and baby blue eyes. Piling her long hair up on top of her head, she scrutinised her reflection with such intensity that her eyes widened, and her nostrils flared. The modern style was to cut the hair into a very blunt cut, level with the bottom of the ears. A heavy shiny fringe completed the fashionable look that silent movie stars like Mary Pickford and Louise Brooks wore so exquisitely. She had already made up her mind to copy the 'bob' as it was known and would visit Madame Yvonne's Salon tomorrow. Long dresses had already made way for short skirts with rolled stockings and her wardrobe contained more than one drop-waisted dress, short enough to bare her sensuous knees. Of course, such outfits were kept for special times when her Mam couldn't disapprove, as Etta knew she would.

Pulling out her best dress in mint green with a vibrant pink sash, she held it in front of her and once more admired the picture of loveliness without any sense of conceit or pride. She had arranged to meet Ernest at the end of the street at 7.30 that night so that they could make the second house at the Picture Palace. She knew exactly what would happen. He would buy the best seats at the back, the sort that accommodated both of them together. It always began with a yawn as his arms stretched above him and then as he lowered them, he gently grasped Etta's shoulder, pulling her close so that her cheek touched his. This of course was only the precursor to a more adventurous move in the dark as his fingers began to rest upon her soft breast until his hand cupped the full swell of her bosom. Etta, feeling the familiar sense of pleasure spreading up into her breast, would close her eyes and melt into his feverish kisses. Squirming in her seat she would unashamedly place her small white hand on his thigh and squeeze hard until Ernie felt that he was about to explode. This was a regular occurrence for the two of them and it was becoming harder and harder for Etta to resist the temptation to succumb to Ernest's advances. She knew exactly what effect she had upon him and enjoyed the power that it gave her when she pulled away leaving him on the brink of sexual release. But she remained adamant that she would never fall in love and certainly never marry.

He, on the other hand, was so frustrated with the overwhelming desire to satisfy his lust that he had already made up his mind to ask her to marry him, if it was the only way he could possess her beautiful young body. At that point in their relationship, he wasn't totally sure that he genuinely loved her, but he wanted her and he was determined to have her at whatever cost. The war had numbed his senses, damaged a young boy barely out of school and real love, the sort of love his dad had for his mam, was something that at that time he couldn't really understand. He knew though, that what he felt for Etta was much more than the animal urgency that overwhelmed his senses in the past whenever he had managed a few stolen minutes with any other lass. But the thumping music coming from the piano that accompanied the silent movie almost erased such romantic notions from his mind and at the same time drowned out his declarations of undying devotion. But even if Ernest didn't know it himself yet, Etta knew in her heart that this young man was beginning to fall passionately in love with her. This made Etta's decision to end things so much more difficult, as every day, Ernie grew bolder and his advances more amorous, eventually building up to his proposal of marriage. It was late on a Saturday afternoon and they had just returned from a stroll around the park.

"I've been thinking, Etta," he said, as he sat upright and proper next to her on the velvet chaise in the best room above the shop. "I've been thinking, we've been walking out together for a while and…"

Minnie, who was sitting quietly with her knitting in the corner of the dark room, smiled to herself. She knew Jack didn't approve of the young man and these modern ways, but he was a likeable lad and Etta could do a lot worse. Ernest seemed completely oblivious of her presence as he gathered up his courage to ask his girl the question that had been lurking at the back of his head for so long. Sensing what he intended to do, Minnie quickly picked up her needles and wool and made to leave the room, giving him a little wink of approval as she did so.

"Oh, what the hell!" Ernie finally bit the bullet and came straight out with it. "Etta, will you marry me?"

Suddenly and very comically, as if the thought had just struck him, he got down on to one knee and repeated the question. Etta was amused by the gesture, but her eyes remained cold as she grabbed his hands and dragged him to his feet. Looking up at his flushed face, his own hazel eyes full of anticipation, she bent her head to avoid his look. Slowly she straightened herself up placing her two hands together as if about to pray and then locked her fingers tightly. Ernie sensed what she was about to say and a mixture of regret and relief filled his head, turning his cheeks red and dulling his eyes. He didn't wait for an answer.

"I don't mean right away; I mean we can wait. If you're not ready, we can carry on as we are."

He tried to smile but his heart was heavy and, in that moment, he realised that he absolutely loved Annetta Ramsey but he wasn't ready to be a husband. He also knew that he couldn't let her go. Every time they were together, she made his very body burn with an all-consuming passion and when they were apart, he couldn't wait to hold her in his arms. He was tormented by the intensity of his feelings for her and it was clear to him that she was enjoying his pain. But it wasn't long before she softened and kissed his sensuous mouth gently with her plump tender lips.

"I'm sorry, Ernest, I do care for you, you know that, but I'll be no man's wife. I have other plans!"

Her pretty face hardened again as she continued, "I will make my own way, I have a talent and I want to use it!"

Rejection finally stabbed Ernest like a knife, the hurt blinding his love for Etta so much that he cruelly turned on her.

"Talent... what talent? You mean those childish scribbles. Grow up, Annetta! You're just an ordinary working lass who needs a man to take care of her. Drawing and such is not for the likes of us. You're a dreamer, nothing but a silly little dreamer and you're a fool!"

With that, he spun round and headed for the door leaving Etta with silent tears spilling down her face. The sound of heavy footsteps thundering down the stairs brought Minnie running in from the kitchen.

"Etta, what's to do pet?" Her voice was shrill and full of concern. "Where's Ernie, what have you done, what have you said to him?"

"He's gone, Mam and I'm glad. I'll never marry Ernest Lowes; never marry any man, never!"

"You silly little lass, our Etta, what do you think will happen to you without a good husband at your side?"

"I will become an artist and live in an attic somewhere and I will have lovers, so many lovers who will all adore me and..."

By now Etta no longer cared what Minnie thought, as her fertile imagination carried her away to a place where no-one could hurt her or destroy her precious dreams.

"Shush your mucky mouth and pull yourself together my girl. Just think on what you've done!"

Minnie violently took hold of her daughter's shoulders and shook her until Etta fell like a rag doll onto the floor, completely hysterical and distraught. The commotion disturbed Jack, who had been sitting by the kitchen range blacking his boots and smoking his pipe and he angrily threw down the polish as he stormed into the front room.

"Can't a man have a quiet smoke on his pipe without all this row going on?"

But Jack was a sensitive man and not at all gruff and on seeing the prostrate girl in a heap on the floor, his tone relaxed and he searched his wife's face for an answer. Although Minnie's face was flushed and tear-stained, it gave little away apart from the pain that she felt. Etta's sobs grew quieter, but she remained where she lay with her head cradled in her arms.

Jumping to the wrong conclusion, Jack looked at Minnie and spluttered out the words like bullets from a gun.

"I'll kill him, the swine!"

"No Jack, Ernie has done nothing wrong. The poor lad has done nothing more than ask this ungrateful wretch of a girl to marry him, that's all!"

Jack ran his hands through his oiled grey hair and then dragged on his pipe, his eyes transfixed on Minnie's daughter. After a moment, he blew out a fragrant burst of smoke and spoke softly.

"She said no, I take it. She did the right thing if you ask me." Puffing on his pipe again, he pondered, "She's far too young to be wed."

"The right thing!" Minnie screamed. "She's ruined her

chances, she has. He was a good lad and he could have provided for her proper, he could, but no, not good enough for this one. Wants to be an artist or whatever and have lots of men to boot. She's nothing but a dirty little slut. She's a whore!"

Jack couldn't believe the venom spewing from his wife's mouth and uncharacteristically and without thinking, he shook her and slapped her hard across the face. As her cheeks coloured and her skin began to smart, a look of horror and disbelief appeared in her husband's eyes. He immediately grabbed her, holding her tightly to his chest.

"Forgive me, Minnie; I'm so sorry, my love," he sobbed.

Etta, who had observed the scene, was so upset by the violence her actions had brought about that she threw herself at the couple and begged their forgiveness.

"It's all my fault. I'm a stupid headstrong ninny, I know I am." She looked from one to the other with tenderness and resignation. "I love you both and I know I'll never be anything but a shop girl, but I need my dreams, Mam. They've kept me alive since I was a bairn, I can't let go now and I can't marry Ernest."

There was an awkward silence when all three of them stood facing each other, trying to find the right words. Jack opened his mouth to speak but nothing came out. Finally, the mother smiled kindly at the child with the remnants of the tears still in her faded blue eyes.

"We'll all have a cup of tea, plenty of sugar. Jack, pet, put the kettle on to boil," said Minnie, as if nothing had happened and all three of them walked together into the kitchen.

Jack placed the heavy black kettle onto the range and then sat down in his chair by the fire. Minnie busied herself by the table, noisily clinking the white crockery while Etta pulled out a wooden stool and sat upright, her fingers nervously fiddling with the fringing on the red chenille tablecloth. Her memory played tricks on her as she imagined the roll of wallpaper spread out on the cloth, the fairies dancing prettily across the paper. Were they dancing or escaping? She decided that they were about to fly off into the unknown to a place where dreams were made. At that moment, she wished with all her heart that she could join them.

Later Etta sat in the front room, looking out through the sash window, as the darkness flooded in from the night sky. Her Mam and Jack had gone to bed to lie in each other's arms and forget the distress of the day. She had long finished her cup of sweet tea but the white cup, painted with pink rosebuds, remained on the saucer that sat on her lap. As she stared at the scattering of tea leaves in the bottom of the cup, she mused on what her future was to be. Thoughts of Ernest remained constant in her mind and she couldn't rid herself of the image of his broken face. Even though she hadn't intended to, she knew she had hurt him very badly. A part of her really did care for Ernest, although she couldn't admit it even to herself, and she desperately wanted to take away his pain. She wanted to lie in his arms and allow herself to be taken passionately and completely so that her body could experience the full pleasure that it yearned. Then she just might abandon her foolish ideas and understand what real happiness was. But something stronger always blocked these feelings, a desire to experience more, to fulfil her destiny and her destiny was not to be someone's wife. She felt sure of this. There was a dark secret deep inside her that wanted to hurt any man foolish enough to love her. Annetta Ramsey was a damaged flower, crushed between the cruel fingers of a father she hated.

Sleep evaded her for most of that night as a myriad of

ideas fought for dominance in her brain, but eventually she succumbed to the exhaustion that came from too much thinking. And after a fitful night's sleep, Etta woke with a decision already made as to how her life would unfold. She had decided to leave the comfort of Jack Dawson's home and find a way to make her dreams come true. Firstly, she would head for Newcastle and visit with her sister, who she was certain would help her. Dossie always described her ladyship as a kind woman, so she felt sure that she would allow her to stay. She could work as a housemaid for a while to earn some money and then take a train to York or even London. Once there, the world would be her oyster, she told herself. She already had experience of shop work, so it would be easy to find a position in one of those big department stores, in Selfridges or even Harrods. She had seen pictures of these magical places in a posh magazine left on the counter by one of Jack's more well-to-do customers. Drooling over the illustrations of long, lean mannequins dressed in fantastically modern outfits, she was convinced that her drawings were as good, if not better. She had practised repeatedly until she achieved the same stylistically perfect sketches that she had seen in the fashion papers. The princesses and fairies of her youth had given way to elegant flappers with exquisitely bobbed hair, adorned with sparkly headbands and feathers. Dresses, no more than flimsy silk shifts with dropped waists and short skirts, barely covered the flat chested bodies of the women who appeared on the pages of her sketch pad. This was her vision of the future; a very modern young woman enjoying the success that her talent would bring.

Of course, she thought about men and her sexuality was never in question. There would be plenty of time and opportunity for her love life to blossom. Without doubt,

Etta was a sensual being with a huge appetite for pleasure, which Ernest had often set aflame, but he also wanted to tie her down, make her a housewife, take away her identity and this was the very thing that she rebelled against. And so she had no choice but to carry out her dangerous plan. She certainly knew how risky it was, there were so many pitfalls into which she might plummet, but her mind was made up. She would leave tomorrow with her best frock and a few belongings, her pencils and sketch pad amongst them. Now all she had to do was tell Minnie and Jack, for she couldn't just leave without sharing her plans with them. She loved them too much to leave them wondering whether she was alive or dead. The decision to go left her feeling bereft but she told herself this mood would pass once she had taken the first step towards freedom. It was hard to motivate herself but even though tiredness threatened to sabotage her plans, she remained determined.

The sun had just come up, sending a sharp ray of light through the chink in the curtains. It was like a spark of life burning into her very being and gave her the courage to do what she had to do. It was still early in the morning, but she knew Jack would be opening the shop in an hour or so and Minnie was always up before him to get a good breakfast on the table. Very soon, she heard her mother moving around in the kitchen and she summoned up the nerve to face her with the news.

"Mam, I have to tell you something really important, so I want you to sit down and listen."

"You don't need to say anything, hinnie, it's all forgotten now," replied Minnie, putting down the pot of strawberry jam before wiping her sticky hands on the wet dishcloth.

"No, Mam, listen. Please listen."

At that very moment, Jack appeared at the door with

an envelope in his hand. There was a buzz of excitement between them as letters were not a regular delivery to the household; bills and invoices most certainly, but a letter was usually a matter of great sadness or immense joy. He held it up to the light, examining the postage stamp carefully.

"Open it Jack, be quick and open it."

But Minnie couldn't wait, so grabbing it from his hand she hastily tore it open leaving Jack and Etta anxiously waiting for the news. The older woman silently read the words written neatly in black ink across the page.

"Well, what is it, woman?" enquired Jack impatiently.

Etta said nothing but held her breath for so long that she felt lightheaded and giddy.

"It's from our Doreen."

Dossie rarely wrote and Mam never normally called her Doreen. Etta looked agitated and Jack wore an expression of concern that he couldn't conceal. He snatched the letter from Minnie and read the words out loud. It was a very short note, informing them of her marriage to Mr George Clifford, the gamekeeper on the estate. He was a good deal older but a very respectable man who had admired Dossie for some considerable time. They had wed quietly a week ago. She was deeply sorry not to have let them all know before now. She sent her love and looked forward to seeing them soon. Minnie slumped down into the nearest chair and covered her mouth hard with her hand to suppress the sobs that were welling inside of her.

"What!" cried Etta incredulously, "Our Dossie, already married!"

"Well, I can't say I'm pleased not to have been there but if she's content with this Mr Clifford and he makes her happy, then she has my blessing." Minnie recovered herself as quickly as she could, smiling weakly at Jack, who nodded in agreement.

But she couldn't hide the disappointment that she felt at not being with her elder child on the day of her wedding. She wiped her face with the dishcloth, smearing the tears that had trickled into the corner of her mouth, leaving a salty taste behind. Etta paced the room, wringing her hands in anguish and doubt. She couldn't quite believe the news. She never imagined her sister would marry, as Dossie had not once spoken of a gentleman friend. It was all too sudden; too much of a change to take in. How would this affect her campaign to free herself, she asked, would it make a difference? Feeling somehow betrayed by her sister's commitment to this man, panic overwhelmed her, leaving a sense of uncertainty for the future. Trying to reassure herself that her sister's marriage wouldn't change anything, she went over the details of her plan, resolving to go ahead and tell her Mam and Jack. But in her heart, she knew this wasn't the right time to spring something else on them and decided to wait till they all came to terms with Dossie's news.

"Don't upset yourself, Mam, this won't change anything. I'm sure this Mr Clifford will be good to our Dossie. Everything will be right for us all. I know it will." Etta tried to sound buoyant but beneath her smile there was a sense of despair.

"You're right, hinnie, I have one daughter wed to a well-respected gentleman and another who will soon be married as well, if Ernest Lowes demonstrates a little more mettle!"

Minnie laughed, happy in her belief that Etta would finally give in to the young man's persuasive attempts to seek her hand in marriage. "Aye, pet, life is good, Etta, we're blessed!"

However, she couldn't have been more wrong. This

was only just the beginning of turbulent times to come. Things were to happen that would transform Etta's life and those who loved her forever.

Chapter 9

Thoughts of starting a new life for herself were still very much in Etta's head, buzzing around like big fat bluebottles but every day that went by ate away at her resolve and she began to wonder if she had the strength to go ahead with her plan. Minnie and Jack were to visit Dossie and her new man at the big house this coming weekend and Etta was to stay behind to open the shop.

"Never mind, lass," Jack said kindly. "We'll send your love to your sister and make some arrangements for you to pay your respects very soon, how's that?"

In a strange way it was a relief to Etta that she wasn't to see the new bride. Her feelings were mixed, and she was confused about the whole affair. It had come as such a shock and at such a bad time for her that she really couldn't face seeing her sister. Her face was drawn, and her eyes filled with sadness, making Jack regret the decision not to shut up the shop for the day. He opened his mouth to speak but Etta's words broke into his thoughts and stopped him from saying another word.

"I know, don't mind me. It'll be good being in charge and I'll manage to find a bit of time to write a letter to our Dossie. It's better when I'm on my own, I can always think of what to say when I catch a quiet minute to myself."

She grinned widely, trying extremely hard to make her eyes smile too. Jack was reassured and busied himself getting ready to take Minnie on their little excursion. They didn't often get the chance of a day out together these days and he could see that his wife was excited at the prospect of the visit. She looked a picture in her favourite hat as she walked down the stairs into the shop.

"Right then, pet, we're off now, we won't be back too late. I'll give Dossie your love and we'll tell you all about it when we get back." Minnie blew a kiss to her younger daughter and with her arm in Jack's they disappeared through the shop door to the sound of the bell.

The morning was slow and Etta took the opportunity to take out her best writing paper and began to fashion a few words to her sister. Unfortunately, they didn't come easily and she found it difficult to put her feelings down on paper. She was indeed happy that Dossie had found someone to love but it only emphasised her own unhappiness with life and tears were beginning to well up in her eyes when she heard a car pull up on the road outside the shop. Looking out of the large plate glass window, she wondered who the Ford Model T motor car belonged to. Recently she had begun to share Jack's interest in automobiles and they had spent many evenings together discussing the merits of the latest machines, much to the irritation of her mother, who found such things incredibly boring. As she wiped her tear-stained face on her work apron, the shop bell rang and the door flung open, revealing a very tall, very handsome young man who pushed his way into the room, his arms full of chocolate and confectionery. Startled, she looked up to find his marble-like eyes fixed upon her pretty face. Catching the few stray strands of hair that fell over her eyes, she tucked them hastily behind her ears before patting the now perfect bob into place.

"Why so sad?" he asked, with a gleam in his eye and a smile on his handsome chiselled face. And with that, he threw a bar of Rowntree's chocolate onto the counter, landing it directly in front of her.

"There you are, my sweet, something tasty for your very own delicious cherry lips!"

Etta picked up the chocolate and laughed out loud at the nerve of the stranger, as she bit the lips that so fascinated him. A deep red stain flushed them until her mouth resembled the sweets he compared them to. As their eyes met, she instantly felt a surge of longing for this impossibly handsome young man. Girls she knew had often talked about love at first sight and she had mocked their innocence. But he was so tall and darkly good-looking with smouldering brown eyes that lingered over her every curve, that her emotions rattled out of control. Was this love?

"Allow me to introduce myself miss, I am Sam Simpson, salesman to confectioners across the north east and I am here to allow you to sample the very best in quality sweets and chocolate." He bowed theatrically and then winked cheekily.

"Well, Mr Simpson, you'll have to speak to Mr Dawson, the owner and my... my father about orders and suchlike." Etta tried to look serious but her eyes were shining and a smile played around her pretty little rosebud of a mouth.

"Well, Miss Dawson, I'm sure you can try out some of my wares and give me your opinion and then... well... you could persuade your father to make out a big fat order for me, couldn't you?"

Etta's face lit up and a broad smile revealed a row of perfectly white teeth.

Picking up on this cue, Simpson continued, "And then, Miss Dawson," he hesitated slightly as he watched the effect of his teasing on the lovely stranger.

"Yes, Mr Simpson, please do carry on!"

Words dripped from his tongue like treacle, "Well, with the commission I earn, I can take you out for a tasty fish supper."

Etta tried not to laugh, crinkling up her nose and pursing her lips.

"Now, how does that sound, eh, Miss Dawson, what do you think?"

Allowing strands of almost blue-black hair to fall lazily over his forehead, he peered at her with just a hint of a smile playing on the wide mouth that was framed by a well-groomed moustache. She was well aware that he was teasing her but she was an expert in that field and she was just about to beat him at his own game.

"I love fish and chips."

"Well then, Miss Dawson."

"My name's not..." she began haughtily, "Oh, just call me Etta, all my friends do!"

Catching hold of his strong masculine hand, she fluttered her lashes and leaned into him seductively, "I am sure we are going to be good friends, Mr Simpson; It is Mr Simpson, is it not, or may I call you Sam, now that we are acquainted?"

The poor man didn't stand a chance. He was an old hand in the art of seduction, as his many conquests could testify, but he had truly met his match in this kittenish little creature. He would have to be on his guard with this one, he told himself.

"I would love to call you Etta, sweetheart and please do call me Sammy." Deep brown eyes melted like his chocolate samples as he deliberately returned the provocative glint in hers.

And so it was that Sam Simpson was to call her Etta for many weeks ahead as she dangled him on a string like a cat with a ball of wool. He fell head over heels for this adorable little flirt but as the months passed, a quite different relationship developed between the two of them that not only surprised but delighted the young woman. She couldn't believe that she could feel like this; it was such a different sensation to those she had felt before. She wasn't playing anymore; this man had captured her heart and the games that came so readily to her were put aside in place of a more submissive behaviour that saw Etta change completely. Perhaps this was what real love felt like and all thoughts of leaving disappeared from her head. He was so confident, so easy going, that he made her feel comfortable and safe with him. It was strange the way she felt, almost how Jack Dawson had made her feel when she believed herself in love with him but Sam wasn't a bit like Jack. He was vibrant and young, so full of life but so much in control for a man of his years. In fact, she wasn't sure how old he was, sometimes he seemed so mature, a man of the world and other times he seemed like a boy, in fact he was probably no older than she was herself.

Samuel Simpson was indeed an enigma, a strange mixture. Etta at times felt she knew everything there was to know about him and at others she knew nothing, other than the fact that he was extremely handsome with a face that somehow was familiar. All this only made him more appealing and attractive and as time went by, she felt a longing that she had never felt with Ernest. She listened attentively to his amusing stories of the numerous tedious shopkeepers and fat confectioners he had met on his travels, giggling coquettishly at all his little anecdotes. But it wasn't very long before Etta appreciated how upset her young man could become when things didn't go his way. The amiable looks and charismatic smiles she so adored could quickly give way to peevish sulks and hostile outbursts whenever she displeased him. Recently she had taken to wearing the sort of outfits that he had admired on other girls and even let her precious bob grow out so that she could fasten her hair back in a style he approved of.

As winter approached, he was making more and more visits to the shop, candied mice and chocolate novelties filled the shelves and on the day before Christmas Eve, Sam was finally introduced to Minnie and Jack as Etta's special friend, Samuel. Proudly taking his hand, she led him up the stairs to the best room where her mother was setting out the fine china on a large, silver-plated tray. Minnie had already guessed that there was someone in her daughter's life other than young Ernest and she had mentioned to Jack that this was no ordinary friend. She suspected that this boy had come visiting with more intention than to wish them all the best for the season. The second Sam entered the room, tall and imposing, Minnie felt a strange heat spread from her chest up into her face. But this was not one of the usual flushes that she had been experiencing recently, this made her whole body shake and she wasn't entirely sure why.

"Good evening, Mrs Dawson, pleased to meet you." A strong hand stretched out to hers and dark marble-like eyes burnt with a light that Minnie vaguely recognised.

A few seconds passed before she glanced anxiously at Etta and then a slight smile and a nod signalled her overly polite response.

"Pleased to meet you, young man."

Noticing the unusual formality in his wife's manner, Jack tried to compensate and nervously flashed a wide smile that almost resembled a grimace, "Come on in, lad, sit yourself down. Don't stand on ceremony, any friend of our Etta's is a friend of ours!"

Pointing at the chaise, he beckoned to Minnie to pour the tea. Her face remained frozen in a civil fashion that gave nothing away. Etta was confused; her Mam was normally so fussy with guests and not at all quiet. Perhaps she had taken a dislike to Sam, although the idea seemed totally inconceivable, as he appeared to be the most charming of men. Ernest, however, was still a strong contender for Etta's affections in Minnie's mind, so this new suitor had a lot of ground to cover if he was to win over the mother. As she passed a cup of tea to the visitor, Minnie at last found her voice and questioned the young man as only she could.

"Etta has told us a lot about you, Samuel, but what did you say your family name was?"

"Simpson, Sam Simpson." His smile was charming, but his eyes seemed so familiar that it quite perplexed Minnie now just as much as the moment she first met him.

The evening passed quite pleasantly with Jack and Sam engaged in conversation about the best sales promotions and the new Christmas lines. Minnie remained quite reflective, still weighing up the stranger. When Sam had gone and Jack had retired to bed, Etta sat her Mam down beside her and stared hard into her face.

"Didn't you like him, then?"

"Oh there's nothing not to like, he's a good-looking lad, well turned out, polite…"

There was a long pause. "And?"

"And nothing, it's just… oh it's nothing!"

Etta was growing angry and the frustration she felt with her mother exploded.

"Well, I like him, Mam and I might even marry him!"

"Has he asked you to marry him?"

"No, but he will… if I want him to!"

Minnie went to bed that night with the young man's handsome features etched in her mind. The strong jawline, the long straight nose, he reminded her so much of… someone!

The relationship between Sam and Etta was becoming ever more serious and as it developed, Minnie became increasingly uneasy with the situation. Sam was always polite and well-mannered whenever she saw him but there was something about that young man that bothered her. On top of that, her daughter had changed from the free spirit who needed no man to feel complete; she seemed now to be a devoted disciple, dependent on Sam Simpson in every conceivable way. One afternoon as Etta busied herself with her hair, wondering whether Sam would approve, Minnie stood behind her and smoothed down the sleek blonde strands that curled around her face.

"What do you know about Sam, our Etta, have you met his Ma and Da yet?"

"No, I think his father is dead and he doesn't say much about his Mam. Why do you ask?"

"Well, you seem to be getting a bit serious, the two of you. What are his intentions? We need to know Et, we know nothing about this Sam Simpson."

"I know all I need to know. I know I love him!"

The words hung in the air like a veil between them until Minnie drew a long breath and sat down at the kitchen table.

"You have to be careful, girl. Things happen when you think yourself in love like that, things that can ruin a young lass good and proper. You need to be sure of your Mr Simpson!"

"I am sure of him. I couldn't be surer. I love him and he loves me. That's all that matters."

She paused, thinking about what she was going to say next but, in an instant, she irritably blurted out the words that couldn't be unsaid.

"And things, as you put it Mam, have already happened and we're to be wed." Etta looked almost hostile as well as proud as she hinted at her lost virginity.

The implication of these words was crystal clear and Minnie Dawson stood up as if to move towards her daughter and then slumped back onto the kitchen chair, grabbing hold of the table as she did so. Beads of sweat glistened on her brow and she took out a lace handkerchief from her pocket and wiped her face. The shame of it was almost too much for her to bear as she thought about the consequences of what her daughter had just told her.

"Has he made you a proposal Etta... has he asked you to marry him already? There was an urgency in Minnie's voice and her words came out as a high-pitched whine. "When will you be wed? He has asked you to marry him Etta, tell me he has!"

"Not yet, but he will!" Etta's reply was determined and cold and she didn't even look at her mother at all, ignoring the tension that filled the room.

Minnie turned away from Etta without saying a single word and shuffled into her bedroom, closing the door quietly behind her. It was a Sunday afternoon and Jack was dozing on the bed, having the usual nap that followed one of Minnie's famous roast dinners. He opened his eyes, squinting up at his wife as she stood bathed in the cold light that flooded in through the sash windows. Swinging his legs from the bed, he placed his feet on the lino that covered the bedroom floor and stretched his long strong arms above his head.

"What's up, lass? You look like you've had a shock, what's the matter?"

Minnie burst into tears and related the whole sordid story while Jack listened with growing concern on his face.

"I'll have words with Sam Simpson, don't you fret my love. It'll all be right, trust me!"

The following night, the Ford drove up outside the shop and Sam sounded the horn to signal to Etta. As soon as she heard the familiar sound, she raced down the stairs grabbing her shawl and hat and ran towards the door. Jack was waiting in the shop and stepped out in front of her, blocking her path.

"I want to speak to that young lad, and I want you, my girl," he glared at Etta, "to go back up the stairs to your mam!"

Jack's words were forceful but inside Etta there was still the spark of the independent, strong minded woman she had always been and she stood her ground.

"No, Jack, whatever you say to Sam, you say to me!"

Etta's young man had grown impatient. Switching off the engine he made his way towards the shop door. As he did so, Jack opened it and firmly invited him to step inside. The charming smile remained fixed, but he flashed Etta a quizzical look as he held out his hand to Jack.

"Good evening, Mr Dawson, so nice to see you again. I hope you and Mrs Dawson are both well."

Without answering, Jack shifted from one leg to the other, refused Sam's handshake and cleared his throat loudly.

"I'll not beat about the bush, Samuel. Minnie and me are anxious to know what your intentions are towards our lass. We believe that marriage is on the cards… is that the case or is this just a bit of fun on your part? We don't want Etta to be hurt, do you understand me?" Jack drew hard on his pipe and then blew out a fragrant puff of blue smoke.

Jack's eyes narrowed as Sam's smile slipped slightly and the young man looked momentarily abashed. It wasn't long before Sam Simpson had recovered himself completely, clutching Etta's hand, he beamed at her before turning to Jack.

"We're both still very young, Mr Dawson and I have to make a name for myself first, but Etta knows that as soon as I have saved enough to give us a good living, we will…"

The pause was uncomfortable and Sam knew it, so he was grateful when Etta jumped in.

"We will be married soon though, won't we Sammy?"

"Yes of course!" Even though his smile never slipped, the previous show of confidence was not quite as visible as it had been and he swallowed hard.

"Under the circumstances, I think we can expect an announcement very soon, can't we? Jack's meaning was explicit as his knowing look burned into the young man's dark eyes.

Sam simply nodded in agreement. Mr Dawson wasn't totally satisfied but he was sure that Sam now understood him perfectly so he once again stared the lad hard in the face. Taking his hand firmly, he shook it before kissing Etta's cheek and wishing them both a good evening. It was to be two long weeks before Sam Simpson called on Etta again after that night when Jack warned him off and he thought long and hard about how the relationship was going. As he left the shop that evening, he had already made his mind up to call it a day and over the next few days he decided to write her a letter breaking off their engagement and telling her the truth. But as the days turned into weeks, the young man had second thoughts and bit by bit, he began to realise the true extent of his feelings for Etta. She was beautiful, so delicate and dainty, a flower of a girl who deserved to be treated well and it came as a shock when it dawned on him that he actually might love her. He had never felt like this before; so protective towards her but at the same time so much in her power. How could such a fragile bloom be so strong? This was not a feeling he enjoyed. He felt almost emasculated by his growing affection for her and anger rose up inside as he once more tried in vain to write another letter. It was at this point he knew for the first time what real love meant and things would have to change: he would have to change but his life wasn't that simple.

Things were certainly not simple for Etta either. Her life had been turned upside down and she didn't understand why. Dropping her head into her hands, she rubbed her brow and screwed up her eyes that had lost the soft blueness, turning grey over the last few weeks.

"What did you say to him?" she screamed at Jack. "I haven't seen him in ages, he's avoiding me, I'm sure he is."

Jack was genuinely upset. This wasn't what he had wanted. Protectively, he laid his strong hand on Etta's shoulder, but she shrugged it away with a stifled cry. Standing up, she stared straight at him but said nothing and then she turned and ran to her room.

"I'll find him, Minnie, by God, I'll find him and when I do…"

Minnie stepped out of the hallway and took hold of her husband's arm, squeezing it gently, lifting his fingers to her lips.

"You're a good man, Jack Dawson, but best let things lie, love… It's for the best!"

But Jack wasn't sure about that.

Sam had finally plucked up the courage to see Etta again and he sent word that he would see her soon. Deep feelings that had surfaced from the very core of his soul had given him the strength to recognise who he was and face his inner demons. He had tried to change her, but he now knew that she had changed him. She was the love of his life and he needed to tell her. Work meant that he would be in Doncaster until the weekend but by Friday night he was determined that Etta Dawson would know how much she really meant to him and he would tell her everything. But when it came to it and he finally plucked up the courage to see her, his good intentions failed him. The decency she had inspired in him was to be short-lived as he considered what he had to lose. Sam Simpson wasn't really a bad man, just a very weak one.

"Where have you been all this time, Sam? I've missed you." Etta 's words bore all the misery she had felt since she had seen him last. "I thought you'd left me!" Her eyes were red and watery and her nose runny. "I must look a sight."

She wiped her nose with her hand, unable to find her hanky in her apron pocket as she tried to tidy up her face by pinching her cheeks and rubbing her eyes. But she knew she was not looking her best.

"What did he say to you? You mustn't take any notice of him, Sammy."

Looking directly at her, he shook his head, "Nothing, he said nothing." He tried to laugh but it was false and Etta knew it.

"Look Etta, I can't stay long... some business I've got to see to, but I'll be back soon and we'll sort things out then. Right, pet?"

Feeling more hopeful, she cheered up and grabbing his arm, she declared with all her heart what she felt, "I love you, Sammy, I really love you."

A weak smile greeted her proclamation and she continued like a schoolgirl. "Yes, we'll sort it all out then, Sam. Don't worry about arranging things, Mam and me can do that. We don't want a lot of fuss, do we? A simple wedding will do."

Terror-struck, he turned away so that she couldn't detect the fear in his face. Marriage: she was talking about them getting wed. She must be a fool. He knew so little about her and she knew even less about him.

"Oh, God!" he whispered aloud, realising how much he had to hide.

Mistaking this blasphemy as a sign of relief that their wedding wasn't going to be a fancy affair she giggled girlishly, happy in her dreams of becoming his wife. Etta's young man didn't know how fast to get away and he didn't even kiss her goodbye. It was during that week that Jack made his discovery about Samuel Simpson. A discovery that made his legs turn to jelly and his mind tried to blank out the secret that he knew he must share with Etta and Minnie. Jack was acquainted with many of the local reps who did the rounds with their confectionery ranges and it wasn't hard for him to find out a bit more about Sam Simpson. Eventually he found out where he lived and finally traced him to Simpson's Sweets in Middlesbrough.

Chapter 10

Jack had walked the streets of Middlesbrough for hours asking strangers the same questions and receiving the same answers.

"Sam Simpson, no not on this street."

Undeterred, he carried on; someone must know him or of him.

Eventually an old fella on his way to work nodded once very slowly and then taking off his cap, scratched his balding head.

"Well there's Simpsons Sweets on the corner, not sure he's called Sam but his missus is usually in the shop. She should be able to help you, mate."

Jack's blood froze in his veins but he gulped hard and with a weak smile thanked the old lad and turned to look down the road towards the corner.

"His missus, his missus!" the words were whispered, disappearing into the cold air without anyone overhearing. Passers-by jolted and pushed against him as they hurried to get home.

Jack was still in shock but his whole body was beginning to tense with anger and an odd feeling of realisation. He had known from the very beginning that Sam Simpson would break Etta's heart and it had been there in the back of his head all along, "He's married, I'll kill him!"

He bumped into a little old woman who was huddled in a thick grey woollen shawl with a battered flat cap on top of her wispy grey hair.

"Sorry, pet," he mumbled and then without thinking "Do you know a Mrs Simpson, lives around here?"

She cackled as a twisted expression etched itself onto the wrinkled old face. "Barker as was, you mean!" she announced, with an air of conviction.

"Barker?" Jack queried.

"No… no… Mrs Simpson, aye that's what she goes by now... No more a Mrs than the man in the moon. Living o'er the brush she is, we all reckon! A disgrace I say. No ring… no nothing. A scarlet woman, that's what I says!" and with that, she shuffled off, muttering to herself.

Walking blindly against the rain that had suddenly and torrentially set in, he marched numbly forward with the old hag's words resounding in his brain. Finally he reached the sweet shop on the corner. With raindrops dripping down his face, he felt for the door handle with wet and frozen fingers. The door was locked and he slowly took in the sign in the window that declared the shop was closed. Looking round, Jack noticed a green painted door that opened into an alley at the side of the shop. Pushing it open, he walked down the earth path that led to the back yard. There was a lean-to attached to the main building and through the tiny window he spied a tall, stately looking woman. She had her back to him but her hair was knotted into a bun at the top of her head and she was busy folding laundry into a wicker basket. It was difficult to tell how old she was but this, he was sure, was Mrs Simpson.

Knocking hard on the back door, Jack straightened up and gulped before a spluttering cough exploded from his throat. The woman turned around swiftly, glimpsing the stranger outside through the glass in the door.

"Who is it?"

"I'm looking for Sam Simpson, I understand he lives here."

The door opened and Jack looked amazed at the figure who stood in front of him. The woman was indeed tall and stately, handsome even but she was definitely middle aged. Surely this couldn't be Sam's wife, he must be wrong.

"Sammy, my boy," she paused for a second. "And who, may I ask, are you?"

"Mrs Simpson, my name is Jack Dawson."

There was a very long silence as the woman scrutinised the features of the man who had just introduced himself. She had no recollection of any Dawsons and certainly didn't recognise this man.

"And... well... what is it, why do you want our Sam? What has he done now?" Her words were spoken slowly and precisely with an emphasis on the word "now."

Jack was uneasy and anxious as how to proceed. He hadn't expected this. So this was Mrs Simpson or was it? Jack remembered the old woman's words. No matter, it certainly seemed that she wasn't Sam's wife, at least.

"You are Sam's..."

"Mother," she interrupted promptly, "I'm his Mam."

"Yes, well, his mother!" Jack stuttered with relief, "I... I... I'm looking for him you see... I need to speak to him urgently."

"Why?"

"It's a bit private."

"Private, eh?" Her face took on a hard curious look. "Well, he's not here."

"I need to see him."

"He's with his brother and my husband at the wholesalers just now. You could speak to him when he gets back later, if it's that important."

"So he's with his brother and his father, is he?"

She hesitated for a while and then looked quizzically at the man, recognising his north-eastern accent. He spoke with that lilting twang that she remembered well, so it could be he was someone from her past but she certainly didn't recognise him. His behaviour was odd to say the least, although something in his manner compelled her to explain herself to this stranger.

"Well… Mr Simpson is my man but… he's not the boys'…" she stopped short, narrowing her eyes. "Look here, what business is it of yours? Who are you?"

"I've told you. My name is Jack Dawson."

She looked right at him down that long straight nose of hers, furiously turning things over in her head and then blurted out, "Did you know Edwin Ramsey, is that what this is all about?"

Jack was slow to recognise the name but wheels started to turn in his brain as she repeated it.

"Edwin Ramsey died in a mining accident. Did you know him? Is that why you're here?"

Minnie had talked about Edwin many times and he knew the story of the disaster that widowed her only too well. She had also told him in times of despair of the widow Barker who had given her husband the sons that she couldn't.

There was an awkward silence as Jack began putting two and two together. He hoped to God that it made five and that he was wrong. The old hag's words came back to haunt him as he wondered could this woman be the same Mrs Barker. There was no other way; he had to know. He pursed up his lips and pushed his hands deep into the pockets of his overcoat as he addressed her by the name he had heard from Minnie's lips.

"Mrs Barker." His words brought a scarlet flush to her face and she took a deep breath in as the fingers of both hands locked together, turning her knuckles blue. Biting her lip and narrowing her eyes, she stood quite still and tall before him.

"Mr Barker passed away many, many years ago before Sam was born. I'm known as Mrs Simpson now. What's this all about? What do you want from me?"

"Mrs Simpson, we have to talk!"

"Just call me Hattie." She sounded impatient. "Now

spit it out, whatever you have to say. Out with it man!"

Jack had never in his life felt so weak in his stomach. He felt near to passing out and the woman couldn't fail to notice his distress. The coldness in her manner melted slightly as she moved closer to the stranger to offer some support.

"You're not well, man. You'd best come into the house and sit down a while and then you can tell me what's going on before the menfolk get back!"

Helping Jack into the parlour, she sat him down before taking herself off to the scullery to put the kettle on the range. A cup of hot, sweet tea revived him sufficiently well enough to ask one simple question of Mrs Simpson, after thanking her for her kindness.

"Just tell me one thing, do you remember Minnie Ramsey?"

"Minnie!" Mrs Simpson went white with shock at the sound of her name. "Minnie Ramsey, a poor sweet thing, she was. I felt sorry for her and her lassies by the time I realised what a..." She searched for the right word to describe Edwin.

"Go on."

"Well let's just say I was sorry for what happened."

"But Minnie said..."

"I'm sure she's painted a pretty picture of me."

"You could say that."

"And it was true." Her face visibly softened, "At the time, I was a fool where that brute of a husband of hers was concerned.

"You stole him."

"Aye, I did and lived to regret it. Things change, Mr Dawson, time changes folk."

A miner's life in those days was hard and it made some men behave very badly, whether from drink or from the misery and danger of a life spent underground. Unfortunately, Ramsey was no exception. He was a tall masculine man with rugged, almost cruel good looks that attracted attention from women. The combination created a dangerous character and Hattie fell for him hook, line and sinker, just as a young Minnie Taylor did before her. They both were to find out what a cheat he was. After his death, Hattie discovered she wasn't the only other woman in his life, there had been a string of conquests. No female was safe from his womanising.

"Was Edwin Ramsey Sam's father, Mrs Simpson?"

The woman began to get angry. What right had this man to ask such questions? Who was he?

"How dare you, man! Who are you, anyway? What's all this to do with our Sam?"

"I'm Minnie's husband, Mrs Simpson, and we know your lad quite well, unfortunately."

"What's that supposed to mean?" she hissed, growing more agitated at his words.

"It's a long story but a lot rests on who Sam really is."

"What are you on about, who he really is?"

"I have to know who his father was. Trust me, so much hangs on it, both for your lad as well as for our little lass, Minnie's bairn, our Etta."

Hattie contemplated the urgency in his words and as the importance of her answer began to dawn on her, she decided to tell this stranger the truth about Samuel's parentage.

"Very well, if you must know, my son is Samuel Edwin Ramsey and I'm not ashamed to admit it. It's the name that appears on his birth certificate, even though Edwin and me were never wed."

"I knew it!"

Becoming quite disturbed by where this was leading, the woman grabbed Jack's hand and stared at him with a softness in her grey eyes.

"He wasn't all bad, you know, at least he made sure the boys had a father's name on the birth certificates." Realising what she had revealed, she pulled herself together and continued aggressively, "Now then, you tell me what our Sam has done. For God's sake man, tell me what this is all about! What has Minnie's lassie to do with our Sammy?"

"I'll tell you what our Etta has to do with it."

There was a long silence as he rubbed at his unshaven chin and sucked loudly on his teeth.

"I'm waiting. Come on, man."

"It's not easy."

"For God's sake, tell me!"

As Jack's story unfurled, the realisation of what it meant became apparent to the woman and her ashen face crumpled as angry tears ran down her cheeks. Her legs turned to jelly and the room began to spin as she wished she hadn't asked for his explanation. The truth of it was too overwhelming to take in.

"Oh my God! My Sam is Ramsey's boy and your lass... Oh, God help us!"

"You know what this means?"

"I'm no fool, I know what's what." Her words shot out like bullets.

Jack shook his head.

"Your Etta is his half-sister," she recovered long enough to whisper behind her hands, unsure if he had heard.

His pale and twisted face was enough to confirm that he had.

"But believe me, Mr Dawson, he had no idea that the girl he was seeing was... well, he knew nothing of any family connection between them, I'm so sorry!"

"How do you know that?" Jack was curious as to what

she knew about the relationship between her son and Etta.

"We knew he was seeing someone and I tried to find out what was going on but our Sam is canny and doesn't give much away but I can tell you this much, Mr Dawson, he had no idea that he was her brother."

"But he is!"

"If he'd known, it would have killed him. He's a wild one and no doubt, but this... no, he wouldn't do such a thing."

"His own sister."

"It's against nature. I just hope that God can forgive them both." Hattie crossed herself as she contemplated the shame of it.

Jack whistled as he blew out a long breath from his dry lips, rubbing the back of his neck with one hand as he held out the other to the woman who was slumped in a high-backed chair. Beginning to feel sorry for her, his demeanour softened towards her but that was his mistake. Rallying, she regained strength and her previous swagger made her turn on him with a vengeance.

"No, I don't believe any of this!"

"You what?"

"I can't accept that he got himself involved with a girl who was his sister. I don't believe that my Sam and this girl of yours have slept together."

She couldn't bring herself to say any more, glaring at this man who had brought such shame to her door.

"Believe me, they have been intimate; I have Etta's word on it." The bluntness of his words made Hattie reel.

"He's asked our Etta to marry him and she's told us that she gave in to him."

"No."

"Ask him yourself."

She laughed nervously and with a hint of antagonism spat out the words that made Jack's blood run even colder, "Well he couldn't bloody marry her anyway, half-sister or not. He's already wed!"

"Oh God," Jack groaned. It was just getting worse and worse but he wished with all his heart that this marriage was the only obstacle facing his stepdaughter.

"We have to speak to your son."

"You can't."

"Where is he, Mrs Simpson?"

"I don't know."

"When will he be back?" The words fell like snowflakes, icy and harsh and Jack remained determined, even though the broken woman was so obviously falling to pieces in front of his eyes.

Remaining mute, Hattie Simpson was still in a state of shock as she distractedly cleared away the teacups into the back kitchen, leaving Jack alone with his thoughts.

Suddenly a motor truck pulled up outside the shop and voices could be heard as the three men began to walk down the passage. They had been to the lock up where they had built up quite a stock of confectionery which they sold at a good profit around the area. They weren't always fussy where that stock came from, though, and Sam wasn't as respectable as the image he portrayed to the unsuspecting shopkeepers on his books.

"We'll do nicely out of this, Sammy my boy. You did well to get those boiled sweets at such a good price and you were very lucky to find those boxes of chocolates just lying there at the side of the road!" he laughed a throaty tobacco-induced guffaw.

The younger man picked up the boxes containing the heavy jars and sloped off into an outhouse at the side of the shop, leaving his brother and father laughing together as they followed him down the path.

"I'll soon shift them; I've got more than a few contacts who I can charm into taking this lot off our hands and more; no questions asked." He thought of Jack Dawson and his gorgeous daughter. The older man was proud of their enterprise and slapped Sam on the back as he grinned back at him, basking in the glory.

"It's him!" she gasped, returning from the kitchen. "Don't tell him yet. Let me tell him. I need to speak to my man first."

"Very well."

"He'll know what to do."

"More than I do." Jack shook his head.

"He's always treated Sam like his own - the boys never knew Edwin as a dad.

"Better off without him, I'd say."

"Our Jim knew about it, him being older but Sam's a Simpson, always has been as long as he could remember."

Her eyes pleaded with Jack, "Don't say anything yet till I get a chance to talk to Fred. He'll know what to say… he'll… sort this little lot out!"

"I don't know how we'll sort this out. It's a God Almighty mess!"

She broke down sobbing, tears rolling down the still handsome face that had stolen Minnie's husband away from his own beautiful daughters.

"I was all set to kill him, your lad, Mrs Simpson, cos I thought he was a cheating son of a bitch but this… well this is much worse."

"I'll talk to him."

"Aye, you talk to him; I've had enough. I need to get home to talk to Annetta. See if I can find the words to tell her the man she wants to marry is her own… brother!"

Sam's mother's brain was whirling like a spinning top. How could this have happened? She knew what her son was like for the women; but this… and what about Eliza? Hattie didn't have much time for the poor soul but Sam had married her, even if it was for her money.

As he turned to leave the room, the door opened, and Sam and Fred Simpson walked in. There was an icy chill in the air and Hattie's face was red and blotchy, her eyes puffy and still watery with tears. Her man took one look at her and then stared hard at Jack, his face becoming purple with rage.

"Who the hell are you and what's been going off here?" He turned nervously to Hattie, "Why are you crying, pet, what's he done to you?"

As if a light bulb lit above his head, Fred's manner to the woman in front of him changed instantly and he screamed at her, "What's going on, lass?"

"Nothing like that, Fred."

"What have you been up to... eh? Eh?"

"No, you've got the wrong end of the stick!" Taking him to one side, she whispered in his ear as a horrified look appeared on his face.

"What the hell are you telling me, Hattie?"

"It's true."

Turning on Sam, Fred's words shot out, "Do you know a slip of a thing called Annetta Ramsey... Etta?"

Jack, still unable to remove himself from this domestic scene, felt uncomfortable and embarrassed.

"Sam you've got to tell us, you've not got this lass into trouble, have you?" The words mixed with sobs tumbled out of his mother's mouth before she even knew what she was saying.

"No."

Unable to restrain himself any longer Jack barked, "You'd better not have, or I'll kill you, I swear, I'll kill you!"

Fred turned on him, ready to use his fists but Hattie pulled him back, her eyes pleading with him to calm down, not sure whether Jack or Sam was the intended victim.

Sam was confused. He looked at Jack, who he knew as Etta's father. Etta Dawson, of course he knew Etta, but she was a Dawson not Ramsey! Words failed him as he struggled to understand what was happening.

"I don't know any Annetta Ramsey."

"Don't deny it, lad! You know our Etta."

"*Your* Etta!"

"Aye, our little lass that you've been leading on all these months."

"But how?" Sammy's eyes widened and beads of sweat glistened on his forehead.

"Years ago, Etta's mother was wed to Edwin Ramsey." Jack nodded and spoke slowly and clearly watching the realisation grow in the young man's eyes.

"But you are Etta's Da." The sweat on the young man's brow began to trickle down his face.

"Jack, tell me you are her father."

Jack simply shook his head.

"Her mam is your wife… Mrs Dawson. Etta's mother is Mrs Dawson…" he repeated as if to make it real.

"Names change, lad - like your own Mam's - she's Mrs Simpson now, isn't she?"

Sammy nodded.

"But she wasn't always so and your father was Edwin Ramsey just as Etta's was!" Jack stared at the young man, trying to decide whether the awful truth had dawned on him yet.

"Do you understand?"

"No."

"No." Jack echoed.

"I mean, yes. I don't know."

Sam slumped into his favourite armchair as if for comfort, his body shrinking with every word he heard. It had been a few days since he had seen Etta and during that time, he had mixed feelings about her. At times he genuinely believed that he had begun to fall in love with her, but he was a coward and he shuddered as he remembered how he had decided to be truthful with her about his wife. But this was something else, something that he couldn't even begin to comprehend. He could and would never see her again. His eyes were closed, his arms folded tightly across his chest. He looked up anxiously as a floorboard creaked in the back room and a muffled cry could almost be heard. His mother also heard the noises from behind the thick chenille curtain and she hurried Jack towards the front door where they faced each other in private.

"Well, you've got what you came for; more than what you wanted to hear, I'm sure, but my lad is a good man with a good wife and we want no more trouble from that lass of yours."

"You what? How dare you insult our Etta!"

"I'll make sure he never goes near her ever again and we'll forget about this whole nasty business."

Jack was not a violent man but at that moment he wanted to smack her hard across her face. How dare she blame Etta? But she was right. Simpson was never going to see Annetta again. He would make damn sure of that.

Chapter 11

In the days and weeks that followed Ernest Lowes's heart attack, his grandson was never very far from his side. They had always been very close but since Elsie, the boy's mother had died, Ernest was mother, father and grandfather to him. David's early years were happy, if a bit different from the other kids in the street. His Grandpa looked after him at night after working at the forge and his mother watched him by day, before setting off to work at the factory after tea. He never really thought about it when he was a child; his life was happy and not at all strange. His Mam was always there when he needed her; when he fell and hurt his knee or when he'd fallen out with Joseph or Harry at school. His grandfather took him to the forge with him every day, where he liked to play with the horseshoes and sometimes he was allowed to lift the big hammer, or rather, attempt to lift it. Grandpa always laughed at his efforts then showed off as he swung the thing high above his shoulder before letting it drop onto the anvil.

In fact, it was rather an idyllic childhood, growing up in such a happy loving home with the two people he loved the most. He never really missed his father but now and then, after some bragging about how big; how strong; how clever their dads were, he would have a fight with one of the lads and the teasing would stop. It was only ever in fun though and they were best mates again the next day. As he moved into the last class before the move up to the big school, he began to wonder about his father and why he was called David Lowes and not by his father's name. His grandfather never really said very much about it, but his Mam told him lovely stories about the bravery of his father in the war. He had killed millions of Nazis and had been decorated by the King.

His father had been a hero; his Mam had said so!

David had been about ten years old when the clothing factory where his mother worked had been subject to an arson attack and many of those working the night shift, like Elsie, didn't survive. Even after the end of the war, emotions still ran high where Germans were concerned and once his identity was uncovered, Herr Schmitt, the factory owner, was tolerated by some but hated by many. He lost much in the fire but not as much as David and Ernest. For the rest of his childhood, the boy only had Ernest, but this was enough for him and he doted on his grandfather. He spent most of his time after school helping him in the forge. His ambition was to be a farrier like him, but the old man had other ideas. Every night after school, he tested the boy with past 11 plus papers and there would be no time for playing about until his homework was all done. The hard work paid off and David passed the entrance exam for the grammar school. His grandfather could not have been prouder.

The years in between turned a delightful boy into a perfect young man and as Ernest recovered, he remembered those special days. When it came to thinking about a career, Ernest had it all mapped out and directed the lad into staying on at school and taking his A levels. After that, a place at teacher training college was the next big step for David and he accepted a place at Doncaster. The thought of a teacher in the family made Ernest brim with pride and he encouraged him to work hard and do his best.

This attack of his was just a bloody nuisance and he was angry at himself for succumbing to an illness. Ernest had always been such a strong man and he felt helpless and useless. He hated that his boy was having to look after him and he was certainly not happy that it meant him missing college. When David asked for special leave to look after his sick Grandpa, there had been no problem, as he was a model student and would soon catch up on any work he missed. In fact, his tutor admired his dedication to an old man who had no-one else to care for him. It took a long time for Ernie to get over such a serious attack and there were dark days when it looked like he might not make it. But he had always had an inner strength and drawing on it one more time, he managed to pull through for the sake of his beloved grandson. The boy had hardly left his side for the last three weeks. He had to get him back to his studies.

"You can't get rid of me as easily as that," he joked with David. "Once I make up my mind to do something, lad, nothing will shift me, and I've made up my mind to do something before I leave you all my money."

David laughed out loud. He was relieved that his grandfather was making a good recovery, but he still couldn't help thinking about that day on the train. Had it all been his fault? Leaving an elderly man like that had been selfish and all for the sake of a pretty face. David knew his own flaws only too well and there was no doubt in his mind that he was foolish and shallow at times but there had been something about that girl, even Ernest had noticed it, he remembered.

"There's something about that one."

"Oh yeah."

"Just like my Etta she is."

"Oh yeah," David repeated with a grin.

"Never gave up on her, you know. Persevered, I did, until she finally made me the happiest man alive."

"I know, you've told me many a time."

"Same with this one… won't give up, I won't."

"Not sure what you're on about, Grandpa."

"That one on the train."

"Which one? Are you still delirious or what?"

In reality, David was quite convinced that he was talking about Lucinda, but why? What was he up to and why was he not giving up on her? She was nothing to them, even if she was gorgeous; neither of them really knew her, did they? There was one thing he did know about her for sure though – she was a genuinely caring person! She had refused to leave them that day, breaking her journey to make sure that Ernest was OK. She had even come to the hospital with them and only left when it was clear that the old man was out of danger. On leaving, she had pressed a piece of paper with her name and address into David's hand, begging him to let her know how the grandfather got on. Of course, Ernest wasn't aware of her concern for him as it was several days before he was fully conscious. When after many months, he finally felt strong enough to recall his thoughts on that day, he found the girl's face had come back to haunt him. He couldn't seem to shake off the beautiful, ethereal image which had so reminded him of his beloved Annetta. How could this girl resemble her so much? It was uncanny and unnerving and no matter how hard he tried to forget her, he couldn't.

"David," he said, as his grandson sat by his chair in front of the roaring fire eating most of the purple grapes he had brought in the day before. The boy looked up and smiled, cocking his head on one side, eager to hear what Ernest was about to say.

"What do you know about that girl on the train?"

"What girl?" he teased.

"You know who I'm talking about, now tell me what you know!"

David was so happy that Ernest was feeling and looking so much better, so he began to describe the girl's appearance, knowing this wasn't what his grandfather meant.

"Well, she was a gorgeous bit of stuff, Grandad. I think even you could see that!"

"Aye I'm not dead yet."

"Fabulous fiery hair and the sexiest green eyes, she had."

Ernest managed a smile and raised his eyebrows, "Stop being soft, lad, you know what I mean."

"Right!" David sucked air in through his teeth and then began, "She's called Lucinda and she's an art student in London."

"An art student."

"I think she comes from some posh family other side of Newcastle."

"She looked like money."

"Plenty of money!"

"Money's not everything, David."

"You're right. She was a nice girl and you know what?"

"Come on then."

"She's got a Dossie. That's all I really know!" he laughed, feeling pleased with himself, waiting for a reaction.

"What?" Something triggered in his brain, "What's that about Dossie?"

"Well, it's a bit of a coincidence, isn't it? She said she had a friend called Dossie and I told her I had a Great-Auntie Dossie once."

"Dossie."

"I did, didn't I? Grandma Etta's sister was called Dossie... that's right, isn't it?"

"Yes... Dossie... that's right!" Ernest paused, "You didn't know her, though."

"No."

"You never met her. I'm sure of it."

"Yeah, you're right I don't think I ever did meet her,

but I remember Mam talking about her all the time."

"I didn't know your mam knew her."

"Yeah, she used to give her sweets and things when she was a nipper, but the name is so unusual, I've always remembered it."

"Well I never. She kept that a secret."

"It just seemed… well, it seemed odd for that girl to know someone with the same name."

"Dossie was just a nickname lad. Doreen, that's her real name. Never knew that she used to see your Mam." The words trailed off and he seemed deep in thought.

"She often talked about her to me. Never knew her real name was Doreen though."

"Your mam never mentioned it to me ever."

"Why was that then, Grandpa?"

"There was some bad blood between Dossie and your Grandma Etta, so haven't seen her in years but I think she's still around."

"Where is she now?"

"Not sure. Married a fella called Clifford, if I remember correctly."

"Didn't you go to the wedding?"

Ignoring the question, Ernie continued. "They both worked on some fancy estate just south of Newcastle. He was the farm manager or something."

"A good job, then?"

He stopped to think, wrinkling his brow and rubbing his chin, "No, he was the gamekeeper."

"Gamekeeper; lots of perks to that job."

"That's it, the gamekeeper. Dossie was some kind of maid to the lady of the house."

"I don't believe it, you old bugger!"

"What you on about?"

"You're having me on," David snorted, but things seemed to be making a strange sort of sense. "I knew she was a cut above the rest of us but you know what, I think that girl on the train, Lucinda, is some toff who lives on a country estate."

"Lucinda?"

"Yeah Lucinda, Lady of the Manor! That's how she would know Dossie."

David looked pensive before grinning at Ernest, remembering what he had said to the girl that day: "You're just a spoiled little rich girl, milady."

The grin disappeared as he carried on in a more serious vein.

"There was never any doubt that she was posh with a capital P but do you think she could be proper.

"Proper what?"

"How on earth can she have any connection to us?"

"There's a connection to my Etta."

"How?"

"I don't know, but the likeness is unbelievable. When I first saw her, I swear to God, I thought she had come back from the grave!"

The whole thing was ludicrous. The old timer must be losing it but even so, David was intrigued and fascinated by it all. He decided to placate him by locating the girl so that he could put everything to rest, including his dead Grandmother's ghost. Suddenly remembering the scrap of paper that Lucinda had given him on the day when Grandpa collapsed, David tried to remember what he did with it. In the confusion of pulling the emergency cord and getting the old man to hospital, it had been stuffed into his coat pocket and completely forgotten about.

"As soon as I'm up and about, lad, we need to go see your Auntie Dossie."

"If we can find her."

"If there's any link between that little girl and my

sister-in-law, then she is the key to this mystery, I'm sure of it."

"You mean Dossie and Lucinda are connected?"

"I just have to find out why some little rich girl is the image of my Etta when she was a lass."

"Grandma Annetta looked exactly like Lucinda? Are you sure?"

"I'm sure."

"You know, Grandpa, the mind can play very funny tricks as we get older?"

David's voice sounded sceptical but never having met his late Grandmother, how was he to know?

"No, David, Lucinda looks like her; exactly like her!" Ernest made it quite clear that he was not to be argued with. "And may I add, young man, I am in full command of my faculties."

"Of course, I didn't mean anything like that. I know your brain is still as sharp as a knife," adding under his breath, "maybe a little blunted, if truth be told."

Reprimanding himself for his unkind thought, he went on, "But you always said she had beautiful blonde hair. Lucinda's hair is red."

"Just like mine was before age stripped it of its glory, Davy boy. I had a shock of ginger hair when I was a young man."

"You don't have to tell me, us kids used to call you Grandpa Carrot Head!" David chortled at this memory and then added, "Only a joke, you know we all loved you even though you were a ginger."

Ernest raised his eyebrows and a half-smile played on his lips. David was laughing but his head was beginning to burst with strange ideas as nothing now seemed to make sense. He thought he knew where Grandad was going with this but it was incredible. After all, he was an old man and he had just had a very serious heart attack; it could be that he was delirious or simply delusional. No matter what, David decided he would take him to see Dossie and settle this matter once and for all. That was if he could find her, of course!

"Do you really not know where she is now, Grandpa? Dossie, I mean."

"Not sure, lad, they fell out, they did... Etta and her sister. Never knew the real reason, she would never talk about it."

"Strange."

"Dossie didn't even come to our wedding, which I couldn't really figure, 'cos she'd always held a bit of a torch for me, I think. Mebbe that's why; couldn't face losing me." The old man gave a wry smile and his grandson bent double in laughter.

"You old Casanova. Bit of a ladies' man, were you?"

"Why aye, course I was. I've not always been an old codger, you know Davy. Believe it or not, I was once as good-looking as you; no... better looking!"

The elderly man chortled loudly, as the younger man huffed theatrically at this remark but then Ernest's face took on a serious look and he continued, "No, there was something that went on that was never mentioned so we didn't really see anything of Dossie for years."

"So, do you think she moved away or did she stay in service?"

"Don't know."

"What happened to her and where was she, last you heard?" Too many questions were confusing for Ernest and he shook his head, brooding on his lack of ability to remember things these days.

"Told you, lad, lady's maid or some such thing in that big house t'other side of Newcastle. Can't really remember where, though."

Ernest's memory was fading these days. He didn't

always know what day it was but he could usually recall things from long ago. But this time the details evaded him completely. His face contorted as he desperately tried to dredge up the information that David wanted.

"I should remember it well, you know. I used to drive her back there most Sundays, in the carriage, after she'd been home to visit with the family."

"The carriage!"

"Aye, lad. Horse and carriage. There weren't many cars about them days and it were a good excuse for me to quiz her about Etta."

"Did she know you fancied her sister?"

"I think she fancied me. I remember quite clearly how she used to smile and giggle at all my silly stories."

"Did she, now?"

"Aye, well, I was a bit of a joker back then. Had a way of making the lassies smile."

David nodded encouragingly and with real enjoyment at the picture of the man his grandfather had once been.

"She was a pleasant enough lass, was Doreen Ramsey."

He laughed a sad little laugh, almost to himself, thinking about those days so long ago. But then an image of Etta's giggling face at the sight of him wearing a tattered old straw hat festooned with flowers that he had grabbed from a horse's head, caused him to grin from ear to ear. The animated way his grandfather relayed these tales from the past with such vigour gave David hope that he was gaining strength and would be back to his old self before too much longer. He would soon be able to return to college. Laughing at his amusing reminiscences, he teased him about his exploits but Ernest was pensive. Why could he remember such a silly little thing from so many years ago, yet couldn't recall the information that they desperately needed to find out more about that girl.

The boy's mind was in turmoil as he thought about the bit of paper handed to him on the day Grandpa collapsed. If only he could find it. He was beginning to think that there was really a connection after all. If they found Lucinda, they would find Dossie and vice-versa. His grandfather was convinced that his Dossie and Lucinda's were one and the same. And David was convinced if they found Dossie she just might unlock the reason for the girl's resemblance to her sister. It was just a feeling but he was sure there was some reason for the remarkable likeness.

Chapter 12

Since that day when she had talked of wedding plans, Sam had kept a low profile and Etta resigned herself never to see him again. She would remain an old maid, just like Annie Hogarth had prophesied so long ago; she would never marry, for if she couldn't marry him, then she... Well that was that! She had heard nothing from her beloved now for days. Obviously, he had fallen out of love with her or had Jack threatened him with actual physical violence? Yes, that was it! Jack must have terrified him into leaving but Sam was no coward. He'd come through the war and from the few details he'd let slip, Etta knew how horrific that experience had been for a lad of seventeen. He was one of the lucky ones who actually survived; came back alive and in one piece. Most of them didn't. He wouldn't be scared off by a threat of a punch in the face from a middle-aged shopkeeper. No, not Samuel!

Jumbled thoughts fought for pride of place in her poor befuddled brain. He had been in an accident - that was it. An accident in that stupid new automobile of his!

"Oh, my God!" Her thoughts spilled out of her mouth in a piercing scream that brought her mother running from the back kitchen.

"Etta, what's the matter? What's happened, lass?" Minnie's eyes were like saucers and her mouth dropped open in sheer terror.

"Sam's motor has crashed, I know it has, Ma, and he could be lying in a hospital bed, not remembering his name, not remembering me."

Minnie sighed with a mixture of relief and anger that her daughter was well enough to have such daft ideas.

"Don't talk rubbish, my girl, he's a wrong 'un, that one. That's all there is to it. Best you forget him once and for all."

The conversation between Jack Dawson and Sam Simpson had been enough to make him think twice about the game he was playing and he had deliberately stayed away for a few days to let things cool down. Etta wept large salty tears, finally taking in the truth. Mam must be right. Sam Simpson was a bad egg and she had to get him out of her life before he destroyed it! Perhaps Jack had done her a favour. Regaining some of her old swagger, she spent some time doing up her hair and preening in front of the mirror, determining to put the man she thought she loved completely out of her head.

Neither Etta nor Minnie knew that Jack wasn't satisfied with Samuel Simpson's response to his warnings or of his decision to find out more about this young man. He had been away from home for hours already and Minnie was getting worried. Little did she know that he was searching the streets of Middlesbrough for Samuel Simpson. He had told her that he had business to attend to but this was the first time they had been apart for so long since the day they wed. Just one phone call had told her that he was fine and that he would be home by supper but Minnie knew there was something more to this business than he was telling her.

"I don't know what he's up to, our Etta. It's not like Jack to be so secretive... well is it, Et?"

The daughter simply shrugged her shoulders and continued dusting the brass scales that sat proudly on top of the shiny shop counter. Etta had thrown herself into her work, filling up jars and stacking shelves but to no avail. No matter how hard she tried, nothing seemed to erase Sam's memory from her brain and she felt the life draining out of her body with every minute that passed. Minnie stared long and hard at the ashen face and felt a pang of guilt that tore at her heart, then suddenly she rushed to the huge wooden press that stood against the wall in the parlour. Pulling out a heavy drawer she retrieved a pad of best quality paper and a tin that rattled with pencils of different hues.

"Here, pet, why don't you take the afternoon off and set about your drawings like you used to? Jack won't mind and I can finish off in the shop. There's not much left to do."

Etta looked at the pad of paper in her mother's hand and felt a tug of want... of need... in her own heart. Without saying a word, she took the art materials and left the room, leaving a smile on the older woman's face. Sketches flew from the pencils in Etta's skilful fingers and faces and figures emerged as real and lifelike as if they were in the room with her. The more she drew, the more she felt relaxed - calm, even - and the memory of Sam's caresses began to fade. Furiously she ripped page after page from the artist's pad as she completed sketch after sketch, each one better that the one before. The talent that had been left to stagnate for so long was still there. Etta was a real artist but where was the dream? It had died when Sam Simpson arrived in her life. He had somehow sapped her creativity and power but now, she told herself he was gone; she could rekindle all her ambitions once and for all. Memories came flooding back and Etta remembered how strong she had been before she met him; how she had planned to run away to London to become an artist. She remembered her dreams.

"Why not?" she said aloud.

"Why not what?" Minnie idly responded to the statement that hung in the air like gossamer.

This was not the time to discuss such matters and Etta simply smiled and shook her head which seemed a good enough response to Minnie, who was only too pleased to see her daughter smiling for the first time in ages. Secretly, Etta started again to make plans of what she could do and how she could get to London, thoughts flooding into her mind, lighting up her face and lifting her spirits. The brightness returned to her eyes and the sparkle that seemed to have died within her slowly resumed its brilliance.

"Why stop at London?" she mused. There was a great big world out there. "Why not America?"

Etta knew nothing of America except what she'd read in the tuppenny Cinema Play papers she bought every Saturday afternoon or seen in the silent movies that sometimes showed at the Picture Palace. She recalled the faces of her favourite stars of the silver screen: Rudolph Valentino, Clara Bow, Mary Pickford, Douglas Fairbanks and Charlie Chaplin. She'd read somewhere that Charlie, the little tramp with the stick had been English. It could happen. Once she had become an artist, she could go to Hollywood. America was a place of opportunity for an artist like her, she told herself, thinking about the wonderful gowns that Clara Bow wore in those films. Those dresses were nothing compared to the ones she imagined and created on paper using just her pencils. Deep in thought, with images of the film stars that she idolised flashing through her head she dreamed of escaping to this make-believe world. Suddenly her expression changed as she realised what a silly stupid fantasy this was. She would never venture any further than this depressing little north-eastern village. She sighed heavily and slumped into a chair with an air of despair etched on her face.

"He's not worth upsetting yourself over, hinnie!" Quite mistaking the reason for her daughter's anguish, Minnie tried to soothe her troubled thoughts.

Etta said nothing. Her mother didn't appreciate any of

this. She couldn't understand the frustration and dissatisfaction that ate away at her.

"Now Ernest is such a good man, I can't think why you sent that one packing. A real catch, was Ernest Lowes, down to earth lad, not a fly by night like… this other one."

Etta remained silent. She was so very confused; she suddenly realised that she hadn't really put Samuel out of her mind, grasping what she felt for him was still there in the pit of her stomach. Ernest Lowes was a good reliable man and she knew how much he loved her. But that was the problem; he loved her too much. He gave her too much power over him and she couldn't help herself but abuse it. She preferred the rogues like Sam, who treated her badly, who made her heart miss a beat and her palms sweat. But Ernest was decent and deserved to be loved, not tormented. A sense of disgust and shame for her behaviour overwhelmed her as she remembered the last time she had been with Ernie. She had treated him so disgracefully. It had been a few days before Christmas, a very busy time for the shop. Children were filled with excitement as they flitted in and out asking for sugar mice and chocolate pennies. Ernest had been very much on her mind at this festive time as she remembered the remorse she felt at the way she had treated him. He had looked so forlorn and upset when she refused his proposal. So, a few days later, she made up her mind to try to make it up to him.

It was a snowy evening when she waited for him as he was stabling the horses. Standing there in the dark with the moonlight reflecting up from the icy ground she looked enchanting, almost ethereal and when she asked him to walk her home, his heart skipped a beat. There was never any way he would have refused her anything and his hopes rose once more. She's changed her mind, he thought, she wants to marry me. But this was not the message she was planning to give him that night. She questioned her motives and found herself to be completely immoral. Why was she drawn to bad men instead of decent ones like Ernest Lowes?

The tack room was warm and deserted for the evening and Etta guided the young man into the darkness, breathing in the heady smell of leather and oils. Saddles and bridles hung on the wall and blankets were piled on top of an old oak chest with a broken lock. Her eyes were twinkling in the half light and sweat was forming on the young man's brow. Etta had always felt something special for this lovely boy who looked at her with such adoration. But she couldn't marry him when her feelings for another were so strong, so sensuous, so dangerous. Looking with half-closed eyes at the pile of blankets on the chest, she smiled the most beguiling smile Ernie had ever seen. He nervously grabbed the coarse horse blanket from the top of the pile and spread it out on a small heap of hay in the corner of the room. Etta looked quizzically at her suitor, feigning modesty and innocence before throwing back her head allowing her carefully coiffured hair to fall over her face, half covering the seductive gleam in her eyes. He could stand no more and Ernest pulled her down onto the blanket where she lay contemplating what was to happen next. This was to be her parting gift to a wonderful man, she told herself, as she finally gave herself to him as only she could. A slight feeling of shame mingled with warm thoughts as she recalled the familiar tenderness that existed between the two of them. She didn't feel the cravings that Sam instilled in her whenever he touched her but when she was with Ernest, there was a genuine fondness that was built on trust and regard for one another. But it was the fire in her belly for Sam that filled her every thought and Ernest Lowes was resigned to the very depths of her memory. Her mind was in turmoil. She didn't know who or what she wanted as she first thought one thing then another.

She had a far-away look in her eyes as she heard her mother repeat his name, "Ernest would make a very good husband, Etta!"

"I've got a headache, Mam."

Minnie, realising that she was getting nowhere with her daughter, gave it up as a bad job and stormed off into the parlour.

After a while of quite intense sulking, Minnie suddenly remembered something that took her mind off Ernest Lowes.

"Oh!" she shouted from the best room, "forgot to tell you, I'm off to see our Dossie tomorrow. She has some news for me. Whatever it can be, I can't think."

"She could be expecting a baby!" Etta's words danced across the room playfully and without much real thought as she giggled at her mother's excited reaction to potentially becoming a grandma.

"No... they've only been married a few months," she mused and then, "No it's been ten months."

"Really, has it been that long?"

"Etta you're right, our Dossie's in the family way. That's what she wants to tell us, I know it."

"Maybe."

"Think, Etta, a youngster."

"Lovely."

"A little baby! Oh, Etta, I can't wait to be a gran."

Whatever had she started? It had only been a bit of nonsense but now she had convinced Minnie that Dossie was pregnant. Could her sister really be expecting a baby? The thought of it actually terrified her but of course it was totally feasible. Dossie was a married woman and it would be perfectly natural for her to be with child but what if she herself was pregnant? She hadn't really thought about the possibility of getting caught herself until now. But it was completely possible. Sammy had never been very careful about their lovemaking.

Oh God, she panicked as she felt at her own belly with a mixture of emotions. What if she was expecting? There was no chance now of Sam marrying her, his absence had made that clear enough and she certainly wouldn't blackmail him into it. Turning over these troubled notions in her head, she reassured herself it had only been a couple of days since she'd seen him, she could just be over-reacting. If she was pregnant, he would want to marry her, she was sure of it. Although there was no longer any certainty as to whether she wanted to marry him. Her senses were all over the place and she didn't know what to think. An unwanted baby would be the worst thing she could wish for at this time. And what was more, if she was in the family way, then she could wave bye-bye to her dreams of ever becoming a real artist. Furious thoughts buzzed around her head like bees in a hive and then she said very quietly, "I won't be going to London. I'll be stuck here forever."

She left Minnie, who hadn't heard that last soft sad utterance, in the front room and rushed off to her own room. Her emotions swung erratically between despondency and elation and it wasn't long before hot salty tears were spilling from her limpid watery eyes. As she threw herself down onto the little bed covered with the pink satin quilt, her pillow was quickly being soaked with a bucketful of inexpressible misery.

"Everything is over. My whole life is over."

As the day turned into night, Etta had recovered herself well enough to open the door to a very weary Jack as he returned from his mission. He could tell she had been crying and his intention to reveal the secrets of the day was thwarted. He would tell her tomorrow when she felt better and when he had found the courage to deliver the news that he knew would destroy her. Minnie was relieved to see him and couldn't wait to tell him her suspicions about Dossie.

"She's pregnant, Jack, I know she is. I'm going to be a Grannie."

Trying his best to sound enthusiastic about the news, Jack muttered something about being very tired and took himself off to bed, leaving Minnie a little perplexed, to say the least. But she was just so thrilled with the prospect of welcoming a new grandchild into the world, it soon passed and she was quick to join her husband in the marital bed. The next morning was taken up with preparations for the journey to Cranfield and there was little opportunity for Jack to speak to Etta alone. She had woken late, still too distressed over her situation to face the overwhelming happiness and joy that her mother was feeling over the news from her sister. Eventually, she managed to return to her duties behind the counter, apologising to Jack and putting her absence down to a sick headache. The shop was busy, which helped Etta to forget her troubles for a little while and her only thoughts focussed on weighing out the boiled sweets and wrapping the chocolates in lovely little packages tied up with red ribbon. She kept a close eye on a couple of scruffy lads who loitered at the back of the shop while filling up some empty glass jars with gob stoppers.

Suddenly she remembered her sister's letter. Self-pity had consumed her thoughts completely but now she suddenly recognised that she was not the only one with problems. Mam was convinced that the news from Dossie was good but something told Etta that it was far from that. If all was well with her sister's pregnancy, she would have come herself or brought George to give them all the good news. She had a strange feeling that all was not well. It was just a niggle but although she desperately tried to shake it off for her mother's sake, she couldn't rid herself of the premonition. Pulling herself together, she shouted to Jack that it was getting late.

"You'd best be off then, Ma." The words greeted Minnie chirpily as she strode back into the shop, where Etta was staring wistfully into space. There was no need to upset her. Not yet anyway. She would find out soon enough if anything was wrong.

"Ta-ra then, pet. It'll be late by the time we get back. Don't you wait up for me."

"No, take care, Mam."

Grabbing her best hat and coat, Minnie kissed her younger daughter on the forehead and set off anxiously to meet Jack, who had gone to get the car out of the garage in the alley at the back of the shop.

"Jack."

"Aye, pet?"

"Jack, we'd better get going. Get a move on!" Minnie shouted out excitedly but her husband seemed miles away, completely lost in thought. How could he tell Etta and Minnie what he had found out, knowing it would destroy them both? That swine had ruined their lives but he just couldn't bring himself to tell them the truth just yet.

The car drove off with a silent Jack behind the wheel and a twittering wife by his side. Left alone, Etta shook herself out of the black mood that had eaten away at her all day. She didn't feel pregnant and even though she and Sam had made love more than just the one time she hinted at to Minnie, there was no real evidence that she was with child. Finding out that Dossie might be expecting had put these strange notions into her head. That was all it was. Even so, her belly still felt a little swollen and her breasts were slightly tender. Her monthly curse had always been erratic so the fact that she was late didn't really mean anything. What a fool she was to think like this. She wasn't pregnant; her married sister was. Shaking away such stupid ideas, Etta reminded herself of the strength, the independence, the passion she possessed and reflected on those early dreams. They could still come true. She told herself it was true. She didn't need any man to succeed in life. She could be whatever she wanted, have whatever she wanted. She would always have her way!

The day drew to a close and the business of the shop subsided, leaving a strange empty feeling that threatened to overcome the optimism that had begun to brighten Etta's mood. The house seemed incredibly still and quiet without her mother and Jack blustering about with their idle chatter and good humour. The silence disturbed her and the previous light-heartedness that had wiped away her gloom over losing Sam threatened to disappear with the last of the daylight. The gas lamps flickered and spluttered, hissing menacingly in the darkening room. She sat down in the parlour, slumping into the red velvet chaise that stood in pride of place under the window. Closing her eyes, thoughts flitted behind her eyes creating pictures of chubby babies and pretty pink infants; the kind she used to sketch when she fancied herself a mother. Her eyelids closed slowly and her breathing deepened until a sweet sense of drowsiness began to consume her. If only her mother and Jack hadn't interfered, she could be married to Sam by now with a child of their own. Every waking moment brought thoughts of him and now even in her drowsiness, he dominated her existence. His tall frame towered over her as his handsome face fragmented in front of her like a magical kaleidoscope pattern. And then she was asleep.

She was woken just before midnight as Jack helped his distraught wife into the front room. Rubbing her eyes and suppressing a yawn, Etta rushed to help.

"What's wrong, Mam? What's happened?"

"It's our Dossie, pet, she's expecting." The words escaped in between sobs, leaving Etta totally confused and perplexed.

"But that's good news, Ma."

"It's not so simple Etta, things aren't quite right." Explained Jack.

"What do you mean, not right?" Etta's face crumpled and she was near to tears herself.

"They've said she must have complete rest and..." Minnie broke down again.

Jack took over the conversation, trying to explain as well and as gently as he could, taking her trembling hands in his.

"The baby could come early, pet, too early even. Do you understand what that means, Et?"

With eyes as wide as saucers, she stared at the man she thought of as a father and simply nodded her head until her chin rested on her chest and her shoulders shrugged.

"And if she manages to go full term, she could give birth to a dead child, Etta. Can you imagine that? I can't bear to think about it. I can't, I just can't. A dead baby; a poor little dead mite. My poor, poor Doreen."

Somehow Etta had known that something had been wrong all along but the realisation of it now was heartbreaking and she clung to her mother as they both wept in total despair.

Jack could only look on, wondering when and how he could give Etta more devastating news. But it had to be done.

Chapter 13

Since the day she was born, Lucinda Addington had been watched over by Doreen Clifford. A poor little mite left to the mercy of the strict and old-fashioned lady of the house. There had always been a connection between them; there had to be! Lucinda was her own dear departed sister's grandchild after all, and she had been responsible for how things turned out. The child knew nothing of her real background or her relationship to the woman who had looked after her from the day she came into the world. This was yet another secret that Dossie was to keep. She loved the little girl as truly as if she had been her own daughter, just as she had treasured Arthur, her sister's son and Lucinda's father.

The day Arthur was born was one Dossie would never forget.

"He's beautiful, Etta," she said, with genuine tears rolling down her cheeks as she passed the child to her sister.

"I don't want to see him. He's a little bastard."

"No, Etta."

"He's… he's cursed!" Etta was exhausted from the birth which had been long and difficult and as she spoke, she thought about the man who had ruined her life, her own brother!

"But he's perfect." Dossie stared down at the child who so reminded her of another man, the one she had loved for so many years in secret.

"How can he be perfect?"

The baby's head was covered in a fine auburn down and his eyes so reminiscent of Ernie's. Everyone always said all babies looked the same but this one was the image of Ernest Lowes, the young man who had so often driven her back to the hall in the little buggy that had been dressed up so beautifully for her Mam's wedding. She recalled that day in every detail. The memory of how his hand had lingered on hers as he helped her down from the carriage flew into her head, making her giddy and lightheaded.

"Etta, I know that you say this baby is Sam Simpson's but are you sure?" her words came out slowly and almost in a whisper.

"I was to marry the man, Dossie."

"I know, but…"

"Of course it's his child. Who else would be his father? I am not a whore!"

Etta became agitated and her head thrashed from side to side. Images of Ernie's handsome and reliable face came flooding into her unconsciousness. His lips on hers, hard and passionate as his hands searched her body, finding it warm and eager for his caresses. That night when she said goodbye to him was to be their first union, an act of love so intensely bittersweet and powerful that the memory would stay within him for his whole life. It would also be the one sweet memory that helped bring Etta through the darkest of times. Shaking the notion from her mind, Etta pictured the man who had ruined her life, Samuel Simpson… no - Samuel Ramsey - her own brother who had seduced her, breaking down her resolve never to truly love any man. But she had come to realise that she never really loved him despite the many times she spent in his bed. Her feelings for him were fuelled only by lust and her punishment was to give birth to his son.

The shame of her actions brought on another violent outburst and she shrieked, "I am damned, Dossie!"

"Shush, my love."

"No, you are right I am a whore and my child is a bastard."

"I'm sorry, pet. Just calm yourself." Dossie stroked her sister's head, wiping the cold sweat away with a muslin cloth.

Once Etta was asleep, Dossie took the baby and popped him into the crib that Lady Addington had provided. It was painted wicker with translucent drapes hanging from a canopy above the child's head. She took a deep intake of breath and looked at him again, very hard this time, taking in every detail of the child's face. She stroked his tiny head and felt the golden wisps of red hair and told herself that all babies looked the same. Of course her sister was right. The child was Samuel Simpson's son. He had to be. Etta said so! As the exhausted mother slept fitfully, Lady Addington quietly entered the room, gliding silently over to the crib, where she stood for several minutes just staring at the beautiful baby boy.

"He looks like such a good child, Dossie, don't you think? So contented."

Tears welled up into her sad eyes, flowing down her cheeks and sending salty drops into the corner of her mouth.

"Yes, he's a bonny lad."

Dossie could imagine just how much her ladyship was hurting. To lose a child was devastating, as Dossie knew only too well, having lost her own precious baby only weeks before. But to know, as her mistress did, that she would never carry a child in the first place was tragic and she somehow wanted to comfort her. Agatha Addington had been widowed early in her marriage and had no desire to be wed again but her very soul ached for a child and Dossie knew it.

"Why don't you pick him up, milady? Hold him in your arms. He feels so lovely and soft."

"The smell of him is quite delicious." The older woman hesitated for a moment and then bent towards the crib to gently feel the little fingers curl around her own. She reflected on the years past when she had tried desperately for a child. Each time there was no pregnancy, she retreated further into a world of her own. A world where time stood still and nothing moved on. Until now. With her husband dead she could never give birth to her own child but this little boy needed a mother. He needed her.

Denying her feelings, Lady Agatha tried to walk away from the little bundle, "I can't, I mustn't."

"Why not milady, no harm in a little cuddle."

Dossie's voice was encouraging, willing her mistress to take the boy in her arms, knowing that she wouldn't be able to put him down.

Agatha's voice was shrill and resolute and seemed to come from somewhere outside the room. "No he's not mine!"

Dossie just looked with disappointment in her eyes as she turned to sit by the side of her poor wretched sister.

There was a stillness in the room as the three women each contemplated their own destinies until it was broken by her ladyship's refined vowels shaping the words that Dossie wanted to hear.

"I think, my dear, I could…"

"Of course."

"I could hold him, just for a moment."

"Why not?"

The words were whispered so quietly that Etta didn't hear them as Dossie busied herself mopping the sweat from her sister's brow.

New-born cries startled the new mother as Lady Addington disappeared with the boy into the next room, swaddling him tight against her heart that was thumping hard in her chest.

"He needs feeding, Etta; can you hear him crying?"

"Let her take him away, I don't want to see him!" she screamed hysterically until her eyes were red and tears flooded her pale face.

Dossie's milk had already dried up after the stillbirth but as she prised him gently but firmly from her mistress's grip, the infant suckled unsuccessfully at her breast. She felt an overwhelming love for the child and gazing down at his beautiful little face, she was reminded of a young man who had so often sat with her on those long buggy rides to Cranfield. There was absolutely no doubt in her mind that this little one was fathered by Ernest Lowes and she was holding his child in her arms. At that moment she felt so close to the only man she had ever truly loved. It was then that she knew what was to be done. She would be his mother. She would love this boy... Ernie's little boy. After all, Etta didn't want him, believing him to be Simpson's baby but she knew better. This child was the image of his father, the man who Dossie had loved secretly and for so long. She would keep him here with her. Suddenly her plan to get Lady Agatha smitten seemed ill-chosen and unfortunate. The days passed in a routine of frantic feeds, cracked nipples and dirty napkins as Dossie spent too much time looking after the new-born. Etta seemed to get stronger and the colour began to return to her cheeks but her spirit was broken and a strange numbness seemed to take possession of her being. After a little while, she was well enough in body to leave Cranfield but a veil hung over the whole household as words were left unspoken and a foreboding embraced the three women. Lady Agatha hovered around the two sisters and the baby, never really saying what she was thinking, making Dossie increasingly anxious. She avoided her mistress as much as was possible but always refrained from looking directly at her whenever they came face to face.

At the end of the second week after the birth, Dossie was in the morning room removing the best china tea things from the pedestal table that stood in the window. Suddenly a voice came from behind and she turned to look into the eyes of the lady of the house.

"Can you go and fetch your sister please Dossie, we need to speak."

At that moment, the two women stared deep into each other's eyes. The cool blue of Agatha's eyes looked cloudy and hard like boiled sweets whilst the deep rich brown of the other woman's betrayed the pain that she felt. Her eyelids stung like nettles but she wept no tears as she simply turned on her heels and almost ran across the courtyard to her own little cottage. She found Etta preparing to return home, carefully folding the few garments that she had brought with her into a battered Gladstone bag. Looking up, she caught her sister scrutinising her every move but there remained a silence between them that spoke more than any word could possibly convey.

Finally Dossie spoke.

"Her ladyship wants to speak to us in the Morning Room. Leave that now and come quickly. Etta, please come now, at once!"

Putting down a crisp white starched nightgown, Etta nodded and wiped her hands on her skirt before patting the untidy strands of her beautiful hair into some sort of order.

She remained silent and resolute as Lady Addington asked very pleasantly, "What are your plans, dear?

"I have no plans, madam."

"Do you have employment to return to?

"Perhaps."

"Are your parents happy to receive you back into their home under the circumstances?"

No answer came back as Etta stared blankly into space.

"Will they allow you to keep the baby?"

"I don't want him."

The questions were clipped and came fast with no pause between them for answers and then came the one question she really wanted to ask.

"What do you intend to do about the child?"

"I don't know, your ladyship." the answer was short and concise.

Dossie opened her mouth to speak and the words tumbled out rapidly.

"Then I will take him, your ladyship, bring him up as my own child, and he can live here with me as my son, I can..."

The mistress looked aghast and cut her off in mid-sentence.

"Your son! What about your husband, how would he feel about bringing up another man's child?"

"It doesn't matter."

"I really don't think you have thought this through, my dear."

She paused and took a deep breath, peering quite unemotionally at the woman who was her servant.

"I am sure you and Mr Clifford are both under a tremendous strain after losing your own precious baby but you must think how such action as this would affect him. It is a ludicrous idea!"

Dossie was quite taken aback at the mention of George; she hadn't considered his feelings at all.

"And as much as I don't want to mention this matter now, I have to ask how you intend to carry on your duties."

"I can still see to everything, milady."

"I have been very patient over these past weeks,

Dossie dear, but you have seriously neglected your work here at Cranfield."

"No, I'm sorry but I will try harder. I will work harder."

"I am afraid it cannot continue." Lady Agatha peered at her servant with no sign of any emotion. "Do you understand what I am saying?"

The message was most clear and the lady's maid was put firmly into place, leaving Dossie feeling aggrieved and distinctly undermined.

Etta looked on with an air of calm detachment, making no attempt to express any opinion at all about the fate of her new-born baby.

Dossie knew how well she had manipulated her mistress into wanting the child for her own and was now regretting her actions. Her feelings for the little boy had grown out of all proportion and she couldn't give him up but what was she to do?

Without thinking she burst out, quite irrationally, "But your ladyship, I must have him, he is my…!"

It was at this moment that Etta broke her silence, turning to her sister with an air of determination and fortitude. "This baby is mine, Dossie, and I will decide on his future, not you!"

Lady Agatha smiled to herself as she put a gloved hand onto the young woman's shoulder to demonstrate support for her words, hoping that she knew what she had in mind. The young mother casually pulled away.

"Lady Agatha, can I thank you for allowing me to stay here with my sister during my confinement?"

"You are welcome, my dear."

"It has been most generous and kind of you and I can only apologise if my sister's attention to me and to the child has inconvenienced you at all. I am ready to go home and I will…"

There was a very long pause as Etta searched for the right words, then said, "I will organise for him to be adopted so my sister will not feel any obligation to leave her position with you."

"You can't do that." Dossie's face was twisted in pain as she clapped her hand against her mouth to stop herself from saying more.

Ignoring her sister's distress, Etta broke in without any sign of emotion, "You have treated us both so very well and Dossie is happy here. I would hate to be the cause of her dismissal."

Etta had a way with her that made everyone take to her, even grand ladies like Agatha. She was able to put such refinement and gentility into her words that she appeared ladylike herself and the older woman had no doubt that she could make a gentleman out of Etta's son. There would be no need to look elsewhere for his adoption. Agatha was undeniably impressed with this slip of a girl and was about to put a proposition to her. But Dossie held up a hand to her ladyship's mouth and she uttered words that were almost inaudible; words that Agatha did not want to hear and would never accept.

"No, you can't have my boy; he is mine!" Dossie's face was white with anger and grief.

"I would give up everything to have him, everything, everything!" This time the depth of sentiment came out of her mouth in a scream so piercing that it brought tears to her eyes.

Her ladyship was appalled at the action and her face was stern and her eyes fixed as she froze Dossie out of any further conversation. How dare this domestic behave like this. She would put an end to this nonsense once and for all and she made a very formal, almost official declaration.

"I have decided that I will bring up Arthur as my own

child. He will live here at Cranfield as my son and heir. It is settled. I will hear no more."

"Arthur… she has already named him," whispered Dossie, as she fought back the tears.

Still indignant at the maid's behaviour, Agatha nevertheless felt an empathy for a woman who had suffered the pain of losing a child and was prepared to forgive her conduct.

"It is for the best. We can give him a very good life here at Cranfield. He will have everything he could wish for and he will be a very privileged child, I can assure you of that."

"But…"

"I hope you can both agree that it would be best for the poor little mite to remain here at the hall as my son."

Etta looked deep in thought for a few moments as she looked first at the crumpled face of her sister and then dispassionately at the grand lady and nodded whilst uttering a single word of consent.

"Yes!"

She fully understood that if her baby was brought up as her sister's child it would be disastrous. He would be forever connected to her. No, he was being offered a charmed life. He would have everything that she or Dossie could never give him. "Yes, it is for the best," she said, not this time to the lady of the house but to her sister as she turned and walked away.

"But… but!" stammered Dossie, almost uncontrollably.

"Leave it, Dossie!"

Not totally insensible to her maid's anguish and grief, Lady Agatha attempted to lessen the hurt, continuing as kindly as her personality would allow.

"I will require the services of a nursemaid, Dossie, and in spite of your atrocious behaviour I am willing to consider you for that position."

Her voice softened slightly and she whispered, "You would be able to spend time with the child that way."

At the same moment, Mr Clifford, her husband knocked and entered the room. It was as if he had been waiting for his cue as he strode purposefully across to his wife's side and took her arm in his huge gnarled and workworn hands.

"Her ladyship has consulted me on this matter and I agree it is for the best, Dossie, my dear. Please, my love, come with me."

He had anticipated this breakdown for days now, as his darling wife had struggled with her emotions at seeing her sister's child alive and well, imagining their own sweet boy dead in the cold ground. There had been several conversations between the gamekeeper and the lady of the house, discussing what was best for his sister-in-law's illegitimate child. George Clifford had been well respected by her husband and with no man in her life, Agatha valued the objective, male opinions that he was able to offer. He had made it clear that his wife was not in a position to adopt the baby and her ladyship was far more equipped to provide for the boy.

"Come away, this can't go on. You must pull yourself together, pet. I know how hard it has all been for you but you can't replace our little lad."

George's words were firm but there was a kindness beneath that demonstrated the strength of his affection for his wife. Dossie's eyelids fluttered involuntarily and she almost fell to her knees but the grip on her arm was strong and firm as the gamekeeper led his trembling wife to the garden, where they sat in silence on a wooden bench beneath the great oak. After what seemed like hours, during which time she had pondered deeply on what was said, Dossie turned to face her husband, the hurt rising to the surface, surging through her veins.

"I don't want to replace him; we can never bring our own dear sweetheart back from the grave!"

The words shot from her very soul, followed by a such a painful howl that it made George shudder.

He knew as he cradled her in his arms that she had never really loved him. He had seen the look in her eyes every time Etta spoke of the young man who declared undying love for her and when she told her how she had laughed at his proposal, Dossie's heart had hardened towards her sister. The relationship between the two women had changed from the sisterly love of their youth into something more disturbing. He had witnessed it himself on numerous family occasions when a jealousy had turned his lovely wife into an unpleasant individual whom he hardly recognised. She had grown pious and self-important but once pregnant, the engaging girl he had fallen for seemed to resurrect and return to him. But fate was to change all that.

She was vulnerable, having just lost their own longed-for child, and he knew that her fevered imagination believed that the new-born was Ernest's. He had to make sure that she was not allowed to claim this baby for her own or he would lose her forever. However, even to a man who thought all babies looked like wrinkled prunes, there was a something familiar about Etta's boy and he was not going to allow his wife to bring up another man's child, particularly if that man was Ernest Lowes. Back in the morning room with the dappled light filtering through the heavy lace curtains which hung at the huge symmetrical windows to the front of the house, Lady Agatha was a picture of confidence. Outlining the conditions of the adoption, she was now in total control and was satisfied that very soon she would have a son of her own. Her head was held high, showing off the exquisite lines of her aquiline nose and forehead and her gaze never wavered as she stared at Etta before continuing in a most unemotional fashion. Her words were clear and typical of her position and Etta seemed to listen intently whilst demonstrating the same level of emotional detachment.

"I will raise the child as my own but he is to have no knowledge of you or any of your family."

"Yes."

"I am not insensitive to Dossie's feelings. She has served me well and if willing, she can help look after him as his nanny but it is imperative that she understands that she can never disclose her connection. I will have my solicitor draw up a legal contract. What do you say?"

Etta seemed to swallow hard yet simply mouthed aloud that same single word, "Yes!"

The one-word answer was succinct and clear and with no apparent sentiment attached and with that, Etta left the room purposefully and resolutely, giving up her son without ever looking back.

Lady Agatha shouted after her, "I will have my solicitor draw up the legal papers for you to sign in due course; there is no need to do it now, my dear."

The triumphant lady breathed heavily and made to return to the child she had named Arthur, her dead husband's name.

Chapter 14

In the first few weeks of Etta's return to the shop after the birth of her unwanted child, Jack Dawson had written to Dossie, asking her to come at once and most urgently. He was not the sort to ever write letters, so when Dossie received an envelope with his name and address on the back she was at the same time both worried and curious. She tore it open without using a paper knife so that it split in two and almost damaged the paper inside. Thankfully, the letter was still in one piece and as she unfolded the white sheet, she looked first at the signature to determine if it really was from her stepfather. It was simply signed "Jack."

She read out loud the few short words that were contained within the letter:

We are very worried about your sister.
She isn't herself. Please come at once.

It was a simple, short correspondence but Dossie knew that she had to leave immediately. Lady Agatha was obliging, if a little belligerent, about being left alone with the baby for the day, but after seeing how upset Dossie was, she quickly arranged for the motor to be made available to her. Doreen Clifford had risen in the world. She was seen as a very valuable member of the household since Arthur's birth and was held in high regard by everyone except Mr Clifford. She didn't even tell him that she was leaving. Their paths didn't really cross very often these days, except to exchange daily civilities. They hadn't lived as man and wife for some considerable time. Dossie dressed quickly but made quite sure that she was wearing her very best finery. A beautiful black hat with a wide brim and a large feather was taken out of the box and placed carefully on her head as she arranged her hair underneath it. Taking a glimpse of her reflection in the hall mirror, she adjusted the seed pearl brooch at her neck and smoothed down the hobble skirt that matched the fitted blouse. She was a fine figure of a woman these days and looked the very picture of respectability, unlike that floozie of a sister of hers who favoured the flapper look.

She greeted the chauffeur, not as an equal in the household, but as his superior, waiting for him to open the door of the limousine for her. A fine automobile arriving outside Dawson's shop created quite a stir in the neighbourhood and curtains began to twitch all down the street. The sound of the engine woke Etta from her sleep, and she walked as if in a daze to the first-floor front window, where she witnessed a fine lady getting out of a car. Puzzling as to the identity of the stranger calling on them, it suddenly dawned on Etta that the fine lady was her sister.

"What does she want?" she said to herself, but out loud.

She listened intently, with her ear pressed to the bedroom door, to the muffled voices coming from the little back sitting room downstairs behind the shop.

"They're talking about me," she sang in a singsong fashion. "She's talking about me. I know she wants to be me. She's always wanted to be me. But I am me so she can't be me, now, can she?"

Etta continued rambling, half-singing the words, half-whispering.

Her face was very pale and her previously beautiful hair straggly and lifeless, hanging over her forehead like a tattered piece of lace curtain.

"Annetta! Are you awake? It's nearly midday. Annetta!"

A shout from downstairs made her eyes widen and her head tilted to one side like a bird. Holding herself very still she breathed in steadily and then pursing her pink lips into a perfect "O" she let out a long silent whistle.

"Etta!" the shout came again. "Are you awake yet? Your sister is here."

"I'm not quite sure if I am awake or not really," she said, again to no one in particular, and then she danced around the bedroom with an imaginary partner.

Footsteps were heard on the stairs and then the bedroom door flung open, and her sister stepped in very slowly and deliberately. Shock froze her steps as she desperately tried to take in the scene facing her. Dossie stared at Annetta for a long time, unable to come to terms with the image in front of her. She looked so ill, so distracted, almost manic. She recovered herself well enough to ask quite naturally, "Etta, how are you?"

Without waiting for an answer, she carried on without being able to stop herself from stating the obvious.

"You look terrible."

Etta wasn't at all upset by the rudeness of the remark and merely replied, "Well, you look lovely my dear, do you think we have changed places? You are me and I am you!" She giggled uncontrollably.

Dossie was shocked and frightened. Was her sister mad? She knew without a doubt that the birth of a baby could seriously disturb some women and they just had to pull themselves together but she had never before seen anyone behave so insanely. In that moment, she knew exactly what she had to do, and she stepped towards the other girl, slapping her hard across the cheek. A red stain began to appear on her face as she put her hand to her mouth. There were no tears, no cries just silence as Etta's mouth opened wide and she exhaled a long slow soft breath. Dossie was taken aback by the response. She had expected her sister to come to her senses, break down even, but she didn't envisage the little scene that was now acted out.

Etta stared straight through her sister with an almost vacant unemotional look on her face.

"Who are you and why have you come here?" She said in a tone that sounded quite lucid now.

Dossie recovered quickly and put an arm gently round her sister's shoulder. "You are not well, Annetta. I've come to help. I think the birth has somehow unbalanced your thinking, my dear. You are not in your right mind, Etta."

"So you've come to put me away, have you?"

"No, no dear sister, I have come to help you."

"Have you, indeed?"

"Look, Etta, I know you are hurting. It was awful the way he left you, but I know his secret."

Of course Dossie meant that she knew he was married but it was another secret that Etta thought she meant.

She screamed and went for her sister's hair, pulling at the tidy bun at her neck until strands of chestnut hair escaped onto her shoulders.

Dossie was bewildered by the assault but tried not to show her distress, "I know that he couldn't marry you, so you mustn't blame yourself," she soothed, as she recovered herself after the attack.

"How can I not blame myself for sleeping with my own brother, Doreen, answer me that."

Annetta's sudden recognition of the stranger as her sister seemed to restore her senses and she became quite coherent.

Dossie reeled at the words. She was not expecting this. This must be yet another figment of her sister's fevered imagination.

"Your brother," she gulped but again, recovered

quickly. "You have no brother. We don't have a brother."

"Samuel Simpson is our brother. His father was our father."

Dossie was convinced Etta was raving and tried to placate her.

"But he isn't your baby's father, Etta. I am sure of that and you should be too."

"Oh, so you think our little Arthur is Ernest's baby, do you? That's why you wanted him so badly. You have always wanted everything that I had, since we were children. You have been jealous of me, Doreen, from the day I was born."

"You're wrong Annetta. Wrong about everything. Think rationally, Etta, we have never had a brother."

Etta only laughed, dismissing her sister's protestations. Her face froze as the smile disappeared and she began coldly and cruelly, spitting out every poisonous word.

"You may have wanted my son, but I made sure you didn't get him, didn't I? He belongs to Lady Agatha, I made sure of that. You may be his nursemaid, dear sister, but you are only a servant. You will never be his mother, remember that. You are not his mother." She emphasised. "You are only a servant and that's all you'll ever be!"

The words cut deep into Dossie's heart and soul and she held onto the door handle as Etta continued to erupt like a giant violent volcano.

In fact, she screamed wildly at her sister until her face was red and twisted, "You are nobody's mother, are you, Dossie? You poor, childless, unloved excuse for womanhood."

She hesitated while she waited for a response and on seeing the tears begin to well up in her sister's eyes, she continued brutally. In that instant Etta Ramsey was a true daughter of the man she despised.

"I pity that husband of yours. Does he know that you never loved him? Of course, you only ever had eyes for those who loved me. That's right, isn't it Doreen?"

With that, she sat down calmly on the bed and watched her older sister, a broken woman crying silent tears, leave the room,

"What's been going on?" asked Minnie anxiously, "We heard shouting and screaming. What's been said?"

Jack looked on helplessly, completely unable to fix this problem in his family. It frustrated and angered him as a man who could usually mend anything, from a leaking tap to a broken chair. But he couldn't put this back together again and there was no doubt about it.

"I'm going, Mam and I won't be back as long as she is under this roof. I know she's ill but the things she said to me..." She paused, remembering the hurt her sister had caused her. It was if she had taken a knife and thrust it deep into her heart.

Jack anxiously tried to make things better and agreed that Annetta was very ill but Dossie wasn't listening.

"She's mad, Jack. Going on something rotten and talking rubbish about a brother. We don't have a brother, do we, Mam?"

Her mother put her hands to her mouth before speaking very quietly and precisely, "I don't know how to tell you Doreen, but you do have a brother." As she looked to Jack in expectation, waiting for him to explain the whole sordid business, she continued in a whisper, "In fact, pet, you have two and one is Samuel Simpson, or should I say Ramsey."

"It's true, Dossie," said Jack. "Please try to forgive your sister. She doesn't know what she's saying right now and that's a fact."

Dossie's face was white and expressionless for a moment, and then it contorted into ugliness as she screwed up her eyes and bit her lip.

Jack revealed the whole story to a grief stricken Dossie, who remembered her father with true hatred at that moment. Flashes of a tall woman with two little boys shot through her brain as she recalled that event so long ago. Remembering how her mother had screamed like a fishwife and how she had dragged her away from the scene brought a realisation that was so deplorable that she put it out of her mind immediately.

"This is all too much to take in right now, Mam. I can't believe any of it!" The words escaped between sobs.

She put her hands to her face and dragged them across her cheeks. Her brain was whirling as she struggled to make sense of what she had just learned.

"I don't know what to think. All this must have turned her mind, I know that, and I feel sorry for her, I really do. She's not well and I can understand why but I still can't forgive her. I will never forgive her. I will never forgive him."

"Oh, you mustn't think like that, Doreen. She's your sister," but Minnie was left wondering who she meant by him. Was it Samuel Simpson or was it her dead father?

"I vow I will never forgive her again, no matter what you say."

And with that, Dossie left her mother's house, returning to the car driven by her ladyship's chauffeur, who had waited patiently outside the house. He had listened with interest to the shouts and bawling yells coming from the upstairs room as he raised his eyebrows slightly. The merest hint of a smirk touched his mouth as the respectable Mrs Clifford slid into the back seat of the limousine, dabbing at her red swollen eyes with a spotted handkerchief that belonged to Jack Dawson. Contemplating the juicy titbits he would enjoy with those below stairs when they got back to the hall, he turned his head to look at Dossie, who barked at him to drive. Without looking back, she swore she would never speak to her sister ever again.

Chapter 15

While Etta was confined at the hall, Ernest fought hard against his feelings for her until he could fight no more and he decided to seek her out. He hadn't seen or heard from her in months, so decided to go to see Minnie and Jack. He asked at the shop every day for news of Etta but Minnie refused to say where she was or give him any hint as to what she was doing. He only knew that her relationship with that other bloke seemed to be over. There had been some gossip in the village about him being a married man. But Ernie knew what it was like. Those old women could turn white to black with their evil tongues, so he didn't really know what to believe and the family were closing ranks, refusing to tell him anything.

"Best forget her, Ernest. I'm only thinking of you, my lad. She's gone and that's that!" Minnie said, with an air of finality.

There was a time, not so very long ago, when she had dreamed of her daughter making a match with this young man. If only things had worked out differently but now it seemed impossible to put them right. She was convinced if Ernest found out about the situation her daughter had found herself in, he wouldn't want anything to do with her. What respectable man would want to take on a ruined woman who had given away an illegitimate child? But worst of all, if he discovered the whole truth, she feared that he would spread rumours that would bring disgrace upon the whole family.

Jumbled thoughts raced through his mind as he listed every single thing that could have happened to his beloved Etta but eventually one inconceivable idea stopped him in his tracks.

"Has she married him? Is that what you're trying to tell me?"

There was such an anguished look on his face that Minnie felt a huge wave of sympathy for the young man who she respected and admired. She was tempted to tell him everything and hope for the best. But before she could say another word, her husband opened the door and stepped inside, guiding her to the comfy chair.

"No Ernest, she didn't marry Samuel Simpson." Jack strongly denied any relationship between Etta and that scoundrel and his words flew like arrows firing into the air with such a force that Ernest was left bewildered at his response.

Regaining his composure, he asked the next logical question, "Has she gone to that fancy art school, then? Is that it? The young man hung his head, "Not good enough for her, now that she's moved up in the world, am I?"

Minnie and Jack remained mute. Minnie didn't want him to know anything of the circumstances surrounding her daughter's predicament. She had managed the neighbours' gossip very well, telling everybody that Etta had taken up a place at the art school in London, but Ernest would dig around for more if they told him anything at all. He needed to let it go, forget all about her and let her get on with a new life once this mess was all sorted out.

Neither of them really knew Ernest Lowes at all. Nothing Etta could ever do would prevent him from loving her, now and forever.

Finally, totally exasperated, Ernest turned and raced off down the street in the pouring rain, throwing his best cap into the wet road in a hot temper. It had been months since that last magical time he had spent with her in the tack room and even though she told him they were finished, he continued to carry a torch for her. But where was she? No one would tell him anything. As he retrieved the sodden cap, he shook it vigorously to remove the wet mud. The coldness he had felt from Minnie froze his very bones as he stood shivering and drenched from the storm. He had come to the end of his tether and he resolved to end this misery even though he knew he would never forget the girl who had captured his heart so completely. It was time to finish it. He couldn't take any more.

Well that was it, he told himself, as he wrapped his muscular arms around his own body and stamped his feet to try to bring a little warmth back into his limbs. Forget Annetta Ramsey; damn and blast the girl. He didn't need her. There were plenty of other fish in the sea.

"You can all go to hell; the lot of you. I don't need anybody, least of all Annetta Ramsey or Dawson or whatever bloody name she goes by these days!"

Not a day went by that Ernie didn't pass the shop, but he didn't go inside anymore and he didn't ask about her. It was as if her world was separated from his, even though the enigma that was Annetta remained buried forever in his psyche. Instead he spent all his time at the stables. He still drove the carriages and waggons now and again, but he was working more and more with the horses. He had always groomed and stabled them, and he certainly had a way with the animals. They seemed to respond to his voice and his touch, and he could get even the most nervous filly to settle.

Images of Etta still flooded his dreams at night but during the long days, he threw himself into work and thought little of her, except to prove to the lot of them that he was somebody with prospects, not just a stable lad. Mr Burnett the farrier regularly visited the stables to shoe the horses and repair equipment and he had taken a liking to Ernie; most people did, he was that sort of a fella with his broad smile and outgoing personality. He treated Ernie like a son and delighted in teaching him the tricks of his trade. They enjoyed a good banter together as Ernie learnt how to do things properly and the young man had a genuine respect and regard for his mentor. He had shoed horses many times whilst working at the stables although it was usually a makeshift job but now, he was realising there was more to this business than he could ever imagine. It was one thing to put a shoe on a horse that fits the foot but an entirely different thing to put a shoe on a foot that both fits and gives the right support. Working with Charlie Burnett, Ernie perfected the skill of shoeing a horse correctly so that he got the right fit of steel on the hoof. It was highly skilled work, but he was a fast learner and his empathy with the horses made the work easier for him than for most others. His arms and hands were covered in burns and nail pricks but he didn't mind.

"You're doing well, Ernest, my boy. You've got the knack alright and no mistake." Charlie patted the young man hard on the back, so hard that he almost stumbled on the cobbles in the stable yard.

They both chuckled loudly as Ernest recovered himself and shook the older man's hand heartily. "Thank you very much, Mr Burnett."

"Nay, lad, thank thee. You've been a grand help these past months and there's no doubt!"

Ernest glowed with pride as he shyly asked, "Can I come to the forge some day and learn more of the trade, Charlie? Do you think I could do it? You know, be a proper farrier, like you?"

The old man smiled and shrugged his broad shoulders.

"Not as good as you, of course; I could never be that good but I'd work hard!"

And he meant every word. He would work every hour

of every day if it allowed him to learn a trade and better himself. He was humbled by the level of skill that was required to shoe a horse well and he began to master some of the aspects of the craft working with Charlie, quickly realising though that a good farrier never stops learning. Burnett was a good man, who supported his wife and six kids very well from his labours and it was Ernest's ambition to perfect the skills that had enabled his master to procure such a level of security. The young man admired him greatly and was determined to model himself on his hero. He was reaching a time in his life when he craved what his parents and Charlie all had. His own folks didn't have much, his father, a collier, never had a lot of money but they had a decent home and they had each other. But Ernest had faith in his ability, hoping that one day he could have the same sort of life as Mr Burnett if he carried on working hard.

It was then that she emerged again, like a spectre. Never really disappearing from his mind, thoughts of Etta intruded into his life once more. If he was successful, she might respect him, marry him; even love him. She was still his obsession and every second away from her seemed like a lifetime. He had lived a thousand lifetimes since their last meeting and no matter what he did or how hard he tried to ignore his feelings for her, she returned to haunt him time after time. Over the many months that she was missing, Ernest Lowes hardly slept. Mr Burnett and his brother Bert took him on at the forge and he did learn how to become a farrier. Learning how to remove shoes carefully as well as shoeing with new ones came easy to him; he was a natural. Repairing equipment and making chains required more dexterity and proficiency and it was hard work, but he mastered the new skills quickly.

He enjoyed the work but the most important thing to

him was that he now felt a renewed pride in himself. No longer was he just a stable lad who sometimes drove waggons and carriages. Now he had the beginnings of a trade that would always be needed. So many more automobiles were on the roads, it was true, and it was only in the very rural areas that you saw the traps and carts that had provided his employment since he was a very young lad. But people would always want horses; for work, for pleasure, for racing and so there would always be a job for a farrier. By the end of the year, he was working full time for Burnett Bros Farmers and Agricultural Farriers and General Smiths and he was earning more money than he had ever seen in his life. He was a man with prospects, with a future ahead of him and when it came to attractive young girls, he could take his pick of the bunch. But there remained only one bloom that Ernest Lowes truly desired.

"Are we off for a well-earned tankard of beer then, boy?" asked Charlie at the end of one very long and hard day. They had worked at the stables at the racetrack in Wetherby and it had taken a long time to get there and back but Burnett Bros were well known across the north as being the best in their trade and their services were very much in demand.

"Aye, I think we deserve a glass of bitter or maybe even two or three," chortled Ernest. "No lass to get back to then?"

"No one special, Charlie. I've got a few on the go through." His face cracked into a cheeky grin. "They can all wait!"

In truth, Ernie had gone out with quite a few bonnie lasses in the last few months but nothing ever came of it, even though many of them wished that it would.

Ernest Lowes was quite a catch, not only was he in excellent employment, but he was also a very good-looking man; tall, well-built and with that shock of hair that sometimes looked chestnut, sometimes auburn like spun gold but never ginger. Unusually though, his beard was almost dark in places with strands of red intertwining and he let it grow as he knew how the ladies loved the way it made him look brooding and mysterious. Undeniably, there was something enigmatic about him these days. Every pretty girl in the county tried to catch his eye at local dances and country fairs but while he smiled and flirted with the best of them, his thoughts were always on someone else. Try as he may, he couldn't get Annetta Ramsey out of his mind or indeed out of his heart.

In the end, as Christmas was approaching, he decided to visit the Dawson's shop one more time. It wasn't far and he walked the short distance, trudging through the thick snow feeling the crunch under his heavy boots. People were chattering in the streets, carrying trees and parcels wrapped up in brown paper and he greeted one and all with a cheery grin and compliments of the season. He felt light-hearted and happy - a feeling he hadn't had for a long time - but he had convinced himself that this would be yet another fruitless visit. However, this time it didn't seem to matter. He would simply wish Minnie and Jack season's greetings and let them know how well he was doing. He was proud of his achievements and he had come a very long way since those days when he simply drove the little trap around the village.

As he approached the shop, the tearoom part of the building was brightly lit and seemed busy as all three of its little tables were full of customers sipping tea and eating hot buttered crumpets. He stood for a while, smiling at the festive scene and envying the way the women were fussing over their menfolk and the way the men were gazing at their lovely wives. As he turned his eyes away from the scenes of marital bliss, he looked up and came face to face with the one person he never imagined that he would ever see again. Annetta was dressed in a very plain black dress with a fetching white apron covering the front. On her beautiful blonde head sat a ridiculous frilly confection that would compete with anything that could be created to adorn the sweet shop window. He couldn't stop himself from laughing out loud; a real guffaw that brought stares from inside the shop. Whether it was at the sight of her in that outfit or the simple fact that she was just there: there, in front of him after all these months; it didn't matter that laugh made him the happiest man in the world. People peered at him through the window and a buzz went around the room, making Etta aware of the confusion that he was causing.

The large picture window was steamed up, but he was clearly visible to her now. A young man with red hair and an unusually dark beard grinning inanely at her through the glass. Screwing up her eyes, she stared back at him, not quite recognising him at first because of the beard on his face but there was no mistaking that hair. It was Ernie. Snow had begun to fall again in the late afternoon of that Saturday in December and flakes were sticking to the dark bristly whiskers. Now it was her turn to laugh. He looked so comical, standing there with a beam on his face and covered in snow. She put down the china teapot that she was carrying onto the counter and dashed out into the street to where he stood. Without a coat to protect her from the cold and still with the silly little cap on her head, Annetta Ramsey fell into Ernest Lowes' arms to the amusement of the customers sipping tea in the little café room in Dawson's shop.

Chapter 16

Returning home from college for the Christmas break, David soon discovered that time had done nothing to remove the obsession to find out more about the girl on the train from Ernest's mind.

"Have you found anything out about that bonnie lass, Davy? You know, that one that looks so much like my Etta."

"Oh, I thought you'd forgotten all that nonsense, you daft old duffer."

In fact, he had been searching for the elusive slip of paper that Lucinda had given him for days without success, knowing full well that Ernest would ask about her as soon as he got back home. It wasn't in his trousers pocket, or in his winter coat. Realising that Ernest wasn't going to give up on his quest, he concluded that it would be easier to play the game, so he continued to try to get his grandfather to recall the grand house where Dossie worked. If they could find her, then he felt sure she would lead them to Lucinda.

"Think, Grandpa, think. Where did she work?"

"Aye, well, I'd pick her up after church and then drive her out to the hall so she'd be there before it got dark. Many a Sunday, it was."

"Go on."

"I always spoke kindly of Etta and asked after her. Then we heard she'd married a man on the estate, Dossie I mean; older bloke, as I remember. Can't remember now what it was he did. Gardener, I think."

"No, you told me he was a gamekeeper."

"Aye, you're right, young'un, he were a gamekeeper. Lived in thon cottage on edge of that big estate."

"Where Grandpa, where?" he urged.

"Aye thon cottage. It was somewhere in the fields

surrounding the big house."

"Somewhere in the fields?"

"I don't think I ever went there, Davy, but Minnie must have told me. I recollect something of the sort."

He was rambling again. It was no good. Grandad couldn't remember where the big house was and they couldn't go to every grand house in Northumberland asking for Dossie, now, could they? It was crazy!

He paced around the room, trying to rid himself of the whole stupid business. His grandfather was old and his mind was wandering; that's all this was. The deluded imaginings of an old man, but he couldn't resist a challenge and if he was honest with himself, he wouldn't mind a chance of seeing Lucinda again. He couldn't quite shift her image from his brain.

Aimlessly, he walked over to the window in the cottage he had shared with his mother Elsie and his grandfather. She was Etta and Ernie's third child, the only surviving one. Etta had miscarried their first baby and given birth to a stillborn boy before giving birth to their only daughter. She was the one who had taken his grandmother's life. His beloved wife had died in childbirth and Ernest had never really forgiven the child who took her life.

The day she was born, Ernie screamed at the old midwife who held the chubby babe in her scrawny arms. She made to present Ernest with his daughter, but he turned violently away, almost knocking the tiny lady into the door as she smoothed down her blood-stained white apron. She began to wash her hands in the blue and white earthenware bowl that had been placed next to the drawer that was to cradle the baby amongst the soft hand knitted blankets. His wife lay on the big double bed completely exhausted by the labour. It had been long and difficult birth and Etta's frail body was almost lifeless as he took her hand in his and kissed it tenderly. In a low soft breath, she begged him to bring her the child to hold in her arms. The midwife shook her head and signalled to Ernest to follow her out of the room. When they were alone, she put her hand gently on his shoulder and smiled weakly.

Still holding the screaming infant in her arms, she gave him the news he dreaded.

"She's had a really bad time, Mr Lowes; lost a lot of blood. I've sent for the doctor but she may not make it."

A feeling of sheer dread overwhelmed him and his legs turned to jelly.

Heading back into the bedroom, the nurse put down the child into the prepared drawer that sat upon the old dark wood dresser and asked quite innocently, "Don't you have a cot or a crib Mr Lowes?"

"Aye, lass, we had a beautiful cradle all ready for the last two but Etta wouldn't have one in the house this time; said it was bad luck."

"I'm sorry."

"Aye, bad luck, she said." Tears streamed down his face, wetting the stubbly growth of hairs that had started growing on his chin and cheeks since his last shave days ago. "I begged her not to try again after the other two babies died but she desperately wanted to give me a son."

"I didn't know about any of this, Mr Lowes. I'm sorry."

It's my fault; all my fault. She wasn't strong enough!"

"Ernest, where are you, my love? Don't leave me. Stay with me, promise me you'll never leave me." The urgent words sent him racing back to the bedside where Etta lay pale and ghostly but still as beautiful as she had ever been to him.

"I'll never let you go," he whispered, as his wife's breathing became more laboured and shallower until it stopped completely.

Anger replaced the alarm he felt a moment ago and he lifted her lifeless body into his arms and let out such a piercing scream like that of a wounded animal that it brought the midwife running into the room.

"She's gone. No need for a doctor now, it's too late." He wept like a baby until he had no more tears left to cry.

Night was falling fast and the light in the room was dimming so that sinister shadows danced across the walls but Ernest didn't budge. It must have been more than an hour since she had sent for the doctor and in all that time Ernest hadn't moved. He was still holding his dead wife in his arms and despite all the midwife's efforts, he wouldn't leave her.

"Will you come away and look at your beautiful little daughter now, Mr Lowes." The old woman pleaded, "The tiny mite needs you. She needs a father."

Take her away, I can't look at her."

"Oh, come now, you have a beautiful little girl."

"She killed my Etta." His voice was loud and filled with hurt and pain. "Take her away. I don't want her. I want my Etta!"

Eventually, the baby girl was sent home with her maternal grandmother, and Etta was taken away and laid in the cemetery. Minnie was to feed and clothe the child and she made sure she was well looked after. She knew her duty. But there was no love left in the old woman's heart. She was a changed woman. The last few years had not been kind to her. The forbidden love that had tortured Etta had also scarred her very badly.

Yet another war had taken its toll and the loss of her beloved Jack almost destroyed everything that was warm and good in her. It was not the bombings that had taken his life; they had all survived the tragic years of homes being razed to the ground and lives shattered by combat. He had died in a flu epidemic, the worst since the 1918 pandemic that killed so many. It was ironic they had both survived the Spanish Flu, only to fall to the latest round of influenza at a time when they were at last realising how to control it. But it was the death of her beloved younger child giving birth to her granddaughter that finished her off. Unlike Ernest, she felt no anger towards the child but at the same time she had no love left in her heart for her either.

Elsie lived happily enough with her grandmother until she was old enough to make her own way in life. Even though she attached no blame to the girl for the death of her mother, she remained a painful reminder of a lovely daughter and Minnie didn't stand in her way when she said she was leaving home.

"Mr Jepson has found us girls some lodgings near to the workshop," she beamed, quite proud of her independence."

"Not far to get into work and Mr Jepson has said that if I work late, he'll pay me more and he'll take me home after."

"Oh yes."

"There's a big order for Fenwick's; ball gowns, Ma. Can you imagine me stitching gowns for grand ladies? Mr Jepson says I could have one."

"What? Those dresses cost a fortune. Why would he give you one?"

"Not one of the good ones, just something that's not just right."

"Not right, what on earth are you talking about girl?"

"He calls them seconds, does Mr Jepson. What do you think, Ma? Can you see me in a posh frock - can you?

"Not sure I can, pet."

Mr Jepson says I'll look like a real lady. Mr Jepson

says I deserve a nice dress. He thinks I'm pretty." The words tumbled out without a pause until Minnie stopped her in mid-flow.

"Enough now, about Mr Jepson. You just take care, my girl. Remember to be a good girl!"

"Oh, I will, Ma," she said, with wide innocent eyes. "Mr Jepson says I am a very good girl."

Minnie's heart sank as she remembered how Etta had fallen foul of that rogue Simpson. "Like mother, like daughter," she sighed.

Elsie was a pretty enough young woman; no way as lovely as Etta but she certainly attracted attention from the wrong sort. She was such an innocent, with strawberry blonde hair and grey eyes, just waiting to be taken advantage of. When she got the job as a dressmaker in a small workshop of six girls that belonged to a wealthy businessman in Sunderland, she thought she had made it. It was a good position and there was no doubt that the girl was an accomplished seamstress. It wasn't just her work that brought her to the attention of the boss, her wide-eyed innocence and her desire to please made her a prime target for his depravity. Mr Jepson was completely lacking in morals and he liked his conquests young and impressionable, so he set about luring the poor young woman into his web. He was older and sophisticated with handsome good looks and an invisible wife. There was never any doubt that Elsie would fall head over heels for him and of course, the inevitable happened.

When she became pregnant, he didn't want to know about it and tried to persuade her to get rid of the baby. He had money and knew people. It wouldn't be difficult to arrange but Elsie refused. She wanted the baby. Not daring to tell Minnie, she was friendless with nowhere to go except for her lodgings, where she couldn't escape the advances of the man who had abused and abandoned her. She had told Aunt Dossie, of course, half expecting her to take her in or persuade her grandmother to let her return. But Minnie was too old and set in her ways to cope with another illegitimate child and Dossie knew she couldn't take her back to the hall; it was all too complicated.

"Go and see your father. He's a good man; he'll take care of you."

Dossie sounded matter of fact and detached; so much so that Elsie felt a sudden coldness towards her. Why was this woman not helping her when she had been there for her, her whole life? And so Elsie reunited with Ernest. The moment she arrived at his door; it was obvious she was in trouble. The old woollen coat she wore was stretched tight across her belly and he knew she was pregnant. He was certainly not a hard man and he wouldn't see his only daughter on the street even though their early relationship was clouded by so much grief and anger. The neighbours were told she had been tragically widowed and she spent her pregnancy growing fat and contented back with a father who she had never really known. Ernest did his duty and looked after the girl as best he could but he couldn't bring himself to feel any real affection until the sight of a bouncing baby boy melted his heart.

"We always wanted a boy," he sighed.

"Are you pleased, Dad?

"Two dead babies and then you came along Elsie and now him. He's a grand lad. What are we going to call him?"

That was the moment that transformed Ernest Lowes. His relationship with his daughter grew and they at last became close as the painful memories of the past disappeared with the birth of his grandson. It was as if things had come full circle, as they inevitably do, and he became a new man with a renewed optimism for life and it was all down to a baby boy named David.

David stared through the paned glass window at the thick covering of snow that lay like a blanket in the cobbled street outside. All of his attempts to find the bit of paper were in vain and his grandpa couldn't remember anything, so it looked like he had hit a blank wall when it came to finding Lucinda. She was a pretty enough girl but she certainly wasn't worth all this trouble and as for Ernest's ridiculous whim, well it was just too fanciful to take seriously. He was beginning to feel irritated with the whole thing. After all, he had come home from training college for the Christmas break and instead of enjoying himself, he was wasting his time on this bloody wild goose chase. As he went to put on his warm woollen overcoat, it suddenly dawned on him.

"Oh my God, what an idiot. It won't be in this coat. I wasn't wearing this coat. I remember now it was a mild September day." He laughed out loud; it had been warm!

He almost ran to the back kitchen, where a row of coats and jackets hung on brass hooks by the door. Grabbing a tweed sports jacket with leather elbow patches from its peg, where he had left it in October, he began searching frantically through the pockets.

He let out a gasp of excitement, biting his bottom lip at the same time as he pulled out a small, crumpled piece of paper.

The handwriting was small and neat and the ink had smudged in the creases but the address was clearly visible.

"I've got it!"

Chapter 17

George Clifford was a man of few words and romance was not really in his nature but he loved his wife dearly and he was saddened to see the state she was in. They had both suffered the trauma of losing a baby but Dossie had endured a long and painful labour only to have a dead, lifeless child dragged from her body. They had been told by the doctors that the baby was dead but Dossie already knew. The kicking had stopped and there was no movement in her belly so she knew as labour was induced that there was no hope. She had held the poor dead little creature in her arms, cradling his blackened and distorted face to her bosom. The experience had devastated her and no matter how hard George tried to comfort her, she remained aloof and cold, until her sister's boy was born and then she seemed to live again. Her obsession with the child and with the man she believed to be his father totally consumed her, changing her from a dutiful wife into a stranger. He tried to understand; to make allowances for a woman grieving for a dead baby but his efforts were all in vain and she seemed to push him further and further away. He knew she had never really loved him but this was unbearable.

"Dossie, my love, you have to pull yourself together. You can't go on like this."

"Why not?"

"It's killing me to see you like this, so cold."

But the more he tried to talk to his wife, the more she retreated into herself, shutting him completely out of her life. It was if he had never existed. Very soon, the way things were between them began to annoy him and sometimes he was so enraged by his wife's lack of respect and affection for him he wanted to end things once and for all. But divorce was out of the question; she

172

would never agree, if only for the sake of her religious beliefs. And George had no real desire to part company with his beloved Doreen; all he really wanted was to have his wife back in the home and back in their marital bed. Since the boy's birth, she had drifted away from him. She had made herself indispensable to her ladyship, who had failed dismally to understand the demands of motherhood. The baby needed feeding and Doreen was the ideal nurse maid. It wasn't long before she had moved out of the cottage and into the nursery. Dossie had achieved her goal: to be there for Ernest's boy.

"Are you quite sure that your husband understands, Dossie, my dear?"

"Oh yes, he understands."

"He doesn't object to you being here to look after the child?"

Lady Agatha had always slept apart from her husband, keeping to her own room, as was the way with the upper classes, but she knew only too well that men like George Clifford enjoyed the comfort of a wife that shared his bed. Smiling sympathetically, she felt she had addressed the tricky issue with diplomacy and tact and left a silent Dossie to her duties without waiting for an answer. If she had asked the question of George, she would have received a very different response, but he was never consulted on the matter. Nevertheless, he had given the matter a lot of thought over the last few weeks and he knew what he had to do.

"If only I could convince her that the child isn't Ernest's, then she'll come to her senses!" His words rattled round and round in his head until finally they spilled out of his mouth in little more than a whisper. Alone as he was, in the fields at the back of the house, no-one could hear what he said, apart from the pheasants that scurried in front of his path. The colourful male bird cocked his head on one side as if to show agreement and then disappeared into the hedges, followed by several drab but devoted females.

He had to find some way of finding Samuel Simpson and making him admit that he was the father. If Dossie believed him, then she could put all this nonsense behind her, if she could only get over this obsession with Ernie Lowes. George had no intention of stopping her from working at the hall, caring for the little lad during the day, but she had to understand that she was just an employee and her priority must always be her husband. He had known when he married her that she didn't love him the way he cared for her. He was older and set in his ways but he had a steady living on the estate and he hoped that she would come to love him or at least grow fond of him. But he could never imagine how infatuated she had always been with another man. If Arthur's true father could be named as Samuel Simpson, then there was a chance he could get his wife back. He knew very little of the circumstances, certainly nothing of the dreadful secret unravelled by Mr Dawson but he knew the name of the cad who deserted his sister-in-law. Women gossiped and he had overheard the conversations between Minnie and her girls on many occasions.

Clifford was a logical man and with a name and an occupation he could find out the rest. Sunday was his day off and instead of accompanying his wife to church, he set off in the buggy to see Minnie Dawson.

The door opened into the little hallway and Clifford stared intently at the whitewashed step before raising his head and doffing his cap to his mother-in-law.

"Good morning, Mrs Dawson." He was too old and set in his ways to address his mother-in-law in any other way.

"My, my, George what are you doing here?" Minnie's smile suddenly disappeared as troubled thoughts entered her head.

"What's wrong, George? Is Doreen alright?"

"She's fine."

"Why have you come here alone? Is she ill? Has she taken a turn?" The day she learnt about the stillbirth was still very fresh in her memory and she felt a deep pain that filled her whole body and sent her senses reeling.

Her son-in-law shook his head resolutely to reassure her that Dossie was well, in that respect anyway. "Dossie is not ill. No need to fret about that."

"Well, it must be the bairn. Is there something wrong with our Etta's baby?" She corrected herself very quickly, "I mean Arthur, Lady Agatha's son!"

"No, no, that's not why I'm here. I've come to ask you to help me find Samuel Simpson."

Minnie was visibly alarmed and beads of sweat formed on her brow. "Come in, lad, sit you down and listen to me," she said firmly, directing the big man to a comfortable seat.

George walked into the immaculately clean and tidy parlour, clutching his cap in his hands. He sat down on the red plush chaise, his huge frame taking up the whole of the seat and watched as Minnie placed herself slowly at his side on a small high-backed chair. Her face was set as she placed her hands together in her lap.

"Best keep out of this one. No good will come of interfering." Minnie studied his rugged, suntanned face and tried to read his motive for searching for Sam Simpson.

"I have to find him, put Dossie's mind at rest."

"Why, what's wrong with our Doreen?"

"She truly believes Ernest Lowes is the bairn's father."

"What?"

"She wants to bring him up as her own. Fancies herself in love with Lowes. She's not been herself since we lost our own little mite."

"Ernest's? Whatever can she be thinking?" The old woman screwed up her eyes and pursed her lips before continuing. "It can't have been easy for either of you, George, but when a woman loses a child like that, well it can do funny things to her head. You just need to give her some time. Be patient with her, lad, and be kind!"

Minnie's voice was soothing but did nothing to appease his anxiety or suppress his determination to locate Sam.

"We've always known of our Dossie's fancy for Ernest, George, but that's all it ever was - a fancy."

"She's out of her mind. She won't have it that Etta's baby isn't his."

But our Dossie must have told you all about the other fella." Minnie couldn't bring herself to mention the name out loud but George knew perfectly well she meant Samuel Simpson.

"The one who got her pregnant."

"Dossie knew well enough what resulted from that fling our Annetta had with yon rotter. He is a no-good scoundrel and best forgotten."

"But is he the babe's father?" There was a hint of anticipation in his words.

"Yes, lad, he is but there's more to it than that and you don't need to know about it. Best not to know."

"What do you mean?"

"Nothing."

"Tell me, Minnie."

"He was a bad man, that's why our Etta has let the bairn go." Folding her arms, she stood up from the chair and made towards the door. "That's the end of it."

"I must find him. I have to, for the sake of my

marriage."

"But what good will come of it if you do find him?" His mother-in-law looked pained, shaking her head in a bid to clear her mind.

"I will force him to accept responsibility for his son, Minnie. That's surely got to be for the good."

"No, no, George."

"But why not?"

"Our Etta wants nothing more to do with him or with his bairn. It's all been settled now." There was panic in her old, tired eyes. "For God's sake, man, leave well alone."

"I have to speak to him."

"Please don't rake up the past. There are things that need to be laid to rest. For all our sakes, George, I beg you to forget about all of this."

"Minnie, you don't know what all this is doing to us."

"Wait and see and our Dossie will get over this silliness before too much longer."

The women in the family had closed rank about the fact that Samuel was Etta's half-brother and had told no-one, not even George Clifford. There was no reason for him to know anything about this wretched business. It was a secret that had to be kept. She had to get him to put this perilous plan out of his head for good.

"Now, you go home to our Dossie and forget all about this nonsense. She'll come to her senses. Trust me, I know about these things. Try for another one, George, and she'll be as right as rain once she's with child again."

And with that platitude, she almost pushed the giant of a man through the door, painting an amusing picture of a tiny old lady manoeuvring an immoveable object out of the room. It would have been laughable if it wasn't so serious but all she wanted was to be rid of her son-in-law as quickly as possible before her husband got home. She would have been pleased to see George in any other circumstances and tea and cake would have been the order of the day but all she wanted just now was to avoid a meeting between George and Jack. She couldn't face going over the sordid facts again and she knew that if George asked him about Simpson, he wouldn't hold back. Jack Dawson had no time at all for the waster who ruined Etta's life.

It was obvious that Minnie had said all she was going to on the matter and he resolved to say no more as he headed down the stairs. Nevertheless, George Clifford left undeterred. He would find the bastard and make him pay for deserting Etta. A germ of an idea had just come to him and he hurried away. He left through the shop, leaving Minnie to her fireside and with a furtive glance behind him, he picked up the order book from the shelf below the counter. There was no one around as he skipped through the pages until at last, he found it... a scribbled name and address, struck through in red ink.

Mr Samuel Simpson
Simpson's Sweets
Albert Road
Middlesbrough.

Just at that moment, Jack came in from the back and on finding George, stopped dead in his tracks. He looked slightly puzzled at discovering him behind the counter before shaking him fondly by the hand.

"Well, well, George, this is a surprise."

Thinking on his feet, George chuckled, "It is, and I'm embarrassed to say you've caught me red-handed, Jack, I just couldn't resist those strawberry creams; they've always been my favourite.

"Help yourself, man, no need to ask. You're family,

after all." Jack grinned amiably and patted the big man heartily on the back. "Is our Doreen upstairs with her Ma? Etta's just popped out, but she'll be back anytime soon. It'll be good to get those two together again."

George didn't utter a sound, creating an uncomfortable silence until Jack continued in an effort to fill the embarrassment between them.

"Well, we haven't seen you in an age, man. How are you? How is Dossie now? After the… well, you know what I mean. Has she got over it? I know its early days but there'll be others."

"Maybe."

"She's still a young woman. Plenty of time for you to have another."

Feeling the heat spread to his neck, an embarrassed George cut the conversation dead.

"Look, Jack, I'm here by myself and I have to get back to Doreen."

"I understand she shouldn't be left too long on her own."

"So I'll be off then. Good day to you."

And with that, he was gone, leaving Jack even more puzzled and confused by the abruptness of his leaving.

George Clifford eventually arrived at the small establishment on Albert Road, pretentiously claiming to be Simpson's Confectionery Emporium. A small group of children was looking through the plate glass window and drooling at all the brightly coloured sweets and bars that were stacked on the shelves. An attractive woman shooed them away with a friendly smile.

"Hey, you lot!" cried George, as they made to run off down the street. "Who's that lady?"

"That's Mrs Simpson, mister, Tilly's mam."

"Mrs Simpson."

179

"She sometimes lets us have a gobstopper for nowt but doesn't look like it today." And with that they all scarpered out of sight.

He was to find the woman, who looked about thirty, standing in front of the brass cash register, ringing in a sale. There was a child, a girl probably six or seven years old, smiling up at him, her head and shoulders just above the high counter.

"Good day, sir, what can I get you?" the woman asked warmly.

"Quarter of Black Bullets please," George said, not knowing what else to say.

"Let me, Mam, I'll get them." The child stood on the top of a small set of steps and reached down a nearly empty jar.

George smiled at the child, then the woman and said with a friendly smile, "She's a canny bairn, that one, I'll bet she's the apple of her daddy's eye, isn't she?"

"Well her da's dead, but aye, he loved her to bits, he did."

"Oh, I'm sorry, lass," George stammered, shocked by the news, and unable to make sense of it. "I was looking for Samuel Simpson. Can't believe he's passed away. Are you sure?"

George suddenly felt very stupid and embarrassed at asking such a question. He didn't know whether to scarper like those kids or stand his ground and apologise profusely. Instead he did nothing, standing uncomfortably in front of her, scratching his nose and dragging off his cloth cap from his thick head of black hair.

She laughed, "Oh, no, you're all wrong, man. Sam's not her dad. I married him when she was small after we lost..." The smile disappeared, "When my first husband died."

"Oh forgive me, I'm sorry, pet... I didn't mean to

speak out of turn." George still felt clumsy and dismayed at his blundering efforts to find out more about Simpson but pushed on with his inquiry. "So this must be Mr Simpson's shop then, is it?"

"No, it's mine, actually." There was a sense of pride in her voice." I've managed this business for years, much of that time on my own.

George acknowledged the statement with a generous nod of his head that demonstrated his admiration for the woman.

Her demeanour changed as if her thoughts were elsewhere." It was left to me by... left to me when I was widowed." She looked genuinely saddened.

George was left quite speechless as he examined the pretty face that was so full of suffering and despair but the kindness in his eyes urged her on.

"Yes, it's Sam Simpson's name above the door though!" there was a bitterness in her voice. "He and that father of his have the run of the place since we wed."

"Right, I see." Said George sensing an anger hidden in the words.

"Wants to carry on the family name, does he? Pass it on to your sons."

"Oh we have no sons and never will have," she sneered.

"I'm sorry, Mrs Simpson. I seem to keep saying the wrong things. I'm not much of a talker. Always putting my size 12 boots in it, I am!"

"You seem to be doing alright to me and please call me Eliza, his mam is Mrs Simpson and always will be!" She liked this big awkward man and felt comfortable in his company, so much so she gabbled on without a thought to what she was saying.

She was lonely in a loveless marriage with no one to talk to except an unsympathetic mother-in-law who could see no wrong in her imperfect son. They all knew that Sam only married her for the shop. She was older and with a child so she jumped at his proposal but every day wished she hadn't.

"We can't have any children, me and Sam. His mother blames the mumps that he had as a boy, that is, when she's not blaming me!"

George was taken aback by such candour and his face visibly reddened.

"I'm sorry, Eliza!"

She laughed a genuine friendly laugh, "Stop saying that!"

"I'm sorry," he said yet again and they both laughed together while the little girl looked up at them both and began to giggle herself.

"Anyway, what did you want with Sam?" she said, folding her arms across her splendid bosom, which George Clifford could not fail to admire. "You're either an outraged father or a cuckolded husband. It's usually one of the two!"

George looked visibly shocked at the unemotional way Eliza Simpson viewed her marriage.

Seeing the look of horror on his face, she smiled very sweetly and with a sense of resignation in her voice, she responded, "Oh, don't fret. I know my husband well enough! I don't worry about it anymore and I don't much care either, if I'm honest with you!" Eliza's face lit up and a pretty smile played around her attractive mouth.

George shifted uneasily from one foot to another, opening his mouth to speak, only to find the words wouldn't come.

Eliza broke the silence, saying, "I'm sorry for embarrassing you, I know my tongue runs away with me sometimes but you're just so easy to talk to. Anyway what do you want with that husband of mine?"

He didn't know what to say to this lovely unhappy woman, but eventually he stammered out, "Well, nothing really, just a bit of business. It can wait. It's been a real pleasure, Mrs Simpson, sorry, Eliza." They both chortled. "Lovely to meet you. I hope things work out for you."

It was a sentiment that he genuinely meant as he felt a real affinity to this unloved woman.

"They won't," she said resignedly, "but don't you worry yourself about me. I have a feeling there's something that you have to worry about that's more important. I just hope my husband isn't involved. He's nothing but a cad and a scoundrel and if he does have something to do with your predicament, then I can only say I'm really sorry."

Not knowing how to respond to such honesty, George simply thanked her for her time, paid for the sweets but left the paper bag full of sugary bullets on the counter, knowing the little girl would not be able to resist them after he'd gone.

Back home, he pondered on the day. He felt such pity for the sorry woman that he felt like beating the living daylights out of Simpson but at least he knew now that Etta's baby was more likely to be Ernest Lowes's than Samuel Simpson's, if what Eliza had told him was true. There was no real reason not to believe her and so he was faced with the dilemma of what to do next. Should he tell his wife and her sister what he had found out and upset all the arrangements with the adoption but worst of all confirm Dossie's suspicions and rekindle her obsession with Ernest Lowes? Any honest man such as George Clifford would have trouble choosing the right path but he eventually decided it was best to lie. It would be for the best if he told his wife that he had definite proof that Samuel Simpson was the child's father and a married man. That way they could all leave the boy where he was best off in a very good home where he would be brought up to be a proper gentleman. But more than that, he hoped that Dossie would give up her ridiculous idea and settle down again as his own beloved wife.

Chapter 18

David was preparing to make the journey to the address given to him by Lucinda Addington. After much persuasion, he had reluctantly agreed to help the old man find the woman named Dossie who Lucinda had spoken of so affectionately. It was incredible but they both instinctively believed that she could be Doreen; the Aunt Dossie his mother had been so fond of. If the search led to his grandmother's sister, he hoped that she might be able to shed some light on why such a high-born lady should remind his grandpa so much of his dead wife. David had never met his Great-Aunt but she had certainly been part of his mother's life, as he remembered her talking about Aunt Dossie, sometimes warmly but at other times with more than a little bitterness.

"I didn't know that your Ma had anything to do with Dossie, Davy. Did she see much of her, then?" Ernest hesitated, feelings of guilt flooding back. "I suppose she must have seen a lot of her in those days when she lived with Grandma Minnie, did she?

"I think so." He dredged up the stories his mother had entertained him with when he was a little lad. "It was funny though, she seemed to paint a different picture of her every time she mentioned her."

"Dossie hadn't any kiddies of her own, as far as I know, but I'm sure she would have loved a bairn, so I suppose that's why she took to your Mam. I didn't know that she had anything to do with her though, I'm ashamed to say."

"Oh yeah, she used to tell me all about when she was little and how much she liked her Auntie Dossie. She must have been very important to her when she was a child but I can never remember ever meeting her. Something changed though, once I was born." David looked solemn, recalling how as a little boy he thought he was to blame for the fall out between his mother and her aunt.

"Something happened between them because she said things from time to time which made me wonder why it changed between them. I don't really know what went on but she didn't mention her so much after a while. I suppose Dossie could have moved away but she'd been there for her when she was growing up. I'm certain of that!"

Ernest felt more than a twinge of guilt and remorse as he remembered the way he had abandoned his daughter. It was no wonder he knew nothing of her relationship with Dossie. He'd had very little to do with her when she was a bairn and he regretted it enormously. He knew how distant Minnie had become and so of course did Dossie but Ernest could never know how much his sister-in-law had cared for his little girl. She was the only person who gave the child any love. She had become a virtual stranger to him since he married her sister and he knew nothing of her life and how his own daughter figured in it. Elsie knew of the rift in the family and thought it best never to mention her relationship with her aunt in front of her father and so another secret was kept.

When she was born, the lives of so many were changed forever. A strong man crumbled and an old woman had a small baby forced on her at a time in her life when she was most vulnerable. Dossie's resilience helped her mother through this difficult time but it wasn't easy for any of them. Ernest tried to block the painful memory from his brain. The truth of it was even more than he could ever have imagined with repercussions for all those entangled in the web of deceit. He tried to picture the relationship between his unwanted daughter and his sister-in-law. Did she love the child or was she simply trying to make amends for what had gone between Etta and herself? Or was she only supporting her elderly mother, who was struggling with a situation not of her making: a dreadful situation that his selfishness had created. He desperately wanted to know what happened during those years when his heart had been so broken that he denied his own flesh and blood. If only he had seen and heard the trauma that surrounded his little girl. Those days so long ago were lost to him now and he could never undo what had been done, no matter how hard he wished for it. It was a lifetime ago when his sister-in-law sat in her mam's kitchen cradling a tiny screaming baby.

"Mam, all this is so hard for you, taking on a youngster at your time of life; it's not fair," Dossie stated the obvious. Minnie found looking after her granddaughter almost too tough in so many ways. Not only was she a constant reminder of the daughter she had lost, but Minnie was not up to the rigours of motherhood at her age. It hadn't been too hard during the first few years, because Elsie had been a quiet baby but now she was older, she was a bit of a handful.

Dossie felt for her sister's child and hated to see Ernest's daughter so unloved but she couldn't take her in. It would upset too much. She had worked hard for the life she now had, well respected by the family and by the other servants. Her position was something she felt proud of and she couldn't risk losing it. But she felt she had to do something to help the poor little mite.

"I can help with the little lass, you know, as much as I can on my days off and in holidays and suchlike. I'd love to and I've much more time now that…"

Minnie's response came so speedily that Dossie's sentence was mercifully left unfinished.

"Oh, can you, pet? That would be great. I'm not so young anymore and she's a good little'un but its hard work for me these days."

It was true Dossie had fewer duties now that Arthur was at prep school and Lady Agatha was happy to spend more time with him when he came home. He was a most handsome and intelligent little boy who entertained his mama with snippets of interesting and amusing facts that he had learnt at school. Now that he was grown, she could at long last really appreciate her son.

Dossie's thoughts were broken as she nodded in agreement with her mother's concerns.

"I know it's not been easy for you, Mam," she soothed, "but Lady Agatha is going on holiday soon and taking... taking the family... with her."

She was cautious when talking about Arthur, so didn't mention his name. Of course, Minnie knew all about the arrangement but had buried all thoughts of the unfortunate business deep in her brain.

"It will be good for them all. They spend so little time together," Dossie continued more confidently now that she had measured her mother's reaction.

This was true enough. Lady Agatha had not turned out to be particularly maternal, although she genuinely loved the boy. As a baby, his upbringing had been left mainly to Dossie, who was assisted by a series of young nursemaids, none of whom remained in service very long. And then there had been tutors and then of course he'd been sent off to school, but her ladyship always made sure they spent time together on an annual holiday to the seaside in Scarborough.

A holiday by the seaside was something Elsie could only dream of when she was growing up but sometimes Dossie took her to Saltburn for the day. The girl grew to love her aunt and her visits were the highlight of her week. She would bring her bags of Parma Violets and lovely melt in the mouth chocolate that she would generously share with aunt and grandma.

"She's a sweet child, Ma. Why can't you give her a little bit of love?"

"I've got none left, lass. It's all gone, swallowed up like that chocolate, only it doesn't leave a sweet taste in the mouth like this does."

Dossie remembered the mother who had given her and her sister so much of everything. So much affection, so much care, so much time. It was a great pity that things had changed her so much. But she couldn't let the bairn suffer. A little motherless girl unwanted by everyone; by her grandmother, even by her own father.

Ernest was still pondering on why Dossie had taken such care of his child without saying a word to him about it. He knew she had feelings for him at one time and wondered if this was her reason for looking out for Elsie. His head was aching with so many strange ideas battling it out in his brain. Of course, he couldn't even guess why she acted as she did. Dossie Clifford was a tormented woman; at odds with Etta and obsessed with her husband. She hadn't gone to the wedding. Too much had gone on between the sisters for her to attend, even though she had toyed with the idea of sitting at the back of the church unseen but neither woman made any effort to make amends and they remained estranged.

Over time, her feelings for Ernest had mellowed. She no longer felt herself in love with him but when Etta died, she felt she should visit him to show her respects and to comfort him. On several occasions, she put on her best black hat and set off on the journey but how could she, when she had kept this bloody awful secret from him for all these years? She had denied him his son, and this was a cross she had to bear. A cross that had ruined her life just as much as it had others' lives. And so years passed with no contact between sister and brother-in-law. No matter what George Clifford told her, she knew who Arthur's father was and it wasn't that man Simpson, that was for sure. Etta had not given birth to a child fathered by her own brother, a belief that had tormented her all her days and forced her give up a son that she and Ernest could have both loved so much.

Doreen was racked with guilt. As Arthur grew, there was no doubt about his paternity. He was the living image of his father and his thick auburn hair was further testament to that. Fully aware of her sister's shame over her forbidden love, she knew that her mind was unbalanced as a result, making her irrational and unreasonable. If she had been thinking more lucidly, she would have realised immediately that the baby was not Simpson's child. There had been so many opportunities when she could have helped her to see the truth, made her think again about her son's father, but she allowed her to go on believing the worst. If only Dossie had been stronger, if only she had tried harder to persuade her sister that the babe was Ernest's. But in her heart, she knew that she hadn't really wanted to. Secretly she wished for Etta to abandon him so that she could have him all to herself; so she could love him as her own and of course, her wish tragically had come true.

At first, she didn't know anything about who Simpson was, but one thing she did know was that he had deserted her sister when she needed him, when she was carrying his child. She'd only met him once but she felt he was a scoundrel who would hurt her sister and she was right. He very nearly destroyed her mind. Then the awful truth came out bit by bit until the whole sordid story of his relationship with them all was finally revealed. George had told her he was married, but that was all he knew, thank God. He had tried to get her to believe that

Simpson was Arthur's father but couldn't marry her sister because he was already wed. If only he knew the real reason. George had been an old fool. Did he really think he could stop her from loving Ernest?

She remembered vividly the day he told her all those years ago. She had screamed at him like a wild thing.

"You had no right to interfere. This has nothing to do with you. Who do you think you are, meddling in our business?"

"I think I am your husband, Doreen, but I'm not sure anymore. Maybe husband in name only!"

This was very true for since the stillbirth, Dossie had refused to share a bed with her husband and on the birth of Arthur, things only got worse. As chief nursemaid to her ladyship's adopted son, she was expected to sleep in the nursery to watch over him. In the gamekeeper's cottage, George slept alone in the brass bed with the feather mattress where their first and only child had been both conceived and died no more than a few minutes old.

"It's not right; you sleeping in the big house and me all alone here in the cottage. We're man and wife, woman, if only you would prove it."

George was filled with the same desire for Dossie that he had always had but his feelings were quickly altering, the longer she kept him at a distance. Images of a pretty little lass, no more than sixteen or seventeen, played in his memory. He had paid little attention to the shy young thing who came to work in the kitchens all those years ago and she certainly paid no heed to him. He was a brusque man of at least thirty years who always had dirty hands and a weather-beaten face. As she grew in years and experience, he began to take more notice of her ladyship's maid, as she eventually became. Her confidence shone in her attractive face and her charming manner was beguiling to a man like him.

It wasn't easy for George Clifford to declare his feelings; he was the strong silent type, who saw any expression of emotion as a sign of weakness. He was also very aware of the vast difference in their ages and he suspected she was involved with the handsome young lad who drove her home every Sunday in the buggy. Nevertheless, they struck up a friendship, with Dossie offering him mugs of tea whenever she had any free time. It was purely kindness on her part, as she felt sorry for the giant of a man who was out in all weathers, but he saw it as an invitation to get to know the lovely girl with the chestnut hair a bit better.

With no chance to meet young men of her own age and realising that Ernest's feelings were only for her sister, Dossie began to admire the honesty and reliability of the man who showed her nothing but respect and appreciation. There was no romancing between the ill-matched pair but a deep attachment connected them and at last he plucked up the courage to ask her to marry him. He was amazed when she accepted. He couldn't believe his luck and he loved her deeply from that day on. But now she was slipping away from him and he was determined to fight for her.

"You say I had no right, but by God, woman, you had no right to take up this position. It's a post for an unmarried wench with no responsibilities to her man." His face was black as thunder and anger was boiling up inside him.

"I have to look after Arthur, you know I do. He needs me, George and I have to be close by to the nursery."

"I need you!" Her husband's voice was urgent and dismissive of her feeble excuse. "One of the nursemaids could see to him during the night and you could sleep here with me as a wife ought to."

"But Lady Agatha wanted me to be the only one…"

"No, Dossie, you wanted to be the only one!"

His fist punched into the big oak door, leaving a mark both on the door and on his fingers, which quickly revealed a purplish bruise. George blew on his hand to take away the heat and the sting but he couldn't take away the throb from his heart.

"He wasn't your bairn, Dossie. He never was. You've given up your chance to have one of our own. We could have had another child."

Ignoring the pain in his eyes, Dossie reflected on his words but instead of thinking of George's baby, she yearned for the child she could have given Ernest. It was her obsession. An obsession with a man she could never really have.

It all seemed like a lifetime ago now but Dossie felt the pain intensely, not just for a lost love but also for the husband she had let down so badly. She cried the day he confessed that he had known all along that Samuel Simpson could not have fathered Etta's child and that Arthur had been Ernest's son all along. After George's death, she came to understand the torment he must have felt and at the hands of his own wife. So many secrets; so many lies. This family had had seen too much tragedy and Dossie blamed herself for much of it. She needed to redeem herself and somehow make amends. It was too late for her and Etta but when Minnie wrote to her elder child begging her to help after Elsie's birth, that's how the relationship began. A childless woman and an unloved child came to be as close as mother and daughter… for a while. And all this time, Ernest was totally oblivious to the link between his daughter and his sister-in-law. He never knew anything about how much Elsie had cared for her aunt. She was a motherless child who craved affection and Dossie was the one person who gave her some tenderness.

"Grandpa, are you listening to me?" I was saying how Mam used to tell me about Dossie. I think she looked on her like a mother, you know!"

"She had a mother, Davy, a mother who died giving her life." The words were little more than a whisper which disappeared without trace.

"What was that?" David turned towards his grandfather, who simply shook his head.

Ernest's face was colourless, his eyes narrow and tired and his breathing seemed a little laboured as he recalled his treatment of his only child. He was so ashamed as he focussed on the unwanted daughter who gave birth to his beloved Davy, he sighed so heavily that his grandson began to stare at him with real concern in his eyes. He could never relieve himself of the guilt he felt whenever he remembered Elsie, even after they were reunited. Her early death meant that there hadn't been enough time for him to really make it up to her for depriving her of a real childhood. Whenever he thought of those days, the pain it brought back was physical, like a stab in his stomach. He felt sick. His face was pale and drawn and he looked so old that David was ready to give up on the whole ridiculous idea. Maybe it would be for the best. Going on some wild goose chase was really crazy and he knew it but there was no way he could convince his grandfather to give up his dream of discovering what mystery lay ahead in the shape of Lucinda Addington.

"You OK, Gramps? Are you up to this? We can forget about the whole thing if you're not well enough."

"Don't be daft, I'm fine, lad, raring to go; that's me. Don't you go worrying about your old Grandpa." He tried to sound keen to get going so as to reassure David but he was more than a little apprehensive about what they would discover.

The more the boy thought about it, the more he realised that he had to do this alone. His grandfather was not strong enough yet. Something told him that there were secrets ahead that would be difficult for all of them to comprehend and he needed to protect the old man, no matter what. It wasn't going to be easy to get him to understand that he couldn't get involved but there had to be a way.

"Come on then, Davy boy. What are we waiting for? If you know how to find out more about all this, then let's get on with it." His old eyes sparkled with excitement. "I just know my Etta's behind all this; I feel it in my bones!"

David just shook his head whilst smiling kindly, desperately wondering how he could protect his grandfather.

Chapter 19

The screwed-up piece of paper with the address that Lucinda had given him was still in one piece in David's top pocket and he kept taking it out and re-reading it to remind himself.

He had an old motorbike that he knew would get him there in one piece but what about Grandpa? There was no way he could ride pillion, so he was going to have to go alone and this would be his perfect excuse.

"Look, Grandfather, I think I know how to find Dossie but to get there, I'll have to take my bike!"

Ernest broke in with an almost juvenile excitement.

"You do... you've found her, then we've nearly done it, Davy my lad. Dossie's the key to all of this, you see and once we get to her; well I know there's something about that bonnie lass, Lucinda. There's a secret there, son and we'll crack it. Aye, we'll get to the bottom of this soon enough. Let me get my cap and we'll be off."

"Well that's the problem, Grandpa, we can't go." David pressed his lips together hard as he screwed up his eyes and emphasised the word "WE."

"What do you mean we can't go? You said you'd found Dossie, so what are we waiting for?"

"I'm going on the bike."

"Aye, but there's room behind you." Ernest's eyes pleaded.

"No, there isn't." David looked away. "Well, yes, there's room on the pillion right enough, but no, Grandpa, it's not safe. I can't take you today. I have to go by myself."

There was a determined look on his face and his grandfather sat down heavily into a worn leather armchair, looking dejected and disappointed.

But then he brightened slightly. At his age, there was

no time for regrets or recriminations.

"Well, alright then. If I can't go, I can't go, that's settled then, son. But off you go and find out as much as you can and then you can tell me all about it over a glass of beer when you get back. Is it a deal?"

David smiled but he knew that his grandfather was down in the dumps despite his efforts to be cheery.

"I'll solve this mystery for you, I promise you that. If this Lucinda creature has anything to do with Aunt Doreen or with Grandma Annetta, I'll find out. Rest assured, my old lad!"

"Cheeky monkey; old lad indeed. Be off with you and don't you dare come back empty-handed!"

When David had gone and he was left alone, Ernest settled down by the fire and began to catnap. Daydreams consumed those waking moments as thoughts of a Christmas long ago brought a warm glow to his face. Perhaps it was just the heat from the hot coals in the grate but slowly he drifted into a deep slumber where the dream was intense and vividly real. He had played out every detail of that day when she agreed to be his wife many times over the last fifty years but he never tired of it.

"Oh, Ernie, I have missed you," she whispered, brushing a snowflake from his nose.

"I can't believe it's you, Etta." He almost hollered to the rooftops, then more softly, "You can't imagine how many times I've been here asking for you, searching for you. I never gave up hope that one day I'd find you again and you would care for me just a little bit."

He stared at the beautiful face, laughed at the lacy cap on her head and kissed her hard on the lips until she could barely breathe and as she fell backwards, he caught her in his strong muscular arms. Staring into his captivating hazel eyes, the embrace was returned so passionately and vehemently without a care or a thought to the onlookers inside the tearoom. Amused faces peered at the two of them through the steamy window as they held on to each other so blatantly and unashamedly there in the street in broad daylight. As she broke free, almost gasping for air and with a purplish bruise on her lips, Etta giggled, imagining what her mother would say.

"What do you think Mam will make of this little show then, Ernest my love?"

Ernie looked a little sheepish as he realised what she meant.

"I am a scarlet woman, I am!" she repeated with glee, "Mam will die of shame."

"The only shame, my love, is that we've been apart this long."

Ernie was what Mam called a real man but at that moment he was crying like a bairn. Wet salty tears were caught in his beard and as he wiped them away with the back of his hand, he gulped hard.

"Etta, marry me. I love you with all my heart, my darling, I love you. I have always loved you."

Not knowing whether to laugh or cry, Etta could only respond with the words he longed to hear.

"And I love you, Ernest Lowes, I think I always have but I never really knew it until just now."

"But where have you been all this time? I know you didn't marry… you didn't marry him!"

Dropping her eyelids, eyelashes fluttering slightly against her flushed cheeks, Etta looked beseechingly at him to stop.

"I don't care about him, Etta, not anymore. It's just you were away for so many months. I tried to forget you: I really did!"

"I know, my love, it must have been so tough for you

but it all seems like another life now. It's all in the past and none of it matters."

"You are all that matters to me."

"It's just you and me now, we're all that counts so please don't ask me about it. It never happened."

"Whatever happened before today doesn't matter to me one little bit, my love."

"But promise me now, Ernie, we won't ever mention this again."

With that, Ernie simply nodded in consent and took her by the hand as they strolled almost in a daze back into the tearoom where the little crowd of customers cheered and clapped. The happy couple grinned and Ernie dropped his head in mock embarrassment while Etta, head held high, flung her arms around him in an impressive gesture of undying love. In that moment, they both shared the same glorious feeling of euphoria that sent their senses reeling and their hearts fluttering. However, it was not all standing ovations for the happy couple. There by the door to the kitchen, with arms folded and a look of disapproval on her face, stood Minnie Dawson, who on returning with plates full of steaming crumpets, had witnessed the scene played out by the two young lovers. She put down the plate onto the nearest table with such force, the china almost broke and the crumpets jumped into the air in an attempt to escape her wrath. The two young people stopped still in their tracks and a hush descended on the room as the onlookers, who seconds before had applauded, now averted their eyes in embarrassment and very busily began to pour tea and butter slices of toast.

"Well, that was an exhibition and no doubt! What do you think you're playing at, the both of you, behaving in such a…a…disgraceful way?"

Etta's unrepentant demeanour seemed to antagonise

her mother even more and her face took on a purplish hue, which made Ernie splutter nervously as he coughed into his handkerchief. She was about to open her mouth again to let out the steaming emotions that were boiling inside her when her protestations were quickly quelled as Etta broke in with the words that Minnie had yearned to hear for so long.

"We're getting married, Mam, me and Ernest, just as soon as we can!"

Ernest woke with a start. It took a while for him to realise where he was. He was disorientated and his face was wet with tears. He was an old man now, the wrinkles on his face evidencing the passing of time but those memories remained permanently etched on his heart. He never did ask why she had gone away and she never told him. It didn't matter.

"Where does time go?" he wondered. "It goes so quickly. One day you're young and fit and so alive. And then it's gone in a flash - it's gone and you're old and worn out."

He didn't really know whether these words had remained in his head or had been spoken aloud. He spoke to himself a lot these days.

"Aye those days are gone, along with my Etta!"

This time he knew the words had been whispered into the room for no-one except himself to hear. "We didn't have long together, really, did we? Only a few short years but they were the best of my life!"

Looking down at his old age-marked hands, the hands that had held her gorgeous face, he knew that even though she was gone she would never age; not like he had done. She would never grow old but would remain as beautiful as ever, as lovely as that young girl on the train who had captivated both him and his grandson so completely.

Night fell as the room darkened and the fire cast a red glow around the room, creating a strange feeling of nostalgia for those heady days when they were first wed and would sit by the hearth in silent appreciation of each other before making love so passionately and uncontrollably as the embers glowed. It was getting late and his thoughts suddenly turned to David, a sense of awkwardness overcoming him as he wondered what his grandson would make of the images that had just occupied his mind. Tittering to himself, he doubted whether the boy could ever imagine his old grandpa as a young virile man. David's generation thought that sex had been invented in the 60s and it amused Ernest to remember his own sexual encounters over the years. Even though he had never re-married, he had certainly not led a monastic life and was sure that his grandson would be thoroughly shocked if he knew of his many conquests. It was hard to believe now that this saggy old body crippled with arthritis could ever have competed in the sex Olympics, but Ernest had definitely been awarded a couple of gold medals in his time. Grinning to himself, he wished that David could have known him back then but for a fully paid up member of the swinging sixties, his grandson was often very prudish indeed, so Ernest Lowes might well have proved too much for him.

As Ernest continued to wait for David to return, he contemplated the reason he had never taken the plunge with any woman other than Annetta. His mood changed dramatically as he remembered the heartache he felt when she died and his vow that he would never feel such a deep pain ever again. And there had never been anyone who came close to her anyway so the situation never arose. He remained unmarried and it was not something he regretted but the more thought he gave to it, the more saddened he became. His life had certainly been tragic and as he sat in the gloom on his own, he was filled with melancholy and wished that David would return. He could never wallow in self-pity when he was around.

It was getting late and as he stared at the clock on the wall, he watched the second hand race round the face. His body was weary and his eyes became heavy as he began to slip back again into that lethargy that brought back so many recollections of times gone by. He seemed to live so much in the past these days, more than he did in the present. If he was honest with himself, there wasn't much for him in the here and now except for his darling boy and he knew he would soon be off to live his own life. The boy was a fine lad and his mother Elsie had been a grand lass. He reminded him so much of her in many ways. His hair was darker than hers had been but his nose and mouth were the same as his Mam's, Ernest recalled. A sweet natured girl with such an innocence about her was prey to every scoundrel in the county and poor Elsie easily fell victim. Her son was just as good natured but thankfully, he had inherited a good brain and sharp wits.

Restlessly, Ernest turned his head from side to side as he dozed in the chair and his legs twitched. He felt a guilt so great it hurt. Poor Elsie. He had let her down so badly. An innocent child couldn't be blamed for her mother's death. Childbirth was dangerous and women died from complications all the time in those days. It was nobody's fault. He had lost so many of those he loved; a wife, a daughter and two more little mites who never even had a chance of life. Life was cruel and unfair. He thought of Minnie. She knew all about that. What a life she'd had with a brute of a husband who'd beat the living daylights out of her and made a fool of her. Then to lose a good one who had really cared and of course she'd lost Etta too.

"But no-one's to blame. We're all dealt different cards in life!" he rambled, as he started to rouse himself from his troubled daydreams.

At that very same moment David was realising that there was one other person who shared the same sense of guilt and believed that the blame was truly hers. She felt responsible for a lot of the tragedies that had befallen the family and it had ruined her life. He had found her, on the Cranfield Estate, an old lady with a secret. David was meeting his Great-Aunt Doreen for the first time.

Chapter 20

The day that Elsie Lowes discovered she was expecting she didn't know where to turn or what to do. She wasn't the brightest of girls or she wouldn't have ended up in this situation, but she knew well enough that it was no good seeking help from Grandma. Minnie Dawson was a damaged woman.

She must be about three months gone by now but she was just a slip of a thing and she wasn't showing. No-one knew anything about it, especially none of the girls at Mr Jepson's. He'd lost interest in her some weeks ago when a new girl came to the workshop. She was young with blonde curls and a very handsome bosom which attracted a lot of attention from all the men, including Mr Jepson.

Minnie would only tell her to confront him; make him accept responsibility, but she knew now about his long-suffering wife and his six bairns and she couldn't bear to hurt them as she was hurt. She didn't love him. Now that she came to think about it, she'd never really loved him. She realised now that he was not the handsome man who she imagined had fallen madly in love with her but was in fact old and rather ugly. How could she have ever been so stupid to fall for someone like that, but he had paid her a lot of attention and that was something she had never ever had before. It was intoxicating to a girl like her to receive so much consideration from a man like him. He was rich and influential, respected in the town. She wondered now, though, if he would be so respected if people knew what he had done. How he had ruined her life. In desperation, Elsie gave in to all kinds of notions from throwing herself in the canal to visiting one of those women who could make a baby disappear if you had the right money. Mr Jepson might give her the cash but she had already made up her mind and she didn't intend to get rid of her baby. She considered all her options again and suddenly she thought of her aunt. Auntie Dossie would know what to do and would help her. She was sure of that, so she decided to make the journey to the small village in Northumberland where she knew she lived. She'd never been before but Dossie had told her tales all about the grand hall and the estate and how wonderful it was. Every time they met, her aunt relayed tales of the wonderful place she called home.

"Oh, yes, Elsie it's a beautiful place, is Cranfield Hall. Set in lawned gardens with trees and flowers. It's got so many bedrooms and there are six bathrooms, all with proper lavatories and running water - hot and cold. You should see it." Dossie enthusiastically regaled the girl with a long list of what was grand about the place.

"Oh, I'd love to see it. Do you think I could come and stay with you sometime, Auntie?" The question was asked so many times year after year, as Elsie grew from a child into a young woman.

Dossie always looked flustered and hesitated to answer but the outcome was always the same.

"Well, I'm very busy, Elsie. You see, her ladyship relies on me for everything."

Elsie remembered the confidential tone in her voice and the knowing smile. "In fact, I almost run the whole place, you could say. I don't know how her ladyship would cope without me at her side."

This wasn't exactly true. Dossie was indeed highly regarded as an employee and, as Arthur's nanny in the old days, she had a special place in his heart. There was no doubt of that, but these days were different to those when she had slept in the bedroom next to the nursery and had almost been seen as part of the family. In reality her life was empty and lonely and her heart bled for the poor little girl but something prevented her from giving in to her desire to give her niece a proper home. And so Elsie grew up idolising an aunt who seemed so wonderful but in reality, so sadly lacking.

Once she had made up her mind to seek help, Elsie set out to visit Dossie, whose address had never been disclosed to her properly, only a sketchy picture of a grand place in the middle of nowhere. However, she eventually discovered the whereabouts of the hall from the landlord of the village pub and after a bit of a trek, she found herself at the big iron gates that protected the grounds from people like her. Looking around, she saw a much smaller wrought iron gate like the ones her dad made, which led into a garden in front of a little two-storey house. This was the gatehouse to Cranfield Hall and was where Dossie had lived since George Clifford had passed away and Master Arthur had grown into a young man with no further need of her services. It was really a lovely little cottage, making Dossie a perfect home but she missed being in the hall in the thick of it. In fact, she felt such a sense of isolation and rejection that she had begun to fantasise about Ernest Lowes again.

Lady Agatha had employed a very young, very pretty maid from France who looked after her gowns and dressed her hair, so Dossie's services as a lady's maid were no longer required either. Of course, she was kept on as an old retainer but there was always the hope there that once Arthur had children of his own, then she would be needed again. This thought kept her going during the lonely days and nights spent in the gatehouse. He was married now, with hopefully a family to come. Not that the wife he had chosen seemed set on becoming a mother. She was a bit flighty, thought Dossie, and she knew Lady Agatha didn't care much for her. However, if they were to have a child, then she would be ready to come out of this enforced retirement. She couldn't wait for that day to arrive.

It was undeniably a very miserable life; a life which gave Doreen Clifford much time to reflect on the past. She had made so many mistakes; hurt so many people and her watery eyes glistened in the half-light as dusk began to settle over the estate.

"I'm so sorry, George," she whispered to an empty chair that had once seen pride of place in the gamekeeper's cottage but had been brought here to the gatehouse when she moved.

"I must have hurt you so much... and for what? Some silly notion."

It was growing quite dark as Elsie stood in front of the green wooden door, ready to pull back the brass knocker that looked as green as the paint on the door.

The resounding clatter of the brass against the wood startled Dossie as she very rarely received visits, other than those from the hall, who nearly always made formal appointments to see her.

Although she was still relatively young, not yet fifty, the years hadn't been kind to her. The early years of her marriage had been very troubled and it seemed likely at one time that it wouldn't last. Losing their only child had been devastating and it had been a traumatic time for both of them, but the dedicated commitment to another man's child certainly didn't help, driving a wedge between man and wife. However, George's perseverance and devotion eventually saved their marriage and Dossie was at last able to at least divide her love between her beloved Arthur and her husband. He was grateful for any scrap of affection she could spare and so their reconciliation saw her set up home again with the man who loved her without question. They were happy enough for those years, until during the war, he didn't come home one night when he was killed in an air-raid. Doing his bit for King and country in the Home Guard, the brave loyal man stood side by side with the professional gunners of the Royal Artillery in the defence of Tyneside when they heard the distant drone of enemy aircraft. Dossie was left a widow, grieving for a man she had never truly loved but for whom she had the deepest affection. She knew he deserved better, more than she could give him and it left her old before her time. She needed spectacles now and her knees creaked a little bit but even so, there was still life in the old girl and there was nothing she liked better than a good old natter. Brightening at the prospect of company, even it was only the grocer or the milkie, she threw off her pinny and opened the door with a cheery hello but almost fell back in shock as she was faced with her niece.

"Oh, my God, Elsie. What on earth are you doing all this way out here, girl?" Recovering quickly, she beamed, "It's grand to see you, pet."

But the way the girl slouched and the pained expression on her face soon changed the ambience of their meeting.

"What's the matter, Elsie, pet?" Dossie, asked with real concern in her voice.

"Just wanted to see you, that's all, I haven't seen much of you lately so I thought I'd just pay a call," she lied, trying to hide the truth without much success.

Dossie knew instinctively that there was something the girl wasn't telling her, "You're in trouble, aren't you? Come in and sit down. I'll put the kettle on."

Over tea, it didn't take much persuasion for Elsie to confide the whole story to her aunt, hoping she would take her in but that was the last thing that Dossie would do. She had too much to lose if a scandal like this got out and Elsie was much too simple a girl to keep things to herself. Her mother was Arthur's mother and this made her his sister. There was no way Dossie could risk the connection being made. Lady Agatha would be furious if the truth came out about her son's real parentage, now that she had turned him into the gentleman he was. No-one except for those immediately involved knew anything of his birth and she desperately needed to keep it that way. Dossie's mind was in turmoil as a poisonous mix of self-preservation mingled with genuine fondness for a poor helpless young woman. She so wanted to help her but she was afraid of the consequences. Since George had died, she had no-one really, Arthur was married with no need of her any longer and it was only her position in the household that kept her sane. She was respected by the other servants and looked up to because of her relationship with her ladyship. This was her world, her life, and she couldn't risk losing it. This unmarried niece was the last thing she needed and her words to Elsie came out as platitudes.

"Don't you fret, hinnie, it'll all be alright, I promise. These things happen all the time and it's fine."

Elsie could tell she wasn't telling her the truth but nodded all the same.

"Babes are born out of wedlock every day and nobody cares. A baby is a baby, after all." Dossie tried to make light of the whole thing.

But really all she wanted was to get Elsie out of her house as soon as possible before anyone could connect the two of them together.

"Well, I'm sorry, pet, but you can't stay here. I'm not allowed lodgers, you see. Her ladyship wouldn't like it." Dossie was lying again. More secrets were being kept and the despair she felt about it grew darker and darker until she couldn't bear to look at her niece.

"Now I think you'd better be getting back home. I'll get you some tea and then you'd best be off before it gets too late. We don't want you going back all that way in the dark, now, do we?" Dossie's voice was anxious and edgy in a strange mix of fear and sympathy.

"Home; What home is that, then? I don't have a home anymore. Do you really think Granny Minnie will have me?" Dossie knew as well as Elsie that Minnie would not have her door darkened by another scandal. Keeping Etta's pregnancy a secret had been hard enough, using up all her energy to cope with the disgrace of it all. Having the boy adopted was a godsend for her and it was not until Etta's marriage to Ernest that she felt she could once again hold up her head in the neighbourhood. Her daughter's breakdown was never mentioned but it took its toll on the old woman and she was never the same again.

The girl was sobbing but against all her better judgement, Dossie had once again hardened her heart as she ignored the misery in the girl's voice.

"I would help if I could, Elsie, but I can't." She had to protect herself but even so she was weakening. After all, this wretched girl was her own flesh and blood, her own dead sister's child.

Moving closer to her niece, Dossie stretched out a hand towards her in a small attempt to offer some comfort but the girl pushed her away roughly.

Straightening her pinny and smoothing her hair, tucking a stray grey hair behind her ear, she took on the manner of a Victorian schoolmarm and firmly instructed the poor girl, "Go home at once and tell your father everything, he's not a bad man. He'll take you in."

Of course Dossie knew Ernest Lowes would look after his daughter, there was never any doubt of that, but she felt a sudden and very real pain in her chest as she realised how she had deserted yet another of those that she loved, for she had genuinely cared for Elsie. Still, there was no way she could have her at the hall. Secrets would come out. Lies would be uncovered. She couldn't risk Ernest finding out about Arthur or Lady Agatha finding out that he had a sister. A sister from a working-class background and with an illegitimate child from an illicit affair with a married man; the shame of it smarted like a hornet's sting deep into Doreen's psyche and she wouldn't allow this scandal to affect her standing in the household. The truth of it all was not the fact that Elsie's situation would offend Lady Agatha, it was Doreen herself who was the genuine snob. Women of Agatha's class were resourceful in every respect and were well used to covering up scandals. Whilst it was true that she would have feigned abhorrence at the mere mention of illegitimacy, it was something that was always dealt with very effectively in her social circle.

Dossie was, of course, right in her assumption that Agatha would never reveal any connection between Arthur and this poor wretch, but in her aristocratic mind, her son had never had any connection with this family anyway. He was a born Addington. That same sentiment was the driving force behind Doreen's actions and she was determined that nothing would damage Arthur's future, not even Ernest's legitimate child.

Sensing the rejection and the tangible air of disgrace that permeated the room, Elsie resigned herself to her fate. After all, she was certainly used to being abandoned by everyone in her family, but she believed Dossie was the one exception. Of course, she was wrong! Remaining as courteous and respectful as she could, she faced her aunt with a doggedness that came from adversity.

"Thank you very much, Aunt Dossie. I'm going now and I don't want your tea. I don't want anything from you ever again. We won't be seeing each other again.

Goodbye!"

And with that, Elsie was gone and out of her aunt's life for good. The two women never met again. Elsie would never forgive the callousness that she had received at the hands of someone who she thought loved her. Dossie was too ashamed to ever contact her niece again.

Years later, those prophetic words came back to haunt Doreen as she read in the newspaper of the horrific death of Ernest's only daughter.

"Oh, my God," she said simply, as she grasped how she could have prevented this tragedy, if she hadn't turned her away so cruelly. If she had been there for the girl, supported her in her hour of need, helped to raise her baby. If only she had been there for her, Elsie Lowes would have had no need to work the night shift.

Chapter 21

David Lowes discovered the gatehouse at Cranfield Hall as easily as his mother had done all those years ago and he knew that he would need to start his search here. There was no other way of passing through those huge metal gates that led to the gravel drive.

What was he going to say? He struggled to find the words. He was a complete stranger looking for Miss Lucinda Addington or a Mrs Doreen Clifford.

He couldn't think what logical reason he could give for his search for either of them. This was a mistake. He hadn't planned it at all well. Some huge brute of a gatekeeper would probably give him his marching orders.

A light bulb flashed above his head as he came up with the solution. He of course was an art student studying with Lucinda and he was home for the holidays, so he thought he'd look her up. That was it. It sounded plausible enough.

As the door of the little house opened, his apprehension disappeared in an instant. A small elderly lady with scraped back dark hair, streaked with grey, stared up at him.

"Can I help you, young man?"

"I'm looking for Mrs Doreen Clifford," he answered, but he had a strange feeling that he had already found her.

"Yes... and may I ask why?"

"I'm her great-nephew. My grandfather is Ernest Lowes," he replied, in a very matter of fact way.

She visibly reeled.

"Ernest Lowes, you say." She hesitated for a while and then muttered as she ushered him quickly into the kitchen. "Come on in, don't just stand there on the doorstep for the whole world to see."

He didn't think he looked that shifty or disreputable

and felt a little offended by the remark but he just laughed it off as an old lady's peculiarity and did as he was bid, stepping over the threshold into the house.

"Are you Elsie's boy, then?"

Dossie scrutinised his face; the shape of his nose, his mouth, the colour of his hair, and shook her head.

"That's right, I'm her son."

"Yes. I see it now." The old lady swallowed hard.

"You knew my mother and my grandfather?"

Another hesitation as Dossie paused for thought before making her reply, fighting back the tears that had begun to sting her eyes.

"Aye, and your grandma. She was my sister."

"Yes, I know. And then he repeated her name, "Etta; Etta Ramsey as was."

Dossie was taken aback at the sound of the pet name everyone had for Annetta and looked clearly shaken. Licking her dry thin lips, she rubbed her nose with the back of her fingertips and then placed them on her mouth as if to silence the words that lurked there. David felt some concern for the woman but decided to pursue his investigation just the same. He had come this far and now was not the time to give up.

"Well, I'll come straight out with it." David coughed to clear his throat before continuing, "We met Lucinda Addington a while ago and we think she knows you."

Miss Lou, she brightened slightly and a light appeared in the faded eyes. "Of course she knows me.

"I have to speak to her - it's very important."

"I've known Lucinda from the day she was born, so what do you want with her and why now of all times?"

There was something in what she said that hinted at some trouble, but David didn't press her for any more.

"Do you think I could see her?"

His great-aunt looked troubled and was silent for a

while before replying. "It's not a good time."

"But it's very important; not just to me but to my grandfather too."

"Ernest. What has she to do with him… with Mr Lowes, I mean?" Dossie felt a pang of fear seize her body but tried desperately not to display any sense of panic to the boy.

"Believe me, there can be no connection between Miss Lucinda Addington and your grandfather."

There was a distinct sense of arrogance in what she said, inferring the class difference between the two of them, which made David uncomfortable. He had come across snobbery all his life but was amazed to discover it in the shape of a woman who came from the same roots as his own grandmother.

"You have obviously made some mistake, young man." Continuing with a smile, intended to convey the fact that she wanted to end this unwanted conversation, Dossie headed towards the front door.

David not noticing the edge in her voice, didn't know what to do next but he had to tell her. It sounded crazy. Surely, she would think the old man had gone senile in his old age. He opened his mouth to speak but before he could say anything the old woman waved him towards the door.

Thank you for coming but I cannot help you, I wish you goodbye now." This time there was some nervousness about her manner that David recognised. There was more than a hint of sharpness in her words. "Follow the drive back to the main road. Take care, goodbye!"

Ignoring her tone, the young man stood fast and was determined to have his say. He moved towards her, trying to remain amiable in the face of her coldness.

"But I need to tell you something and I have to see

Lucinda. Believe me, it will sound quite incredible." His smile was so like his grandfather's, it could melt the iciest of hearts. "I can't make sense of it myself, but Ernest is convinced you would know something, he believes that you can help."

The way he referred to his grandfather as Ernest and the fact that he remembered her made the old woman catch her breath. "Why is it so important that you see Miss Lou and what is it that you think I know?"

Dossie's resolve was beginning to weaken and David saw his chance.

So he just went for it and told her everything about the meeting on the train, the likeness to Etta and about Ernest's heart attack.

The old woman put her head in her hands, remaining quite still and silent for several minutes before regaining her composure.

"I'm sorry if it's come as a shock. He's fully recovered now though, so you don't need to worry."

"No… no lad, it's not that, although I'm glad that he's well." She beckoned to him to sit with her before continuing.

"So you do know my grandfather, I take it?"

"Oh, yes, I know Ernest and I knew your mother." Memories of Etta and Elsie flooded her mind but disappeared quickly as she remembered what the boy had said about the heart attack.

"And you're sure he's well now? Your grandfather, I mean? I knew him a long time ago, you see, and you are so like him when he was a young man." She smiled a half smile and then continued, "I know you too. Well, I knew of you, to be more precise. I was there, you see, when your mother was expecting… I knew it would be a boy!"

Dossie was wittering but stopped sharply as she caught David staring at her in a strange, concerned way.

"So, Ernest is in good health now, is he?"

"Oh, yes, he's quite recovered, thank you."

David's voice was polite but he was intrigued by her incoherent ramblings and he spoke out abruptly, "You don't know me! I've never met you before."

Dossie sighed, both in relief at Ernest's recovery and in anticipation of what she was about to reveal to this confused young man. Inhaling deeply, she paced the room before sitting down anxiously next to David. There was no point in evading the issue any longer; the stress of covering up all these secrets for so long was too much for the elderly lady and she was ready to disclose all her lies. He had guessed so much already; it was inevitable that the truth would come out. No matter how painful, she determined to confess her sins.

"Well, I'm glad you've found me at last."

There was a hesitation and then she began again, "It's time for me to get it off my chest. I have to tell you a story, David, and I'm sorry to say that it's not a very happy one."

"I don't understand. What's this all this about?"

"Let me begin at the beginning, it all happened a long time ago before you were born." She breathed heavily, gathering all her strength for what she was about to divulge. She needed him to understand the whole sordid story from the very start. After all, it concerned him just as much as Ernest. Their lives were all inter-twined and Lucinda was just as much a part of the web as any of them.After settling herself down on the comfortable sofa in front of the fire, she beckoned to David to pull up a wooden high-backed chair and sit before her so she could study his face carefully. He was a handsome lad but his hair covered his eyes and his collar, as was the fashion those days, and she couldn't help thinking he needed a good haircut. She searched his features for some resemblance of Elsie but found none, although she fancied he had inherited his good looks from his grandfather. David waited patiently for her to begin her story as she had whetted his appetite for what was to come. Finally she lifted her face to the ceiling and breathed in heavily through her nose, before letting out a long, slow sigh.

"I had a younger sister, David, your grandmother. I'm ashamed to admit that I was jealous of her from the day she was born. She was a pretty little thing with light blonde hair and fine features. Mother loved us both, I'm sure of it, but she doted on Annetta and of course she was very clever and knew how to get her own way. I resented the way she manipulated… people."

She broke off as she recalled how Ernest had absolutely adored her sister. "She got everyone to dance to her tune. She was just so bloody appealing to everybody. Everyone adored Etta!"

David didn't know where this tale was going but she told it in such a captivating and enigmatic way that he was enthralled from the start. "Please go on!"

"As she grew into an even prettier young girl, I am embarrassed to say…"

She went on with David listening intently, "I was still very jealous but at the same time I was ashamed and envious of her in equal measures."

It was true, Etta was everything that Dossie wasn't.

"I was plain, David, plain and boring and she was beautiful and exciting."

Doreen had never been unattractive; she had a pretty face and lovely eyes but in comparison to Etta, she had always felt like the ugly sister. Of course, her nature had in truth always been cautious and some might have found her profound sense of practicality a little boring.

Annetta, on the other hand, was unconventional, a true

creative in the fullest sense of the word.

"Our Etta was a free spirit. You know the sort - she never cared what people thought - and she had such dreams as a young woman. Yes, David, I was jealous but the way she carried on with men made me blush to my hair roots." She let out a long sigh, "But I'm sorry, I shouldn't be saying such things about your grandmother. It's not proper."

David was not in the least shocked and showed no sign of the outrage that Dossie had anticipated. He simply shook his head and willed her to go on.

"Her behaviour was embarrassing to me." Sensing she hadn't caused him any offence, she carried on. "Probably not to you, a modern young man, but in those days and to me it wasn't at all respectable, the way she carried on."

"But she did nothing wrong," declared the grandson who was beginning to know more of the woman his grandfather had adored.

"Well, not in your eyes perhaps and if I'm honest, there was a big part of me that wished I could have been a bit more like her. If only I had the nerve to fall in love like she did, feel like she did."

As the words formed on her lips, Dossie felt self-conscious and she pulled herself up sharply, smiling an embarrassed smile that encouraged David to ask, "Were you never in love, then, Aunt Dossie?"

"In love?" she looked into space.

He wanted to know more of this story. She relaxed as she took in the familiarity of his address to her. The only other person to call her aunt had been his mother. It sounded so intimate that she let down her guard even further, revealing things to this stranger that she had never told to another soul.

"I married a man old enough to be my father because he was respectable and because he was the only one who ever asked me. I could never imagine any man loving me the way your grandfather loved my sister, but George Clifford did; only it was too late by the time I finally grasped the extent of it."

The words were now flowing as freely as if in the confessional box. Doreen was not a particularly religious woman anymore, but this was her confession, The only trouble being that David wasn't a priest and he couldn't absolve her of any sins.

"I'm a wicked woman, David. I have done some very bad things!"

Sobs escaped from her chest as her face was stained with wet tears that dripped from her nose and into her mouth.

"Ernest would have had his son if not for my interference. They wouldn't have kept on trying for a boy after those stillborns and Etta wouldn't have died bringing your Mam into the world. Well, there you are, lad. You have the truth of it."

David was more than a little confused. What did she mean? Who was this son and what had he got to do with her? By now, he was actually near to tears himself; tears of frustration as well as those shed for this distraught creature. As he handed the old woman a clean white handkerchief, he yearned for her to give him the answers.

"But I don't understand… a son… who… where?

The whole sordid story came to light as Doreen related everything to him: Her sister's affair with the man who turned out to be her own brother: Ernest's baby given away to a rich childless lady and Annetta's breakdown.

None of this could be true. It was more like the plot of a film he might see at the local flea pit on a Saturday night than real life. But it was true and his grandfather had been ignorant of the facts for all these years.

"There's more, I'm afraid; worst of all for you, I

believe I was responsible for your mother's death.

"What!" he gasped, "But you couldn't have been. "My mother died in a factory fire."

Weeping until her body was wrung out like a dishcloth, she gulped down the tears and began again.

"She came to me when she was expecting you and I sent her packing. I should have supported her, David; an unwed mother, begging me for help. I could have helped to bring you up but there were too many secrets that would come to light if I brought you both here, so I rejected her."

The sheer tragedy of it was beginning to dawn on David.

"I sent her away. I'll regret it to my dying day."

"You couldn't have known…" he tried to finish but the words stuck in his throat as the whole range of emotions fused together in his head, thinking over what she had just said. What did she mean an unwed mother? His father died in the war.

"My father died in the war," he said aloud.

"Oh, God. I'm sorry, David, I thought you knew." It was too late now to take back what had been said and seeing the doleful look on his face, she made the decision to tell him the truth.

"Your mother got pregnant by her boss, a married man. She was never wed herself."

He shook his head as he paced up and down the little room, dragging his fingers through his long hair. It all made sense now. He could never quite understand how his father had died in the war as he was born a year after it ended, but as a child, he preferred to believe the lie. As he grew into manhood though, thoughts of his own illegitimacy were pushed further and further into his subconscious until he never even thought about it. But why had she told him this now? Why? Maybe she was guilty, guilty as sin of ruining lives. Maybe she took a delight in hurting others. She had certainly hurt him! His whole childhood destroyed in a few short words. As a boy, he had created the story which painted his father as a war hero and this woman had just torn it all to shreds in a matter of seconds.

Immediately regretting revealing this secret, Dossie tried to apologise but couldn't find the right words.

After what seemed like an age with neither of them saying a word, Dossie broke the silence.

"You see, I just don't seem to be able to help doing the wrong thing. I shouldn't have said anything just now. But I thought you knew. When she came to me for help, she told me about Mr Jepson."

"Jepson?"

"Her boss!"

If only Dossie had helped his mother. He pondered on everything she had said. If his mother hadn't been at the factory that night. If the factory owner, Mr Smith hadn't really been a German; If people hadn't been overcome with fear and hatred: If she had never met Mr Jepson, if he had never been born. A tremendous anger bubbled inside him and he thumped his fist down hard on the oak table. Pain pulsated up his arm as he rubbed his bruised fingers with his left hand. Dossie rushed to his side in a bid to comfort him but he pushed her away and averted his gaze. He couldn't look at her.

"Oh, David, I'm so very, very sorry. I don't know what to say. Please forgive me, I beg you, forgive me for everything."

After a couple of minutes of silence with the searing pain still throbbing in his hand, he recovered himself enough to let out a strange laugh that spoke a thousand words. After the shock of finally acknowledging he was illegitimate, he appreciated she had actually done him a favour. At least now, he could face up to the truth instead of living a lie as he had done for the last twenty-odd years. He never questioned why he was known as Lowes; he just accepted it because he loved his grandfather so much.

So many lies; so many secrets; so many bloody tragedies. How could he possibly reveal all this to his grandfather? It would kill him. The day that they'd met Lucinda Addington heralded the opening of Pandora's box and it was going to be impossible to close it again.

Doreen lay in a crumpled heap on the horsehair sofa, but he didn't know at that moment whether he would shake her or offer her comfort. She was just a poor old woman.

"I am so sorry. I never wanted any of this. I loved your mother like the daughter I never had; I truly loved my sister and mistakenly loved your grandfather."

He looked straight through her as the words burned into his brain just as fiercely as the flames in the grate ate away at the logs. "How can you say you loved my mother?"

"My love was all mixed up and it came out wrong. I should have saved it for the only man who loved me. Instead I threw it away and created one hell of a mess."

"I can't even look at you now. You've hurt everyone I have ever loved. I hate you!"

The more he tried to make sense of everything he'd heard that afternoon, the more disgust he began to feel for this elderly woman who was completely broken by guilt.

"Please, David!"

The heat from the range made him shift suddenly and his aunt looked up at him with such a pitiful look on her face. A picture of his mother sitting by the fire toasting pikelets popped into her head. As David looked deep into her eyes, she could only hope that the hatred he felt might melt from him like the butter spread on those toasted crumpets. At this time of year, it had been a treat that they both shared and the image brought back such sadness that her face crumpled.

But it wouldn't be easy for the young man to get over the pain he felt and even though he was beginning to feel sorry for the old lady, he just couldn't forgive her. In reality, she couldn't really have influenced her sister's decisions. From what he'd learnt about Annetta, no-one could have done that. It had been her decision not to tell Ernest about the baby, for whatever reason. Doreen had lived with guilt for most of her life. Perhaps she had been punished enough. As for his own mother, she was a victim of a society that had been perverted by war and hatred. It was the dawning of a new age now; a new world where people were free to love. Mothers didn't need to die in childbirth. The stigma of illegitimacy was being lifted and independent women could follow their dreams.

His thoughts turned to Lucinda. She had a right to know who she was. Eventually he put his feelings behind him and tried to get back on track. There was a reason he was here.

"We have to talk to Lucinda. Please, you have to take me to see her."

"I can't do that." Dossie blew her nose loudly and wiped her tear-stained face on her apron. "Not today, boy. It wouldn't be right. Her grandmother is on her deathbed."

There didn't seem to be any more that could be said that day. It was getting late and they were both emotionally exhausted, so David simply left without another word, leaving the woman to try and come to terms with what needed to be done.

Chapter 22

David finally arrived back home to find Ernest fast asleep in the chair. The fire had gone out, but the embers were still orange and warm. Dragging a crocheted blanket from the back of the settee, he threw it over his grandfather's legs and in doing so, woke the old man from his dreams.

"Oh, you're back then, are you, lad? I must have dozed off. Sorry," he apologised.

"No, I'm sorry, Grandpa, I've been so long, you must have thought I'd got lost." David paused, sucking in air through his teeth. "Things took longer than I expected."

Nothing much got past Ernest and he knew straight away that David was upset and worried. "Out with it, boy. Tell me what's troubling you."

There was no way that he could face reliving the events that had taken place that evening in the gatehouse. "It's very late. I think we should sleep on it and I'll tell you everything in the morning."

David was trying desperately to find a way of breaking the news to Ernest and at that moment in time he was failing miserably. After a good night's sleep, his head might have cleared enough for him to find the right words.

"Tell me now, Davy lad. What have you found out?"

The young man was adamant and he stood his ground firmly, as if going into battle. Picking up on the cue, Ernest faced him square on.

"We've got a fight on our hands, have we, lad? It's war then, is it?"

"Don't talk daft and shut up!" he uttered, with more directive than he had intended and the old man was visibly upset until his grandson hugged him with such force that he shifted in his chair.

"Come on. Bed, you old crock, and I promise I'll give

you all the details tomorrow."

They laughed but Ernest was sure Davy was hiding something and although he did as he was bid and turned in for the night, sleep evaded him and strange thoughts whirred in his brain. His mind took him back to the war and he saw David dressed in khaki with a gun in his hand. The gun was pointing straight at him. It was nonsense, Davy had never known war and for that matter, neither had Ernest really. He was 41 years old at the start of World War 2, too old to be conscripted. Instead, as a farrier, he tended the horses and pit ponies that kept the coal moving in the mines. Of course, many miners were exempt from duty but without them, the war couldn't have been won. Oh, he'd played his part during those dark days well enough, but he'd longed to see some real action like his younger brother Lance. While drilling in the village hall with the rest of the old men and the young boys, Ernest dreamed of being in the RAF, a brave pilot fighter, no less, but he knew that in all probability, he would have been a rear gunner like Lance. His brother was one of the lucky ones who came back. Not many rear gunners actually did!

Trying desperately to sleep, he tossed and turned, threw the blankets to the floor and punched his feather pillow into submission until finally giving in to Morpheus. David woke him early the next morning with a mug of hot sweet tea. As he perched on the edge of the bed, Ernest pulled himself up onto the pillow and rubbed the sleep from his eyes. Neither of them had had much sleep that night but David decided that if the deed was to be done, he may as well get it over with now and quickly. And so he began at the beginning.

More than a week later, Ernest was still reeling from the shock of the revelations of the previous Friday. His son had been born and died without him having any knowledge of the events. He had never known about Etta's pregnancy, but it all made sense now. The secret she would never reveal about those missing months had finally and tragically been exposed.

Even now, he couldn't bring himself to blame her and, in his heart, he knew with certainty that if she'd confessed all, they would have done nothing about it. How could they have denied their son the life of privilege she'd allowed him by giving him away? His only regret was that he'd never even seen him, not even a photograph. However, he had something better than a picture in the form of a beautiful grandchild Arthur had created for him. He couldn't wait to see her again but knew this time the meeting would be difficult. They were no more than strangers really, but she had his blood flowing through her veins and he instinctively felt a surge of affection for the young girl they had met on a train.

Having finally recovered from the previous week's revelations, David had persuaded him to be patient, outlining his plan of action.

"Once we get there, Grandpa, I think it would be best if you see Dossie on your own." He wasn't ready to speak to his great-aunt again just yet.

"Try not to get upset." He was worried about his grandpa's health and knew how painful this was going to be.

"I'll speak to Lou. We need to break it to her gently. After all, she's just buried her grandmother. Another shock so soon afterwards won't be easy for her to comprehend, to take on board, I mean."

"You're right, Davy boy. You always were very clever with all these big words; you'll make a brilliant teacher. You understand people the way I used to understand horses." There was a genuine sense of pride in the way he poked fun at his grandson.

"OK, you get to know Dossie again. You'll be alright, won't you? Or do you want me with you?" He questioned with his eyes, raising his eyebrows almost to his hairline. "I'll try to help Lucinda to make some sense of all of this, if you're sure you can handle it."

"Of course I can, I'm not daft, not yet anyway!"

David just grinned. He had still to come to terms with everything he had learned but he knew he had to help his grandfather.

"I've booked a taxi to get us there, so get yourself ready. It'll be here in twenty minutes."

In little more than an hour, Ernest Lowes was drinking tea with Doreen Clifford in the parlour of the gatehouse.

There was a tension as they caught each other's eye over the china cups decorated with pretty pink roses. She was older, of course, but he recognised something about her immediately. Those lovely green eyes, though a little watery now, were still as twinkling as ever, even though her hair was faded and there was a washed-out look about her whole appearance.

After a few minutes, Ernest put down his cup and looked pointedly at Dossie, who was dreading what was to come.

"He's told you the whole story, has he? "She pointed in the direction of the big house where the lad had gone to meet Lucinda.

"Yes, he's told me everything." Ernest was feeling embarrassed and began to wring his hands.

Even though they had known each other for years, they were strangers now. Strangers with a secret.

He couldn't bring himself to look at her but she couldn't help herself from feeling a fondness for this man and she found herself gazing at him affectionately. Scrutinising the familiar handsome features, which age hadn't totally diminished, she held the stare until he finally returned her look and they both instantly turned their heads away. But her eyes were drawn back to the dimple in his chin and the chiselled cheekbones that had become more pronounced as he had grown older.

"What did he tell you?" she asked directly.

"The whole sorry story." He paused, trying to judge her reaction as he revealed the bit she was dreading.

"All about Arthur, my son!"

His name on Ernest's lips made her waver, dredging up all those feelings of guilt that had blighted her life for so long.

"I know about Etta's fling with him... the one..." Ernest's mouth was dry but he continued, "the one who turned out to be her..."

"Her brother!" Dossie finished the sentence. "It was disgusting!"

Ernest looked aghast. "But you told David she didn't know who he really was."

"There was no way of telling when they first met but how can you be...well, intimate like that with your father's son. Surely you can tell."

"That's ridiculous, she had no idea that he was her half-brother," Ernest sprang to Etta's defence and it was obvious to Dossie that he still cared very much for the dead woman.

"It was disgusting," Dossie repeated, upset by the force of the feelings that were still there for her sister, "her own brother; she was a slut."

She had no idea why she was talking like this but meeting Ernest again like this brought back strange memories and there was an anger that came from her own self-loathing and bitterness. A look of sheer disbelief and outrage appeared in his old eyes and his face was white with shock and anger. He had come to meet her with an open mind, determined not to lose his temper, as David had instructed, but her words were cruel and uncalled for.

"You witch, how can you say that about your own sister?"

"She took you away from me!" As these words were finally spoken, Ernest looked shocked at the meaning that lurked behind them, but without acknowledging her feelings, he simply stated the truth.

"I loved her, Dossie. I loved your sister."

"And I loved you!" she cried, blurting out the words before she realised what she was saying.

Completely disregarding this declaration, shaking the words out of his head, he screamed, "You stole my son; you persuaded my Etta to give up our little lad."

Everything he had learnt made his head spin and an uncontrollable resentment led him to act without thinking. He wasn't a violent man but he couldn't stop himself at this moment from taking her shoulders in his still strong arms and shaking her forcefully until she let out a shrill cry from the pain. It took all his willpower to stop himself from slapping her, imagining the pink bruises to her cheeks. He let go his grip and she collapsed to the floor, leaving him bereft and confused. Glaring at him with hurt in her eyes, she remained silent as he pulled her into his arms and held her tight. She hadn't slept since all this had come out and her mind was in turmoil. She was mad with guilt - she must have been - to say those terrible things. As soon as he realised what he had done, he regretted his actions immediately. Her testimony of love for him was too much on top of everything else and he'd just snapped. How could she say she loved him when she had destroyed his life? But he was wrong to do what he did and he knew it. His emotions were swinging like a pendulum and he no longer felt in control of what he was saying or doing.

"You've got to forgive me, Dossie. I'm so sorry. Please forgive me," he was distraught.

"But you can't really believe what you've just said!"

"It's me who should be sorry, Ernest. No, I don't know what made me say it. I loved my sister; she was a sweet, wonderful woman. When she found out about Sam Simpson it just sent her crazy. She didn't know what she was doing." The words spurted out spasmodically between sobs.

"She thought that devil Simpson was the father!" Dossie spat out his name. "In her disturbed mind, she could only see evil in that beautiful baby and wanted rid of him. She wouldn't believe he was yours, but I knew from the minute I saw him, I knew!"

"Why? Why, if you were so sure, did you let her go ahead with it?" His heart was heavy, thinking about what might have been.

"I'm so sorry!"

"You bloody stupid woman, I can't bear to look at you. Why didn't you help your sister? Why didn't you come to me?"

"I couldn't stop it. Lady Agatha had lawyers draw up papers and suchlike. It was all too late. Do you think I haven't regretted for one minute what happened?"

"I'm going. I can't stand to be in the same room as you. You destroyed my life. You took away my son. Our son; Etta's and mine; our baby!"

Ernest staggered to the door as his legs felt like jelly forcing him to grab the back of the seat that stood in the hallway. Dossie immediately rushed to his side and helped him onto the chair.

"Oh, my God, Ernest are you alright? Let me get you a drink."

For a few minutes, the old man sat in silence as his sister-in-law hovered anxiously before bringing him a glass of water. As she handed him the glass, she pleaded with all the emotion that had built up inside of her for years.

"Please say you forgive me. I know I don't deserve it but please, Ernest, try not to hate me!"

Contemplating her sad old face, Ernest realised just how pointless it was to hate her for what had happened. Perhaps he couldn't forgive her but he had to forget or it would drive him mad. He couldn't bring back Etta or Arthur but he could meet his granddaughter. His son's child.

"What's done is done." he said philosophically. He was so tired and there was no point dwelling on the past. They were both well past the first flush of youth and to waste time on things that couldn't be changed was futile.

He had thought for so long about all that happened in his past, his relationship with Etta, her death, his treatment of his only daughter, believing that he had come to terms with the guilt. And he realised nobody was to blame. How many times had he said this to himself over the past days? Now he had to forgive his dead wife's sister. He was still smarting from the injustice of it all, but he had always been a tolerant man and was prepared to try to forgive and forget. His relationship with Etta was testament to this attribute. Not many men would have forgiven her for the way she treated him.

"You weren't really to blame for any of this, Dossie."

"Oh but I was!"

"It was nobody's fault. I'm sorry for hurting you. I shouldn't have done that."

"I deserved it for what I said and you know Ernie, in a funny way, I feel as though the guilt's been lifted from my shoulders."

"Two wrongs don't make a right!"

"I know, but it feels like punishment for my sins!"

"Punishment."

"Oh, believe me, I've lived a life of punishment. I've hurt everyone who loved me. My husband died thinking I never really loved him. But I did, Ernest. In my own way, I did."

Ernest didn't know what to say as he took her hands in his. He wasn't sure whether the gesture was a sign of forgiveness or of frustration but his grip was strong until he loosened his fingers. There had been so much pain in his life and in hers. It was time to put the past behind them. There had to be forgiveness. For the sake of his dead son's child.

"I have a granddaughter who doesn't know who I am. In fact, she doesn't really know who *she* is, does she Dossie?"

"You're right."

"But hopefully, she soon will."

Dossie smiled a slow, mournful smile but there was hope in her eyes and she felt that their lives could be changed and for the better.

"Our Davy says that there's a blood test we can do that will prove once and for all if we are related and I think we should do it."

"You must do whatever you need to do, Ernest, but I can tell you now, Lucinda may be Addington by name but she has Lowes' blood and your test and time will tell!"

The two of them sat together by the fire, neither saying a word for what seemed like an age. Then suddenly Ernest broke the silence.

"You know it's been a long time since I've sat with a woman like this."

"You've been lonely?"

"Oh, I've been lonely!"

Any feelings of hatred towards his sister-in-law began to subside and memories of how she was when they were young flooded into his head. She had been a good woman whose only sin was to love the wrong man.

"Are you alright now, Ernest?"

"I hate to admit it but I feel comfortable somehow."

"Oh, Ernest."

"I know I should hate you, but no matter what's happened, you and I have something in common."

"We do?"

"Yes"

"And what's that, may I ask, Ernest Lowes?" A sense of optimism began to grow in Dossie's breast. There was a chance he could forgive her. Her words were light and the hint of a smile was visible on her thin lips.

"We're both very lonely and we both loved the same girl."

"Oh, Ernie, you're so right; so very right. I am and have been a most lonely woman for my entire life."

"But you were married. Were there no children?"

"I've only ever loved other people's children because I had none of my own."

"I'm sorry."

"But yes, I cherished my sister in spite of all the hurt we caused each other." There was a hint of Annetta's attractiveness in the old face proving the blood relationship between them.

"I knew you two had been close."

"I suppose it was because I cared so much that I was so upset when she got pregnant out of wedlock."

"I had no idea."

"Mam always laughed at my prissiness but with a father like ours, I craved a decent life. I think that's why I married George. He was such a good honest man."

"Were you happy?"

"Happy?"

"With George?"

"I could have been, should have been. He tried so hard, bless him."

"He sounds like a decent bloke."

"Oh yes, George was a good man. Decent!" Her eyes glazed over and her expression hardened. "I was disgusted with our Etta. It wasn't decent what she did."

"It wasn't her fault."

"I know. I should have been there for her but it wasn't my fault either." Dossie stared pitifully at the man she adored. Looking at him for approval, she went on, "You can't imagine what it's like to hate your own father."

"I know. Etta told me all about him."

"He was an immoral man."

"But Etta?"

"I was scared."

"She wasn't a bad lass, just wanted too much."

"I was scared that she'd inherited his bad blood. I couldn't bear to see her ruin her life."

Ernest was deep in reflection as he processed her words. "I can't for one minute imagine hating my own father, though I know what he would have said about a child out of wedlock."

"It was shameful."

"But times were very different then, Dossie."

"I know, but when Arthur was born and he was the image of you..." She started to cry at the memory of the beautiful baby boy who so reminded her of the man she loved. "I just snapped and that's when everything simply fell apart." She collapsed in tears again, burying her head in her hands.

"My God. Why didn't you tell me?"

He immediately went to her side. It was the kind of

man he was. After everything she had told him, he couldn't bear to see her so distraught no matter what she'd done.

"I couldn't. I wasn't thinking straight and I didn't think you would believe me."

"But why didn't Etta tell me?"

"She really thought she was carrying her own brother's child. How could she tell you that?"

"I loved her."

"She was too ashamed."

Ernest was deep in thought with a faraway look in his eyes.

"You know, you could be right. I don't know whether I could have taken it."

"But he was yours. I knew it and I didn't tell you."

"I know."

"You don't."

"What?"

"I loved you, Ernest. I wanted your baby for my own." Tears flowed freely again leaving Dossie gulping for breath, her whole body consumed with a sense of guilt and shame.

Gently lifting her to her feet, Ernest stared her full in the face with such an air of compassion.

"You were both under such a strain," he murmured, finally beginning to understand.

"She didn't want him. I hated her for that."

"No."

"When my baby died, it was if my whole world ended and here was my sister with a child she didn't deserve."

"It's no wonder you each acted the way you did, with everything that happened." Ernest was beginning to understand. "But you were sisters."

"Yes, she was my baby sister."

"I remember how you were when you were just girls.

You were so close. Etta looked up to you so much."

Nostalgia softened her as she admitted her true feelings without ever taking her eyes from his sympathetic face, tears still visible on her lashes.

"Yes, I know!" she sobbed. "Etta was my little sister but things went wrong, that's how it was."

"But why desert her?"

"Believe me, once I'd come to my senses and she was over the breakdown, I tried again. I tried desperately to build bridges. I did try, Ernest, I did!"

Dossie seemed to regain composure after Ernie's apparent sympathy and she blew her nose loudly on the handkerchief that he handed to her.

"I knew of the rift between the two of you, of course I did, but she never really spoke about it. Etta was like that with secrets, she kept them very close to her chest."

"She never told you any of this?"

"She wasn't one for opening up. I suppose that's why she never once told me…" Ernest's sentence remained unfinished.

"You know everything now though, don't you?"

"Yes"

"I'll regret the part I played in it to my dying day; please believe that, Ernest."

"I don't know, Dossie."

"But you mustn't blame her either. She was very ill. You didn't see her the way she was."

Dossie clearly remembered the images in her head of her dear mad sister in those months after she gave up her baby.

"Oh believe me, Dossie, I saw that side of her many times during our marriage."

"You did?"

"Oh aye. When our babies died, she went into terrible depressions but she seemed to get over it after a few weeks."

"Oh, no, Ernest it wasn't like that."

"No!"

"It took months and months before she was really well again after Arthur was born. It was hell and I tried to make it up with her, I really did."

"So why did you give up on her?"

"She was set against me, Ernie, wouldn't have anything to do with me ever again. I lost my sister long before you did but I never stopped loving her."

Any feelings of resentment that he had previously felt towards her disappeared in that moment and were replaced with tender sentiments for his sister-in-law, whose wistful face looked so appealing in the firelight. "Maybe we can get through this, in spite of all that has gone on in the past."

"Be friends."

"In time, maybe."

For the first time in years, she felt a yearning for a man; for this man, the only one she had always believed she loved.

If friendship was all he could offer, then that would be good enough for her. In fact it was more than she could have ever wished for after all that had gone before.

"Do you really mean that, Ernest? We can be friends. You forgive me!" her face transformed in that moment and she became almost pretty again. "I don't deserve it but thank you; from the bottom of my heart, I thank you!"

"Steady, lass. I can't promise anything yet."

His eyes twinkled and he looked like a young man again sending her heart racing and bringing a rosy flush to her cheeks, but there was more than a sense of apprehension in her eyes as she wondered how Lucinda would react to discovering her true identity.

"I think, though, it's time I met my grandchild. I've

got a lot of catching up to do and I'm going to need your help."

Chapter 23

While Grandfather and Great-Aunt reacquainted themselves, David was busy trying to find a way of telling Lucinda the truth about her parentage.

"This is not going to be easy," he mumbled to himself, as he walked across the cobbled courtyard to the main entrance. "How do you tell someone their whole life has been a lie?"

Somehow, he found the determination to come out with it and he stood tall, stretched up to his full six foot and puffed out his chest like some male bird showing off its feathers.

Within seconds though, this bravado had deserted him and he was all set to turn on his heels and return to the gatehouse when she walked across the courtyard, leading a beautiful black stallion by the nose. Lucinda, head bent low and shoulders drooping, looked so forlorn and dejected, only brightening slightly as the horse gently nuzzled into her. Pulling out a carrot from her pocket, she raised her head and almost immediately she caught sight of the young man who she recognised as the boy from the train. It had been nearly three months since that day when they had first met, but it had been such a traumatic encounter, she couldn't forget him or his grandfather.

She was back from college for the Christmas break; like him, she supposed. A time for most students to make merry and forget the workload, at least until after New Year. But for her, it had been the worst time of her life since the day she lost her parents. She had just buried her grandmother and now she had no-one left.

"You!" she exclaimed, excited to see him again. "What are you doing here?"

Suddenly, pretending to dredge up his name from her memory she repeated herself, "David, it is you, isn't it?

What on earth are you doing here?

"I er… well, I wanted to see you." This was true, of course, but he wished with all his heart it was under different circumstances.

His voice was shaky and she detected the anxiety that he was desperately trying to hide.

"Your grandfather," she gasped, suddenly thinking of her own dear grandmother." Is he OK? he's not ill or anything, is he?"

"No, he's fine. Very well, in fact. He'd like to see you, Lucinda, or can I call you Lou again?"

"How lovely. I'd love to meet him again," she beamed, suddenly so relieved. I'm so pleased he's fully recovered now and do please call me Lou."

"Yeah, well…" David was again lost for words. She was such a well-bred young lady, quite unlike anyone he'd ever really known, and he was unsure how to proceed in such a difficult situation. But Lucinda continued the conversation, giving him time to recover himself.

"Is he at home at the moment? I could drive out to your house, if you like. It would be delightful to see him again. I am so relieved he's well."

"Mm… well, he's actually here right now. He's with Dossie."

"What!" Lucinda laughed for the first time since she had returned home from London.

The sound of her laughter seemed to summon a small weedy looking lad, as the groom came from nowhere and led the horse away to the stables.

"Thank you, Harry, he'll need a good rub down," she shouted back to him.

The lad simply nodded.

"We were sorry to hear about your loss." David bowed his head and looked genuinely upset.

"Oh, is that why you came? I didn't think you knew Grandmama."

"No, we didn't, but Dossie told us."

Lou's eyes widened, trying to make some sense of what was going on here.

Trying to offer some clarification, David explained, "You see, your Dossie is actually my Dossie too. She is my Great-Aunt. She was my grandmother's sister.

This was incredible. What a coincidence! She thought back to that day when they teased each other about Dossie. Then a warm glow came over her as she thought about the old woman who had been there for her since the day she was born.

"She was my nanny, so not related at all, but she was Mother and Grandmother to me; more than my real one in fact!

A sudden and overwhelming sense of guilt and grief overcame her as she thought of her poor dead Grandmother.

"No, I don't really mean that. Sorry, it came out all wrong."

"Don't worry."

"My Grandmother adored me, and I her, but she wasn't the motherly sort, if you know what I mean. She was never one for kisses and cuddles, but Dossie was.

This was his cue and if he didn't follow it now, he would never divulge the truth to this lovely young girl, who was so completely unaware of her real identity.

He breathed in deeply and gulped so that his Adam's apple visibly jumped in his throat.

"But you are related."

"Related? What do you mean?"

"I think Doreen Clifford is your Great-Aunt as well as mine!"

There, he'd said it, and all he could do now was watch

and wait as the information he had just thrown at her seeped into her consciousness.

"My Great-Aunt? But how?"

She staggered toward him, her head in a spin as she grabbed at his arm to stop herself from stumbling on the cobbles.

A moment before, she had fretted about having no relatives left, feeling orphaned and alone, but now this stranger was telling her she had a Great-Aunt and what was more a Great-Aunt who had looked after her all her life without ever revealing who she was.

"No, you're kidding me, aren't you? This is a joke and not a very funny one."

"No joke, Lou."

"Don't you realise I have only just lost my Grandmother? This is cruel. Why have you come here?" The words all ran into one as she struggled to cope with the information he had just given her.

"No, listen, please just give me a chance to explain everything. I don't want to hurt you."

She wasn't listening. Instead, she screamed at David to go away and leave her in peace but at that very instant, Dossie and Ernest arrived in the courtyard.

Lucinda ran at Dossie, the one person who she trusted to care for her.

"He's mad. Send him away, Dossie. He's crazy."

Soothing down her hair, as she had done since she was a little girl, Doreen took a hysterical Lou by the hand and led her in through the huge double doors to the magnificent entrance hall. David and Ernest followed like lapdogs. A manservant came out from a side door and awaited instruction, only to be shooed away by Dossie with an air of authority.

After twenty minutes or so, all sitting in the morning room with cups of tea in hand, Lucinda had calmed down enough to beg Dossie to tell her what was going on. It took almost another hour for the whole story to be told. Dossie began, only to be superseded by Ernest and then by David, each one of the little trio adding another dimension to the story until the whole truth had been revealed.

"We have no definite proof that Arthur, your father that is, was Ernest's son but David says there are ways of proving such things these days," Dossie said, as kindly as she could.

"I can't take any of this in."

"I was there at his birth, Lucinda, and I watched him grow into a man and there is no doubt in my mind that Ernest Lowes was his father."

"But how?"

"This man was your father's father. He is your grandfather."

Lucinda had just buried her grandmother, or the woman she believed to be her grandmother and now she had just listened to the most remarkable story that she had ever heard. Her head was all over the place and struggling to come to terms with it all, she threw herself at the one person in the world that she trusted implicitly.

"Dossie, I just can't understand any of this." The words escaped from her lips in between sobs. "Please help me. Who am I?"

"You are your father's daughter, child and always have been. You've felt that since you were in the cradle."

"I know. I am everything that he was!" Her face lit up with pride and a genuine sense of love for the man she'd barely had time to know.

"And your darling father was everything that this man and my sister were!" declared the old woman, with a sense of remorse for denying them the right to their son.

"It's all just too much."

"He was my sister's son, born out of wedlock and brought up by your grandmother as her own!"

"So, you're telling me this man was his father?"

Dossie didn't reply but simply looked across at Ernest.

"Which means that I am his granddaughter," she said, contemplating the old man sitting at her side.

"That's right, sweetheart." Ernest's eyes smiled.

"This is all too incredible to believe!" Lucinda sank her head into her hands, waiting to hear more of the story. Suddenly she shook her head and stretched out her hands.

"No, no more. Are you after money? Is that what this is all about?"

"Lucinda, how can you think that?"

"But Dossie, this is insane. I don't know what to think."

"We are telling you the truth, my love. I wouldn't lie to you."

"I know you wouldn't. I'm sorry but I just can't take any of this in right now."

"It must be hard for you but listen to what we have to say. Hopefully, things will begin to make sense."

It took a while for the whole meaning of what was being revealed to her that day to sink in, but the more she considered the facts, the more she began to believe what she had heard.

"So, it's true, I am your granddaughter."

"I believe you are that, pet and I knew the first day I set eyes on you that we had some connection."

"I have to admit, I felt something too."

"You never met her but you are the image of my wife, Annetta, your grandmother."

"No, my grandmother is… was… Agatha."

"Forgive me, girl, of course she was, but my Annetta's blood flows in your veins, just as mine does."

Lucinda looked fondly at this old man, her soft blue eyes glistening. A stranger who claimed to be her grandfather was smiling back at her and at that moment she hoped with all her heart that it was true.

He reached for her hand. "I only wish you could have met your..." He hesitated. "You would have loved her and she would have worshipped you."

"Oh, God. My world has just turned upside down."

"We haven't come here to upset you, pet, but you are so like her."

"Am I, really?"

"You are the image of my sister." Dossie couldn't resist finally admitting the truth to the girl she had cherished since she was born.

"I wish I could have met her." Lucinda reached out for the old lady who she loved as a mother.

"And I wish that I could have met your father." Ernest's eyes were red and watery with tears. "My son."

"You would have adored my father if you'd met him!"

"I would."

No matter how unbelievable the story was, the girl felt a strange sense of belonging. She had felt something for this old man from that first meeting on the train. There had been an instant connection. Why else would she have felt compelled to go to the hospital with him?

They both took a few silent minutes to take in what they had said to each other and after a little while, Ernest smiled sadly and looked deep into Lucinda's beautiful blue eyes.

"I would have loved to have seen him just once... my son... my boy."

Lucinda's heart went out to this frail old man and she blinked away the stinging tears that threatened to spill down her face.

"Do you have a photo I could borrow? I never knew what he looked like."

This was madness, here she was in the midst of a family gathering that could have been played out every Sunday teatime in every home in the country. Sitting here drinking tea and making small talk amongst strangers who claimed to be her long-lost relations, Lucinda felt absolutely bewildered but at the same time quite comforted. It was taking a while for everything to sink in but somehow it seemed to fit together. Her father was never really like his mother, they were so vastly different and so was she. Her values and opinions were so unlike those possessed by her late grandmother. It seemed obvious now that they had never shared the same genes.

"You have a photograph?" Prompted David, who up to now had listened in silence to the unusual family reunion. He had seen a very different side to his Great-Aunt.

"Oh, no, sorry," she quickly gathered herself from her reverie, "Grandmama never showed me any but we have something far, far better, don't we, Dossie?"

"In the attic!" Dossie whispered, suddenly realising what Lou meant.

The self-portrait was mounted in a gilt-coloured wooden frame that held the wonderfully executed oil on canvas painted by Lucinda's father. A handsome young man of about twenty stared out from the picture, his hair as fiery red as Ernest's had once been. His sharp eyes were a mixture of blue and grey, flecked with brown. Dossie was so right, it could have been Ernest himself in his younger days staring out from the gilt frame. As she carefully scrutinised the painting, Lucinda couldn't fail to notice the likeness, even now, decades later. The shape of the face; the line of the nose and there was no mistaking the hair and the eyes. Ernest was speechless. He looked first at Lucinda and then at David, his face fixed with amazement. They both returned the look with nods of affirmation. This was the first and only time he had seen his son and he was overcome with such emotion as he turned to face Dossie. He said nothing, his face frozen but she knew what that silent stare meant. He genuinely believed everything she had told him. There wasn't the slightest doubt in his mind that Arthur was his son. He turned to the woman, whom just hours before he had hated with his whole being but now was the only one who could give him what he wanted. Trying to smile, he spoke quietly and gently, hoping that she would tell him everything he needed to know.

"Would you mind spending some time with me, Doreen? I want you to tell me everything about my boy."

"Oh, Ernie!"

"I want to know all about him; like when he was a baby; what was he like as a youngster?" His whole body was quivering with anticipation. "What kind of man was my son?"

The questions streamed out of his mouth just as the tears ran down his cheek. Happiness shone from the old lady like a golden beam of light. There was nothing she would like more. Lucinda hugged them both. It came instinctively and naturally as though it was something she had waited for her whole life. Even though Ernest was a relative stranger to her and Dossie had only ever really been a servant in the household, they were her family now and she felt warm and secure in the knowledge that she was genuinely precious to them. David suddenly became very aware of the fact that Lou's mother hadn't been mentioned at all during the revelations and not wanting to cause his newly found cousin any further hurt, he jumped in quickly in his usual chirpy fashion.

"Did he paint your mother, Lou? I'm partial to a pretty face," he said, winking at Lou, "and I'd make an educated guess that she was a very beautiful woman."

It obviously did the trick and the girl became animated and excited.

"Oh, yes!" she exclaimed enthusiastically, delighted at the prospect of talking about the mother she was too young to really know, "she was lovely, she was a glamorous actress, you know. There wasn't time for her to become famous but I know if she had lived, she would have been one of the greats."

"An actress, wow!"

"Daddy painted lots and lots of pictures of her. I'm going to get them all out of that dusty old attic and hang them on the walls so that I can see them whenever I want!"

Lucinda's whole demeanour had brightened and there was a lightness about her that they hadn't witnessed so far that day. She was so pleased that he had brought her mother into the conversation. They must all learn to love her memory as much as they did her father's. Her grandmother never liked her mother but she was sure that her new grandfather would have loved her. As the four mis-matched individuals huddled together in the formality of the morning room at Cranfield Hall, the newly formed family couldn't have been happier but Ernest began to feel uncomfortable in these surroundings and longed for the comfort of his own hearth. A niggle began to form in his brain. They were from such different worlds and he wondered whether this happiness could really last. It would take time to forget the pain of the past. Yet it was unbelievable the way that the four strangers had come together so quickly and in such a traumatic way. Even David managed to forgive and forget. Perhaps it was because of the tragedies that they had all endured that they were able to bond in mutual respect and trust for one another. Dossie never believed that she could be absolved of her sins but both Ernest and David finally understood her torment and allayed her fears that she would be despised for what she'd done. There was no hatred in any of the four lost souls who came together as if by magnetism; there was only love. Lucinda had found a real family at last and David, who had also missed a mother's touch, eventually found it in his Great-Aunt's embrace. And as for Ernest, he had discovered that real affection was possible even at his age and with a woman who had been responsible for such heartache. Amazingly, he was able to put it all behind him and embrace a future that he never believed could exist for him. But most of all, the cement that held them all together was the realisation that Lucinda had been the reason they had discovered each other and they all loved her, each in their own separate ways. This was the beginning of their story, a story that would see secrets revealed and put to rest; a story that would let an old man and an old woman live again and two young people enjoy a life that they truly deserved.

More than three months later, Cranfield Hall was up for sale and Lucinda was preparing to come home for the Easter break. She caught the train from Kings Cross station and settled down for the journey back to Newcastle. David was picking her up on the motorbike and intended to take her to Grandpa's for a few days before returning to the hall. She would be an extraordinarily rich young woman, having inherited her grandmother's estate, but she had never had any airs and graces and she was more than happy to spend time in the four bedroomed house in Kimberley Terrace that belonged to Ernest Lowes. It may have been a terrace but it was considered rather grand in the village, as it was much larger than most and had a lovely garden which led down to the outbuildings which housed the forge. He no longer worked as a farrier but all his tools were neatly stacked or hung on the walls and he would often spend time reminiscing in the darkness of the old building that still smelt of smoke and of horses.

Lucinda adored horses and had the same knack with the animals as her grandfather had.

"Take me down to the sheds please, Grandpa," she asked as soon as she arrived at Ernest's comfortable little house.

"What do you want down there, lass? It's a bit of a mess."

She felt happy amongst the tools, the tongs, the rasp and the anvil; she drank in the atmosphere and the smells filled her nostrils.

"I love it."

"Never mind all this. How's the art coming on then, lady?" he teased.

"I'm doing alright, I think. My next assignment is a portrait."

"Etta would have been so proud of you, lass," he sighed, "You have brought all her dreams to life."

Lucinda had made up her mind to paint Ernest's portrait but suddenly she changed her mind.

"I want to paint her, Grandpa! I want to paint Etta!" She almost glowed as she made the announcement.

Ernest looked puzzled but at the same time as proud as punch. "You want to do my Etta's picture, lass? I can't believe it."

"Yes, I really do."

"I only have a few faded old photographs of her." Sucking on his bottom lip, he rubbed the grey stubble on his chin," They weren't very good in those days, not really clear but I guess you'll get some idea of how lovely she was."

"You know what, the best portrait of Annetta is in your head," she encouraged. "You can give me every detail of her appearance, every shade in her hair, every feature of her face and the shape of her body and I will paint what you see in your imagination.

As they reached the forge, Ernest chuckled with real pleasure as they both imagined the enigmatic woman who had been her grandmother. They stood together in the semi-darkness and with a strong smell of horses mingled with cold dead ashes, Ernest remembered a night long ago in a tack room… the night Lucinda's father had been conceived.

A call from the house broke the reverie and Dossie came bustling down the garden path from the kitchen.

"Why didn't you tell me Lou had arrived?" She was hard of hearing these days and didn't hear the spluttering din from David's bike as he pulled up outside the front door.

She had been busy upstairs preparing the guest room for their visitor, making sure the bed linen and the towels were good enough for her ladyship. She mused at the thought of Lucinda Addington staying here at Ernest's humble home.

She and Ernie had grown very fond of each other since his granddaughter had gone back to London and they had spent a lot of time together. Somehow, the past that had separated them had now brought them back together and despite all that had gone before, Ernest had grown fond of Dossie. They were more than just friends but he still needed to take things slowly and Dossie was happy enough to let him. One day they might take it a step further but for now she was content with her lot.

"The upstairs room is all spick and span and ready for

you, Lou," Dossie announced proudly. "I've put a bottle in the bed, child, just to take off the chill."

"Thank you. I'll stay tonight but then I must get back to the hall. The estate agent rang yesterday. Someone is interested in buying Cranfield."

David had been sitting quietly by the fire, giving them all time to chat and catch up but now he felt he should at least try to find out Lucinda's plans for the future. It would devastate his grandfather if she decided to leave now that he was beginning to really get to know her.

"What will you do once the place is sold, Lou?" he enquired casually, but secretly hoping for the right answer.

"Well, I've been giving it a lot of thought, Davy. I aim to buy a house in Newcastle, somewhere with an attic or a basement where I can set up a studio for when I graduate. Until then, I'm going to need someone to look after the place for me and then look after me as well once I'm back." The young woman caught his eye as she grinned cheekily.

"I might be quite clever, David, but I've not got much common sense or any domestic abilities to speak of. I shall certainly need someone sensible to make sure I don't starve or burn the house down or something equally stupid. I hate to admit it but at college, I leave all the practical things to my flat mate. I know I'm useless!"

David nodded in agreement, whilst giving her a most disapproving stare.

"She doesn't mind, honestly! Feeling very embarrassed by her confession, Lou stuck out her bottom lip like a petulant child. "But I will really need someone to help me out when I come back here to live."

"Got anybody in mind?" he joshed. "Who could possibly look after such an incompetent as you?"

"Well, a respectable elderly couple would be my first

choice and I can quite see you in a chauffeur's uniform, young sir, or possibly you could be my butler." Her eyes were teasing as she fluttered her lashes seductively.

David returned the look with an indignant stare, raising his eyebrows but it wasn't long before a guffaw escaped from the pressed lips. He was such an attractive young man, the thought of a peaked cap on top of that handsome head quite tickled Lou and she smirked at him, suppressing feelings that she knew were not quite proper, given their relationship. Kissing cousins might be rather nice, if somewhat inappropriate, particularly given the circumstances of her grandmother Etta's disastrous liaison with Sam. Did it run in the blood? she thought to herself. David made an exaggerated attempt to clear his throat, coughing loudly in order to break the uncomfortable sensations brought about by this playful discourse. His cousin was grateful for the cue to reinstate the now platonic relationship that existed between the two of them. They had too good a rapport to spoil it all by allowing silly amorous ideas to cloud their friendship. She just needed to test the water by asking for his opinions on her plan for them all to share her new home.

"Seriously though, David, I want Ernest and Dossie to come and live with me."

She paused, searching his face for any hint as to his feelings on the matter. "As family, of course, not as servants and I want my best and only cousin to be part of the family as well. What do you think?"

Giving nothing away, he nodded his head in acknowledgement. There was an electricity in the air as he processed her suggestion, delighting in her obvious excitement over the proposal. She would always be incredibly special to him and there was no doubt that he wanted her to be part of his life but there could never be anything romantic between them. It wouldn't be right!

"Ernest would love it and so would Dossie but you know how proud they are!" And just to clarify the situation, he added, "And as for me, my dear Lou, well, I have my own life to lead, you know."

Lucinda looked downhearted. "Oh, of course, I didn't mean anything. I just want to help you all. Once the money comes through from the estate, I want to share it with my family."

"But we can't take your money, Lou, it was your grandmother's and she left it to you."

His cousin smiled fondly at David's concern for her but remained determined to look after them all. "Listen, you have all given me something so precious since we all met, no amount of money can ever repay it, believe me."

"We'll see," he said, simply.

Chapter 24

The weeks turned into months and the months into years as Lou's student days came to a successful end a little after David had gained his teaching certificate. Coming back up north with a first class arts degree under her belt, Lucinda felt that the world was her oyster and she was on cloud nine. The property she purchased with her inheritance had been renovated to an extremely high standard, the work thoroughly overseen by her grandfather and great-aunt who looked after the place while she had been away in London.

Now only two years later, Lucinda, Ernest and Dossie were all settled in comfortably to their new home in the best part of Jesmond, just outside of Newcastle. It was a three-storey Victorian building with a huge attic where Lou worked. She had turned the empty space into an artist's studio and it was perfect. Light streamed in through the little windows but also flooded in from the skylights in the roof. The room was strewn with canvases and smelt of oil paints and turpentine and no-one, not even Dossie, was allowed into her sanctuary. The house was big enough for all three of them to live happily together with enough space to enjoy some independence when it was needed. The extensive grounds which the house was set in were well laid out with a lawned garden surrounded by high hedges and edged with flower borders. Ernest just about managed to keep it looking tidy but Lou made sure he had some help with the heavy work. Whilst the grounds were no match for Cranfield Hall, there was still a lot of land to maintain and she hadn't brought her grandfather to live with her as a gardener. Likewise, with Dossie, who kept the house like a new pin but Lucinda had engaged a daily woman to come in to take on the majority of the housework. Of course, her aunt didn't like the idea of another woman doing what she considered to be her job but once it had been explained that she would oversee everything, she was perfectly happy in the role. In fact she rather revelled in the idea of being mistress of the house.

Lucinda never once missed Cranfield. In fact, she was glad to be rid of all the unhappy memories. She had established her identity within these walls - a new identity. She was no longer a ladyship or even Miss Lucinda but simply Lou Addington Lowes, an artist of considerable repute for one so young. Dossie continued to fuss over her darling girl and Ernest watched them both rub along together like two peas in a pod. He hadn't been as happy for a long time and was made even happier when Davy came to stay, as he frequently did during the school holidays. He had secured a particularly good job as Maths Master at a boys' preparatory school near York.

Ernest could never have imagined that one day he would have such a wonderful family as this. His one regret was that Etta wasn't around to enjoy it with him. Thoughts of the past were never far away these days. He remembered a time long ago when they were newly married - such a magical time when time stood still and they simply possessed each other - the smell of Etta's scent; the trace of smoke in his hair. A memory of her washing away the stench in the old tin bath caused his whole body to tingle. The touch of her hands on his scalp, the nearness of her presence and the heady perfume of the soap all blended together in his mind, making him dizzy with a desire to hold her just one more time. He had a good nose and was susceptible to certain smells. Etta had told him this so often. Even now, all these years later, the hot odour from a fire evoked memories of the furnace. He would miss his forge. With the money he got for his house on the terrace and the outbuildings, Ernest invested in the art gallery that Lucinda purchased shortly after graduating. This made him feel more at ease about accepting the share of the estate she gifted to him and others. He could never accept charity, not even from his rich granddaughter.

"It's the opening of the gallery tonight, Grandpa. You and Dossie will be there, won't you?"

"Well…"

"David is picking me up at six sharp 'cos I need to be there early but he can come back for you later."

"No, Lou, I don't think so. We won't fit in with all those fancy toffs but we'll be thinking about you."

"But you've got to come," she said, tearfully.

"No, I don't think Dossie is very happy about it."

"But why?"

"Thinks she might bump into one of those toffee noses who used to visit your Gran at the hall. She doesn't want any of those posh ladies to recognise her as one of her ladyship's retainers."

"That's just foolish and you know it!" She felt quite angry about this show of inverted snobbery.

"She doesn't want to show you up, love, in front of her betters!"

"Grandpa, I will not stand here and listen to such rubbish."

"You and I both know that you and Aunt Dossie are worth so much more than any of those so-called betters."

"Well, child, I won't argue with you but if we don't make it, you know we will be there in spirit if not in body."

She had dreaded this moment when the difference in their social class would come between them and in one desperate attempt to persuade him, she pulled out her trump card.

"But I'm unveiling the portrait of Annetta this evening."

A sad smile came to his lips as he merely nodded his head and bent to kiss her on the cheek.

"You can't miss the unveiling. You've not seen it yet; nobody has and it's my best work yet."

"I know, pet. You've worked on that painting for nigh on two years, off and on. You put your heart and soul into it."

"I just couldn't quite capture her how you described her, Grandpa."

"I'm sorry, love."

"I just kept trying to get the right expression, the right smile, the right look but Etta was elusive right up to the very end."

"But it's finished now?"

"Yeah, I finished the portrait of Annetta in time for my exhibition tonight so you've got to be there."

He had mixed feelings about seeing the picture. There was no doubt he was immensely proud of his granddaughter. She had real talent and he knew that the painting would be a masterpiece but an image of his beloved wife might be just too much to bear. He couldn't bring himself to look at the few old photographs he had of her. Sometimes even looking at Lucinda brought back memories that were so painful.

"Give it up, you silly old fool!" he told himself.

As Dossie entered the room, she couldn't fail to notice the melancholy that radiated from him.

"What's the matter, old fella?" she asked jokingly, but instinctively she knew he was thinking about Annetta.

"She'll never leave you alone, will she? You see, Ernest, she never grew old and ugly like the rest of us."

Suddenly it dawned on him that she was right. If she

259

hadn't died so young, then maybe this obsession with her memory wouldn't be so real. After a while, with the old lady staring at him full of sympathy and fondness, an expression of determination and resolve fixed on his face. In all his years he had never felt such an attachment to any woman, not even Etta. The warmth that enveloped him when he held Dossie was intoxicating, knowing that she loved him exclusively with every beat of her heart. He had never felt that with Etta. It had taken him nearly fifty years to come to that realisation but his eyes were open now and as old as he was, he had to take this last chance of happiness.

"By God, Dossie, you never said a truer word. It is time to let her go." His voice was shaky and as he took her hand in his, he asked without any hesitation, "Will you marry me, Doreen?"

"What, at our age?" The words questioned his proposal even though in her heart, she meant, "I will, without any reservation; I will!"

Dossie couldn't believe that the man she had loved for the whole of her life had proposed to her and her heart skipped a beat.

Suddenly an awful thought dawned on her. "You do mean it, don't you, Ernest? You don't just feel sorry for me?"

A huge grin sliced his face as he grabbed her hands.

"Of course I mean it, you silly lass, but let's just keep it to ourselves for a bit, just until after the opening. We don't want to steal Lou's thunder tonight, do we?"

Dossie agreed but secretly her head was bursting with the thrill of it all and she was just dying to tell their secret to the whole wide world. She felt like a young girl again.

True to his word, David dropped Lou off at the gallery at six on the dot and as she strode off into the foyer, she turned to look directly at her cousin.

"Drive home now and bring them straight back here, will you please, Davy?"

"I'll do my best."

She peered over her shoulder as he stepped back over the threshold and into the road, where his car was parked.

The gallery was empty except for a couple of girls dressed all in black busying themselves polishing champagne glasses. She smiled over to them.

"Everything OK?"

"Yes, Miss. We've got the fizz in the fridge, cooling!"

This was going to be quite an event, she thought to herself, "I can't believe it… my own exhibition!"

Her style wasn't at all in the modern vein of art. She liked people and things to look real and her work seemed to be popular, in spite of the criticisms she received from some of her tutors at college, who had favoured the abstract. Strolling leisurely around the room, she stopped at each piece, scrutinising the workmanship of every brushstroke. Once satisfied that her paintings were good enough, she stood back to admire the effect, occasionally straightening the odd frame that was not exactly at ninety degrees. Soon this room would be full of friends, admirers, collectors and critics but there was just one person she really wanted to see come through those doors. By 8 o'clock, the room was buzzing. Men and women with varying opinions chatted loudly and without inhibition.

"It's so old-fashioned, darling!" said one very tall, very skinny, incredibly old female with scarlet lips and matching nails that looked like claws. Her hair was scraped back so tightly, her eyes looked quite cat-like.

"Meow!" giggled Lou to one of her college friends.

And then there came a loud high-pitched voice from across the room.

"I simply adore her work, sweetie, don't you?" A short, plump lady grabbed another drink from a passing tray and guzzled it down in one gulp.

The tall, flamboyant young man with her wore a floppy hat and a flowery tie adorning a purple Ben Sherman shirt with a button-down collar.

"You must see this portrait, my dear. It's quite the best thing I have seen in years. It is just so alive, the subject seems to be seducing me with her eyes."

"Oh, Sebastian," his companion crooned, "you are such a card!"

"No, no, you are wrong; she's not a temptress!" said another in the crowd. "Her eyes are deep and melancholy. She really speaks to me."

A woman with a silk turban wound around her head opened her mouth wide, revealing a tongue stained with red wine. Her arms flailing like the sails of a windmill, she spoke of the angst and heartache that she saw in the painting.

Everyone who viewed the portrait had their own interpretation of the enigmatic face but there was no doubt that Lucinda's painting was extremely well received by the critics.

Remaining as calm and serene as she could, even though in that very instant her heart was beating so fast she thought she would faint, Lucinda turned to her friends with a look of sheer joy on her pretty face.

"Oh, my God, did you hear that?" she breathed. "It's my Portrait of Annetta… they love it!"

And then, no longer able to contain herself, she clapped her hands together loudly and let out an excited squeal.

Her friends collapsed in hoots of laughter and downed another glass of champagne. "You are a success, Lou. Cheers, love!"

An enormous sense of pride and happiness filled her very being but as she threw back her head in absolute rapture, she noticed the clock on the back wall and a sudden gloom threatened to dethrone her triumph.

"He's not coming," she whispered, almost to herself.

Gulping yet another glass of Moet, Lucinda felt a little dizzy and very giddy. She certainly knew how to drown her sorrows and almost fell into the arms of the young man in the adorable hat.

"Whoops a daisy, darling girl!" he teased. "Can't have my favourite artist breaking an arm or suchlike, can we? Can't have you out of action, now?"

"Certainly not!" echoed the companion, who faltered slightly and then asked what she called an impertinent question.

"Is it a self-portrait, my dear? I know you have named it 'A Portrait of Annetta' but the subject is so like you. There is an unmistakable resemblance, do you not see it, Sebastian?"

Lou burped and giggled outrageously. At that very moment, David caught her arm and dragged her off into a corner.

"What the bloody hell are you playing at, Lou? You're making an exhibition of yourself. Granddad's here. Pull yourself together."

Tears had begun to spill down her cheeks as he passed her a paper napkin grabbed from a passing waitress.

"Wipe your face," he ordered. "Dossie's here as well. They've got some news for you."

Of course, Dossie hadn't been able to hold her tongue but after fifty years of loving the one man, maybe that was totally excusable.

"Oh, you've come, I'd quite given you up."

Ernest walked slowly and unsteadily with his stick until he reached a chair at the side of his granddaughter where he gingerly sat down, supported by David. Dossie, who was just a little way behind him, peered at Lucinda over the top of her spectacles.

"So we see." The old man was not at all amused by the drunken spectacle that swayed before him.

"You've just got to see my portrait." She collapsed in a fit of giggles again. "Well, it's not *my* portrait, not a self-portrait, I mean. Of course, you know that, but do you know some of these lovely people here actually think it's me!"

Ernest and Dossie looked embarrassed.

"So, you see Grandfather dear, you were right all along. I am the image of the woman who gave away my father. The bitch who ruined your life!" Stumbling, she grabbed David's arm to steady herself. "Hopefully, some fool will buy her and take her out of our lives forever."

Ernest was speechless and white with shock. Seeing his distress, Lucinda began to cry and made to apologise. "I'm so sorry, please ignore me, I'm just so bloody drunk!"

"Lou, dear, I think you should have some coffee; David, fetch some black coffee please."

Dossie guided her niece into a secluded corner away from prying eyes and as she did so, Ernest took some time to pull himself together. He hadn't realised how much Lucinda had been affected by everything that had happened. He almost felt responsible and he scuttled off to find the painting, which hung in pride of place. Staring up at the beautiful face of his dead wife, the old man wheezed as he caught his breath.

The perfect mouth was turned up at the corners in a pretty smile but Ernest detected a sadness and a cruelty that only he could see. The painting was well executed but it disturbed him greatly. He stood, for what seemed like an age, staring at the woman he had loved with a passion. Then suddenly he realised that the passion was gone. He no longer felt anything for Etta.

Presently, he was aware of the others behind him.

"What do you think?" An anxious tear-stained Lucinda waited for his answer.

"It's perfectly painted." He lingered a while over the words. "You've captured the spirit of your grandmother. Well done, lass."

The young woman was delighted. "Thank you so much. I am so glad you like it." Then, turning swiftly to her aunt, wiping away the black mascara streaks from her face, she asked, "Now tell me, what is this news that David spoke of earlier? You see, I wasn't so drunk after all!" She laughed and hiccoughed at the same time. "What is it you've got to tell me?"

Chapter 25

The next few months were busy for all of them. Dossie was fretting about wedding arrangements, Ernest was busying himself with what he was going to have to wear. David was trying desperately to get him into a new suit for the occasion and Lou was excitedly arranging meetings with prospective art collectors.

Of course, she was also helping with the wedding plans. She had designed the most elegant outfit for Dossie and had organised one of her friends to make it. It was a beautiful shade of buttermilk and the fabric was pure silk with pearl embellishment. A simple dress with bracelet length sleeves was expertly cut and fitted to Dossie's matronly figure, giving her an elegant silhouette. The matching coat was slightly shorter, revealing the embroidered hemline of the frock. She hadn't chosen the hat yet but Lucinda had one in mind: a quite modern look, made entirely of silk rosebuds clustered together to create a halo of peach coloured flowers. She was in her element, working out designs, choosing fabrics and deciding on exact shades. Dossie was only too happy to leave such frivolity to her niece, as she concentrated on baking an enormous fruit cake that would be the centrepiece of the wedding breakfast.

In the midst of all these preparations, Lucinda was managing deals with several high-profile dealers and in a few days' time she would be in London to seal a deal with an American collector. Her work was fast becoming the latest thing in the art world, where many were becoming bored with the abstract pieces that dominated the market. The realism that she created in her paintings was much sought after by several discerning collectors and her name was bandied about in some of the smartest circles in town. The American collector was interested in the portrait of Annetta and although she had decided not to sell, Ernest had persuaded her to let it go.

"We don't need a picture of her, Lou!" Smiling at his granddaughter, he held her pretty face in his rough old hands."

"But I thought you would be upset if I sold it."

"We have you, Lucinda. You are everything to me and to your aunt. We don't need an image on canvas, no matter how well-painted it is. I want you to sell it."

That was that. Her mind was made up; she would sell her best painting to the highest bidder. And at that moment in time, the American offer was on the table and for an amount at which she could only marvel. It amused her to think that Etta would achieve her ambition of ending up in America at last, even if it was only as an image on canvas. The days were flying by at breakneck speed and the old couple were anticipating their forthcoming nuptials with a mixture of delight and apprehension. Marriage at their stage of life was daunting and they both wondered if they were doing the right thing. Ernest was set in his ways and Dossie had been used to a life quite different from his. However, a strong bond had developed between them and an affection had grown steadily since that traumatic meeting in the gatehouse. Even in the middle of such happiness, Ernest felt a strange sense of gloominess and he was pleased that Etta's portrait was going to be sold.

"What's on your mind, my old love?" Dossie was a transformed woman. Finding him had changed her into someone compassionate and full of love. Of course there was still a little snobbery lurking deep in her character but her current lifestyle allowed her that small luxury and it didn't hurt anyone. In fact it tickled David and Lou to think of the lady of the manor as they had both named her.

Ernest didn't answer, remaining mute as his thoughts flashed back to the day he married Etta. It was a winter's day, just after Christmas, and he pictured her there by his side. She was wearing white velvet, trimmed with rabbit fur. The dress was cut low in the bodice and reached her ankles but her modesty was protected by a full-length cape with a hood that protected her beautiful blonde curls from the snow. It was a quiet affair with few guests: Minnie and Jack, Ernest's younger brother Lance and his family from Doncaster and Jack's brother Daniel and his wife. That was it. No sister... no Doreen.

What would Etta make of all this? Did their forthcoming marriage have her blessing or her curse?

Dossie, sensing his angst, gently touched his arm. "Are you having doubts, pet?"

Reassuringly, he beamed at his wife-to-be and shook his head with real conviction.

David had no doubts that they were doing what was best for the both of them; two lonely individuals in the autumn of their lives. What did they have to lose? After many days of searching, he found the right suit for his grandfather and actually managed to persuade him it was perfect in every way.

"You'll look like a real toff in that outfit. You will, Grandpa, believe me."

"Aye, a right dandy you'll make of me, won't you, lad?"

"No, you 'll be dapper - not dandy - there's a big difference!" David roared with laughter.

"Well, I don't want to outshine the bride, now, do I?"

"No fear of that. Lou has delivered something that will make your eyes pop."

"Well, say no more. It's bad luck and we've had

enough of that in our lifetime."

"Hey, no more of that sort of talk. Let's just look forward to a great day, shall we?"

And with that, the pair of them linked arms and decided on a pint or two at the local pub.

When Dossie tried on her new wedding outfit, she filled up with tears. It was the most stunning thing she had ever worn in the whole of her days. She felt like a queen and the rosebud hat felt like a crown. Tucking stray strands of grey hair under the hatband, she cooed as she took in her reflection in the wardrobe mirror.

"Oh, Lou, it's gorgeous; you've made me look almost beautiful."

"You are beautiful and Grandpa Ernest will think so too!"

Doreen felt a chill and her whole body shivered, even though it was a warm spring day. Her sister's face seemed to glare at her from the mirror but as Lucinda smiled lovingly at her, it disappeared in a flash.

The day before the wedding was a Friday. Guests, although there were very few of them, were looking forward to a good old-fashioned knees-up over the weekend. Some of Ernest's old cronies were a bit in awe of his new surroundings and wondered if the 'do' would be a bit too posh for them but they had no need to worry. Ernest had made sure that the reception was going to be an affair worthy of his north-eastern roots, no matter what David or Lucinda thought. There would be plenty of Newcastle Brown Ale as well as the bottles of champagne ordered by Dossie. Caterers had been booked to serve the three-course meal in the dining room of their home. It was big enough for the twenty guests and would be much cosier than some ostentatious hotel. The doubts of the previous days had lifted and Ernest and Dossie were beginning to relax over breakfast as Lou bustled into the kitchen. Grabbing a cup of the treacle that Dossie called tea, she gulped it down then stuffed a slice of hot toast into her mouth. With butter dripping down her chin, she swallowed the food quickly as Dossie gave her a disapproving look. This was not the ladylike way to eat breakfast and certainly not what was expected of Lucinda Addington Lowes. Resisting the urge to laugh out loud, which she knew would just irritate her aunt even more, she apologised profusely. Ernest caught her eye and winked. This was just what she needed to summon up the courage to give them both the news that she knew wouldn't go down too well.

"Listen, you two, I have to take the train to London today for a meeting. It's all set up and won't take more than an hour and then I'll get the first train back tonight."

Dossie looked startled.

"Don't worry, I'll be back in plenty of time for the wedding. You know I wouldn't miss that for the world."

"But why do you have to go now, today of all days? I need you at my side, Lou. You know I can't do myself up the way you do it." Dossie's eyes watered.

Ernest said nothing but there was something severe about the way he viewed his granddaughter.

"Look, this American buyer has instructed his London dealer to seal the transaction and it has to be done now."

The two elderly relatives looked puzzled.

"He wants to buy the portrait."

"Then you've got to go, but just you make sure you are back tonight, my girl. You can't let Dossie down."

"Of course I will." And she blew a kiss to the pair of them as she left for the station.

"How do you feel about Lou selling Etta's portrait and to the other side of the world?" asked Dossie, uneasily.

"Do you know something, Dossie? I never really liked that painting," Ernest confessed. "Oh, it's a brilliant painting, don't get me wrong. Lucinda is talented, but there was something sad about it that... well, now that it's off to America..." The sentence was left unfinished.

The implication of his words didn't register in Dossie's brain, as her only thought was on how much Ernest had loved her sister. It still worried her, even now that he had asked her to be his wife. But Etta was gone, dead and buried, and Dossie was very much here with Ernest, the man she loved. She could live with his memories so long as she had him.

"Really, pet, I thought it upset you too much to look at it; brought back too many memories. I know you'll never get over her."

"No, nothing like that," he sighed. "Annetta is long gone, Dossie, and we need to start living. We have to make the most of what little time we have left. I will never forget Etta, as I'm sure you won't, but it was a lifetime ago. She's nothing but a distant memory and I've got Lucinda to thank for that."

He bent to plant a gentle kiss on the old lady's forehead. Dossie felt such a surge of emotion in that second that she threw her arms around his neck and wept silent tears into his collar. This was the moment when she finally understood the depth of his feelings for her. He loved her. The day drew to a close as night began to fall. The thought of the long day ahead made both of them think of sleep.

"We need an early night. Best get ready for bed."

"She's not back yet!"

"Don't worry, hinnie, she'll be here. She won't let you down. She's worked too hard on that outfit of yours to leave you to dress yourself. She knows you'll never get that hat right."

271

"What do you know about my hat. My outfit, Ernest Lowes, is a secret until tomorrow." Tutting in an exaggerated petulant way, she sounded like a slip of a girl instead of the matron she actually was. A cheeky smile lit up her face, adding to the illusion.

He knew nothing but was good at winding Dossie up and enjoyed watching her flap. There was no malice in it, of course, and he patted her hand affectionately, chortling to himself at her reaction.

She switched off the lights downstairs before heading for the bedroom.

"I didn't hear Davy go up; did you, pet?"

"He went up early on. Said he had some reading to catch up on."

"That boy, he'll wear out his eyes before he's finished." She smiled. "Do you know, I think he's working on his speech for tomorrow. That's what he's up to, Ernie!"

Without saying a word, he dropped a kiss on her lips as he started up the stairs. He was well aware of what Davy was up to. There wasn't much that Ernest didn't know about his grandson and the lad knew it. He had never been able to hide anything from the old dude and tonight was no exception. Lucinda was a different matter, though. Ernest hadn't quite weighed her up completely yet. She was an enigma just like her grandma. He couldn't help thinking about what she was up to.

Lucinda was feeling great. The meeting had gone even better than she had expected and the deal seemed to have been wrapped up well and truly. The American collector had come up with the dollars and was now the proud owner of the painting. After downing a quick glass of celebratory bubbly and grabbing a half-stale vol-au-vent, she thanked everyone and set off in a taxi for Kings

Cross. Her thoughts were all over the place as she sat in the back seat of the cab. She was overjoyed with the sale but a sense of regret lurked somewhere at the back of her brain. There was nothing left of her grandmother Annetta now, except for a few faded photographs that didn't really picture her loveliness. Maybe she should have kept the painting but it was too good an offer to refuse. Reassuring herself, she checked her watch.

"How long till we get to the station, cabby?"

"Traffic's bad tonight, Miss."

A sudden panic overcame her as she feared she might miss her train.

"Can't we go a little faster? I have a train to catch."

"Sorry, love, it's not up to me, ask this lot in front to get a move on."

Lucinda fiddled with her gloves and tried to calm herself but thoughts of Dossie and Ernest wondering where she was did nothing to curb her alarm.

"Soon be there now, Miss." The cab driver tried his best to reassure his young fare but he was also growing impatient with the ever-increasing traffic and tutted to himself, whilst beeping loudly on the car horn. Traffic jams were the bane of his life.

Cuddling together in the big double bed, Ernie and Dossie felt warm and comfortable but sleep evaded them both.

"Don't you worry yourself about our Lou, my old lass. She'll be back soon enough."

How did he know what she was thinking? It was true, she was anxious about Lucinda but there was something else on her mind. Here she was, snuggling in a bed with a man she wasn't married to. Doreen Clifford, prude of this parish, living in sin... Well, only till tomorrow. She raised her eyebrows and giggled. How she had changed;

how they had both changed; and it was all down to Lucinda. Suddenly her mood reverted as she looked at the alarm clock on her bedside table.

"She's late!"

The train was standing in the station as Lucinda ran from the taxi, throwing a ten-shilling note and some coins into the cab. She left him counting his money as he held up his hand in a gesture of thanks. Racing through the crowds, she headed for the platform, her heart in her mouth. Flashing her ticket at the man at the gate, she rushed past him without waiting and proceeded to the platform. She could see the train and her spirits lifted. She was going to make it!

Sleep was creeping up on Dossie as her eyelids began to close. Ernest, however, suddenly felt very awake and as he gently pulled his arm from behind her head, he sat up gingerly in bed. Dossie sighed softly and turned over. Staring down at her, his brain mulled over the events of the past. The years had been hard to both of them and he was glad that they had found each other, despite what had gone before. Vivid, spiralling pictures filled his thoughts; images of Annetta, of Arthur, of Dossie, and he began to feel restless. Regretting the cheese he'd had for supper, he reached for the antacid pills by the bed. As he tossed and turned, Dossie stirred, half asleep.

"What's wrong, pet?"

"Go back to sleep love, I'm fine."

"Night-night then, my sweet," she murmured dreamily.

Chapter 26

The long journey from London seemed endless as the train rattled along the tracks towards Newcastle. Feeling agitated, Lucinda tried to relax herself by picking up the Agatha Christie she had tucked away in her bag. After reading a few pages, her eyelids grew heavy and her head lolled against the padded headrest in the first-class carriage. It wasn't long before she was asleep. Her dreams were troubled and separate images of Annetta and Agatha merged into one. It was a strange combination but the grandmother she had conjured up was smiling at her, soothing her as if she were a child. She felt warm and safe as the woman smiled benevolently, stretching out her arms in a tender embrace. Liquid blue eyes almost drowned her in their intensity and gentleness.

The train jolted and she half woke with a start. She'd never really known a proper grandmother, the sort that her friends at college spoke about. Perhaps her dream of one was what she had always wanted. Dossie was the only one who came near to this image and she was worried she was letting her down. She imagined how upset she must be, wondering whether she would be back in time for her big day. There was no one else in the compartment but she verbalised her anxieties drowsily to the empty seats.

"I'm such a selfish cow. How could I have arranged this meeting, today of all days? It could have been re-arranged, postponed till after the wedding. They both have such little time left!" She thought fondly of the elderly couple who had found love at the twilight of their lives.

"Dossie needed me. They both needed me. Oh, God, please let me get back in time!"

The words vanished as sleep threatened to overcome

her again.

But the portrait seemed to consume her every thinking moment, as if Annetta was willing her to disappoint Dossie and upset Ernest's wedding plans.

"What the hell am I thinking?" Lou shook herself fully awake as she sat bolt upright in the padded seat, marvelling at the nonsense that was filling her head.

She reassured herself with the thought of the hundreds of dollars she was to receive from the sale of the painting and of the boost to her reputation as an artist. Feeling better, she put the book back into her bag and took out a bar of Nestle's Five Boys. Unwrapping the layer of silver paper from the bar, she anticipated the smooth velvety taste of the chocolate. Checking the time on her gold wristwatch, she knew it wouldn't be long before the train pulled into Newcastle Central. And then it would only take ten minutes or so to get home by taxi. They would probably be asleep by the time she got in, but she would be there for them both in the morning. She just hoped they hadn't worried too much. It was going to be a big day for them tomorrow and they both needed a good night's rest.

Ernest struggled to sleep, tossing and turning as he lay next to Dossie. He tried desperately to lie still so as not to wake her but sweat was running down his forehead and his back was wet through. She stirred and let out a soft sigh as she turned in the bed to face Ernest. Struggling to open her eyes, she reached out her hand towards him and felt his cold clammy chest. Suddenly wide awake, Dossie sat bolt upright in bed, fear and a sense of unease filling her brain.

"Ernie, what's wrong? Are you ill?" Racing out of bed, she grabbed her dressing gown and sat on the opposite side of the bed next to her fiancé. Feeling his head and noticing the dreadful ashen look on his face, time stood still as she screamed for David.

Time seemed to be passing so slowly for Lucinda. She wasn't very far from her destination, but the train decelerated and came to a halt. There was a delay, something on the tracks but no announcement came and she began to grow angry as the strain showed in her eyes.

"What's happening now? Why are we bloody stopping here?" The question was again addressed to the empty compartment and no answer came back. Looking at her watch for the umpteenth time, her heart began to pound in her chest and the dryness in her mouth made her swallow hard.

It was intolerable, totally unacceptable, she would write a letter of complaint to British Rail as soon as she got home. Rising to her feet, she peered through the rain-streaked window but there was nothing to see. She was about to go and seek out the conductor when the train jolted back into life and threw her down onto the chenille covered seat. She was feeling so apprehensive, she reached for one of the tranquillisers prescribed for her when her grandmother died. Popping the tiny white pill into her mouth, she waited for the calmness to transcend the anxiety. She waited and waited.

They both waited for what seemed an eternity. David had called for an ambulance as Dossie held on tight to Ernest's clammy hand. The young man fought to remain calm for the sake of his aunt, but his brain was whirring so much that he felt nauseous. This was not happening; he would not allow the old bugger to die. Tears began to sting behind his tired eyes, but he blinked them away and as he tried and failed to smile reassuringly, he blew his nose hard. Men didn't cry like little girls or old women.

Feeling like crying but refusing to give in to such silliness, Lucinda blew her nose into a Kleenex. The train picked up speed again and chugged and rattled towards the tunnel. She knew once through, they would be nearly there and her anxiety started to die down slightly, although the dryness in her mouth remained. What she wouldn't give for a cup of tea right now; a cup of strong dark brown tea, the sort Dossie brewed in the big aluminium teapot. Staring through the window, the rain persisted to block her view and Lou strained to see where they were. Raindrops ran in little rivulets down the pane.

Dossie's tears fell like raindrops, streaking her face and running down her throat until they soaked her nightgown.

"Don't go, you can't leave me now." The words were hardly audible but as she spoke, she squeezed his hand so hard, she left finger-marks on his pale freckled skin. Her pain was physically visible. It contorted her face and bowed her body so that her back arched and her knees gave way.

By now, David had given in to his own unbearable misery and he echoed his aunt's sentiments with such an anger that the force of it frightened the old lady. She tried to hold him back as he lurched towards his grandfather but there was a strength welling inside of him that refused to be quelled. Losing her grip on the young man's arm she felt the smooth cotton of his shirt sleeve slip through her fingers as he pulled away from her. She was left paralysed with the smell of fear and anguish in her nostrils, unable to move or utter a cry. All she could do now was to watch as her nephew's heartache defeated him totally and completely. The boy was wrecked! He let out a harrowing scream that seemed to come from the pit of his stomach.

"Don't you dare die, you old man. Don't do this to us." And he buried his head in the blackness of his grandfather's chest.

As she peered into the shadows, Lucinda was aware of the change to the train's rattle as it headed into the tunnel. The window was now a mirror, reflecting images back into the compartment. Scrutinising her tired, unkempt appearance, she tried to tidy up her hair. Dragging her hands across her face, she attempted to bring back some colour into her pale cheeks. Searching in her bag for some powder and lipstick, she turned away from the window but a sudden stabbing in her breast made her sit up sharp.

"That vol au vent," she mouthed explaining away the pain as indigestion from the stale offering consumed at the gallery.

Rubbing her chest, she casually looked back at the glass, the face of her grandmother stared back at her. Wet streaks ran down the cheeks but her mouth was smiling. Lucinda's heart missed a beat and her lips, so dry, stuck together until she licked them apart. She felt a fear so real she almost fainted.

Pulling herself together, she checked her Rolex again in a bid for normality. She sighed heavily.

"It's so late. I can't believe it's so late!"

The ambulance arrived too late. David and Dossie were prostrate across the lifeless body, both silent and exhausted. The old woman's grip on Ernest's hand was still strong as her fingers were physically unfurled by the ambulance men.

"She's won, Davy. I always knew she would never let him go." The whispered words disappeared into the drama of the room as his body was torn away from her

279

grasp. Men in uniform were unpacking equipment, one breathing air into Ernest's mouth as another was thumping on his chest. There was no response but it was in their eyes; just hanging there, waiting to be spoken. To be announced. The end of life.

David was in such a state of shock; he didn't even hear what she said. His heartbeat was pounding in his head as his beloved grandfather's body was lifted into the waiting ambulance. They were still working on him but he knew it was too late. He had never known an emotion so extreme, so intense as this. It penetrated his whole body making him feel physically sick. Suddenly thinking about his aunt, he rubbed his hands roughly over his head, blinking back his sorrow and turning to find her huddled in a corner like a frightened child.

Pulling her up into his arms, she felt like a rag doll - all limp and lifeless. Her breathing was slow, but he could feel her rapid heartbeat against his own chest. She held up her face to his, her eyes pleading with him to turn back time, then feeling the depth of his pain, she watched helplessly as he gave in to his overwhelming grief and let the tears run freely. Feeling like a small boy again, he remembered his cries the day Elsie died but this didn't even compare; he had just lost the one person who had been Grandfather, Mother and Father to him. Wallowing in self-pity, he pulled himself up sharply as he felt the warm wetness seep into his shirt. Dossie's face was streaked with her own silent tears as at that moment, she thought only of David's misery.

It seemed like time had stood still with not a word spoken but then, eventually, the silence was broken as Dossie finally found the strength to speak out in a loud clear voice.

"I always knew, Davy. He could never marry me. Etta wouldn't allow it. She always had to have her own way!"

There was an air of conviction and conclusiveness in what she said that made David believe, despite the illogical implausibility of her words. Etta was dead and buried and it was a fact, but somehow, he knew Dossie was right. Never knowing the woman who had been his grandmother, David found it incredulous that he felt such a bitterness towards her now; but he did. She had robbed his grandfather of his last few years of happiness and there was something in his aunt's words that rang true. It was pitiful the way her life had turned out and a real sense of regret teemed inside of him.

"She was here. She came for him, David." A shiver ran down his spine, leaving him feeling weak to the stomach.

Both numb from the trauma, they wrestled with the mystical notion that Dossie had expressed. David, a modern young man, struggled to understand but whether it was fate or destiny, he had the strangest feeling that the spirit of the woman his grandfather had adored had played some part in this tragedy. He could almost see her face as clearly as Dossie could but almost instantaneously, she was replaced with a mirror image of her granddaughter. It was then that they were both brought back to the harsh reality of Ernest's death.

"Oh, my God, David," Dossie cried, "how are we going to tell Lou?"

The train rattled noisily along the tracks, shaking the girl in her seat as her eyes fixed unnervingly on the spectre still there in the window. With an air of increasing trepidation threatening to seize hold of her, Lucinda blinked furiously as she tried unsuccessfully to remove the image from her brain. Then real panic gripped tight as Etta's face lingered in the glass, holding her gaze, refusing to let her go. Eventually, Lucinda turned her head sharply away from the window in a bid to take back control. Soon after, her brain whirred into action, slowing down the racing pulse and quickened heartbeat. It was just tiredness or it could be the Valium, she told herself, trying to rationalise what she had seen. It was only her own reflection in the window; it was rain, not tears. She covered her face with her hands, leaving them there as she took in a deep breath of air. Hardly daring to remove her hands, she gingerly let them drop into her lap but kept her eyes focused on her inter-twined fingers as she continued to compose herself. At last, she felt a calmness return and she laughed nervously as a sense of relief replaced the terror that had almost conquered her a few minutes ago.

Finally, the train emerged from the tunnel, as this time she caught a glimpse of her own reflection mirrored in the rain-splashed window. It was still raining hard as she smiled back at herself, a familiar smile that quickly disappeared as she realised they weren't raindrops streaming down her face in the glass; they were real tears. Tears of a sorrow to come.

About The Author

I am a mother and a grandmother who has enjoyed creativity in many forms throughout my life. My love of writing began at school and I wrote poetry and short stories throughout my time at college. I studied art and English literature, qualifying as a teacher in the seventies, which led me into a long career in education. After working in the classroom for a number of years, I became a headteacher and then worked as an education consultant before retiring. I started writing again at that time to combat boredom and keep my brain cells well oiled. It was then that I decided to write "So Many Secrets," my first novel.

Born in County Durham, I left the area at the age of eighteen and only returned four years ago after living and working in Yorkshire for many years. I live in the beautiful village of Brancepeth, surrounded by green fields and wide open spaces. My cottage is set in the grounds of an Elizabethan manor house, which is steeped in history. There is no shortage of inspiration for writing, from my immediate environment with its castle and beautiful Norman church to the rich industrial heritage of the north east which offers endless opportunities to explore.

Born into a small mining community, I grew up surrounded by strong characters and life-changing events. My parents knew the value of education and gave me loving encouragement throughout my childhood, ensuring success at school. My father, a talented artist himself, was unable to pursue his dreams but was determined to ensure I was able to make the most of the chances that life offered me.

www.blossomspringpublishing.com